Love and Sin

LOVE and SIN Copyright © 2018 by Tempestt Luckett. All rights reserved. Printed in the United States of America. For Information address info@tppublish.com

www.tppublish.com

The Library of Congress Cataloging-in Publication Data is available upon request.

Second Edition: February 2018

This one is for my most dedicated real supporters.
I can't express my gratitude in words.
-TL

CONTENTS

CHAPTER ONE

"**Y**ou forgot, didn't you?" Lovely's assistant Sasha asked her. Lovely looked up at Sasha with a blank expression on her face. "Forgot what?" Lovely asked Sasha. "I'm not about to tell you so you can cover up. But your Mother is on line one boss" Said Sasha. Lovely rolled her eyes upward trying to figure out why her mother could be possibly calling her at work when she knows she hates being interrupted with shenanigans from her family. Don't get her wrong she loves her mother it's just her mother tends to overreact to incidents or bother her constantly about her settling down and having children. Lovely having to hear her mother constant pestering about reproduction was going to drive her insane. After all she was still so much into her career and with her business getting off the ground a year ago, Lovely's focus was basically being an entrepreneur, a business woman, a successful one at that. She didn't have time for dating and babies, especially out of order. She sighed as she reached for the phone to speak with her mother.

"Hey mom, is everything alright?"

"Yes, honey I was just calling to make sure you didn't forget about today." Her mother said. Lovely pondered on what she could be possibly forgetting about.

Her mother chuckled on the other end. "You forgot, didn't you?" her mother asked

"Of course, not mom, I remember today I can't wait for it." Lovely tried to play it off

"Oh good, I can't wait for you to meet Travis, he is such a handsome man, well rounded, good head on his shoulders, stable. I've told him so much about you Love, all wonderful things of course."

Lovely closed her eyes and held in a scream. She couldn't believe she had agreed to this. She couldn't remember when she had agreed. Now she would have to go along with it.

"Great Mom, I'll be there, can't' wait to meet him." Lovely said with sarcasm.

"Love now I really know you forgot. You and I both know you wouldn't agree to a blind date. Today is your father's retirement party." Her mother expressed with a sigh

"Oh shit, I mean shoot."

"Yeah young lady, you are so busy running your company that you forgot. I had half a mind not to call you and remind you but I know your father would have been crushed if you didn't show up."

"I'm sorry Mom, I will be there with the best gift and a big smile"

"Love, seriously, slow down you are twenty-six years old you are still young, you don't have to conquer the world overnight. I understand that the investment business is cutthroat and it's a male dominated field but you need to live your life too. When is the last time you went out and enjoyed you? When is the last time you had sex honey, because I only know one man that you have been intimate with and that was four years ago?"

"Mom seriously let's not discuss my love life right now, I am not ready for a relationship. I am too focused on getting D&B Investment Management on the map in a major way. It's getting there but I want it to be better, like you said it's a male dominated field."

"I understand Love I do; I know what it's like to want success for something that you are putting your all into. I was the same way with my business I wanted to dominate the court room. But then I also understood that I wanted a family one day and when your father and I got together I knew even more that I wanted it with him. All I'm saying honey is you can have it all the successful business, marriage and family."

"I understand Mom. I will try to make more time out for me."

"No Lovely don't try, do it. Your life will pass you by before you know it and you will regret not doing more things for yourself. I will see you tonight seven p.m. sharp no lateness ok."

"Yes, mom seven sharp, I will be there. Love you."

"Love you too Lovely, I'll see you tonight."

"See ya mom."

Lovely hung up the phone and released a sigh; her mother was always getting on her about something. Lovely had time to ponder on her mother's words about dominating the investment business. She knew her mother was right on some things regarding slowing down and taking in the fruits of her labor. She hadn't thought about a relationship since Michael. While she was in her second year of law school she dated Michael Davis, he was a charmer the type of man you would want to introduce to your family. They were together for two years until he showed his ass. Michael was older by four years and she was 20 years old when they met. Her intelligence and determination allotted her to graduate high school at sixteen and college at nineteen she took a year off before applying to Law School.

When she was accepted into Cornell Law School her mother and father were so proud of her, she was making goals and accomplishing them at an early stage in her life. Michael had been her one and only relationship so far, she tried dating after her relationship ended but she was still harboring feelings of how she was treated in her relationship, if she was going to start dating and be in a committed relationship the man of her life would have to understand and support her dreams.

She was thrown out of her thoughts with a knock on her door. She responded with them to come into her office. The door opened and she was greeted by her business partner Desmond Bryans. She took a few seconds to take him in, his business attire were pleated coal black dress pants, crisp grey dress shirt with an abstract themed red, black and grey tie. Desmond strolled into her office with a smile on his face. Desmond was attractive no doubt about it. What woman wouldn't want to take a ride on him? With his chiseled jaw line, high cheekbones and piercing blue eyes and a smile so bright and tempting she was sure he left several women in their office and building alone with soaking wet panties. She couldn't deny her attraction to him he was gorgeous, he should be on a cover of a magazine instead of doing investments and money management. The two have known each other from working at one of the biggest investment company's together during an internship, when Lovely wanted to branch out and start her own company Desmond was supportive and more than willing to jump on board.

"Hey Des." Lovely acknowledge him.

"Hey Lovely, how are you this morning?" He asked she slightly shrugged and stated "I could be better. I have a lot to get done today and I probably won't get to finish it since I was just reminded of my Father's retirement party today."

"Oh really, is it anything that I can take off your hands?" He asked as he sat down on the couch that was inside of her plush office space.

"Anything that I can help with darling you know that I'm more than willing.'

"No, I'll manage I know you have more than enough work and meetings on your own I don't want to pass mine off to you. I don't want to seem like a lazy business partner." she stated with a slight chuckle. Desmond looked at Lovely and laughed.

"Sweetheart you could never and should never use the word lazy with you in a sentence. You are far from it and I actually know that you over work yourself. Hell, I feel like the lazy one with all the man hours you clock. I would be glad to take any of your bearings on as mine.' he stated.

Lovely just smiled a little and began to rotate and try to work out the kinks in her neck. She was stressed and tensed, Desmond saw this and got off the couch and started to approach her. He walked to the back of her chair and started to gently message the kinks out of her neck.

"Geesh sweetheart you are way to tense, you need to relax, Love." He continued to knead the tense muscle in her back and neck.

Lovely had let out a slight moan as she began to relax. The moan registered in Desmond mind as well as to other body parts. He knew she didn't mean to release such a sexy moan but damn if he could help his reaction do it. He continued to work on her neck hoping to hear another moan.

"Des your hands are working magic right now. I think you are in the wrong profession." she said jokingly.

Desmond cleared his throat before he responded because he knew that his voice was going to sound too husky, he couldn't help that the pleasurable sound she was giving off was doing to him. He licked his sexy lips before responding

"Well Love I have been told that I can give much pleasure with these hands."

Lovely caught the innuendo from his words. Lovely's breathing started to change as she imagined what he could possibly do to her and her body with those hands. Slowly she felt his fingers caress her shoulders and collar bone the light feathery touches a sensation crawled up and down her spine. She imagined his hands going lower until it reached the top of her breast where his fingers brushed upon the firm curve, she envisioned his palm slowly clutching her breast into his wide palm, his fingers tweaking her taunt bud. She laid her head back and slowly bit her bottom lip and she let another moan escape her mouth. She was throttled out of her thoughts by the abrupt entrance of her assistant Sasha. Lovely jumped as if she had been caught with her hand in the cookie jar. She looked up at Desmond who had a slight smirk and a naughty gleam in his eyes. Lovely's body became hot and she knew her face was red. She cleared her throat as she sat up straight in her chair.

"Ms. Daniels sorry to interrupt but you have your conference call with Ms. Jermyn in ten minutes and I wanted to remind you that you need to get a gift for your dad for tonight." Said Sasha

"Thanks Sasha, Call Ms. Jermyn and see if we can push her meeting to three o'clock, I am going to need more time to get my dad's gift."

"Sure, that's not a problem boss." Stated Sasha.

As Sasha walked back out the room her eyes connected with Lovely's again with a questioning look in her eyes then her eyes scanned from Lovely to Desmond then back to Lovely. Lovely just gave her the 'we will talk later' look and Sasha exited the room. Lovely swung around in her chair to look at Desmond who had an innocent look on his face but that naughty gleam was still there. As she stared at him she could only wonder why she allowed her imagination to get the best of her like that. Yes, she thought Desmond was attractive but she would never mix business with pleasure; that would be a sure disaster on her part. She watched him walk back to the couch with a slight swag to his walk. One would never guess that he was biracial an African American mother and Caucasian father; since he looked more on the white side that he inherited from his father along with the blue eyes.

"What do you plan on buying your dad?" He asked "I'm not sure actually, I could use a man's opinion, what do you think I should get him?"

"Depends on what he likes, does he play any sports? What hobbies does he have?"

"I know he likes golf and basketball, football he watches but he's more into the other two sports. I don't want to buy him something so cliché for his retirement, you know.'

"Go to Barney's they have a selection on nice things, I'm sure you'll find him something from there.'

"Thanks I'll try that, listen about what just happened I-I'm not sure, but it shouldn't have." Before she could finish she was cut off by Desmond approaching her desk. He leaned on the corner of her desk and turned Lovely's chair to fully face him "I already know what you are going to say, but before you do let me just put this out there, I have had feelings for you since we've interned together, I understand the type of woman you are and what you want to accomplish in life and I don't want to get in the way of that. In the past few years that I've known you, I haven't seen you in a relationship. I understand that you want to focus on building your empire, I want to be that man that gives you the best of both worlds; you can have the empire and a man that fulfills your every desire, fantasies and gives you the ultimate pleasure. I want to keep a smile on your face and that support you need. With all that said I would like to ask you out on a date just to see if we can take this business and friendship to another level." Lovely couldn't believe her ears her mind was racing fast; she wasn't sure if Desmond had telepathically read her thoughts before he came into her office, the words he spoke were exactly what a man would have to understand if they wanted to be in a relationship. She took a deep breath before she began to unleash her words.

"What happens if it doesn't work Desmond, are you willing to risk our friendship and business relationship for it. Because I'm not, I don't mix business and pleasure, what just happened was an in the moment thing. Don't get me wrong I think you are an attractive, intelligent and sexy man, I just don't want to ruin what we have for something that could have never been'

"I thought you were a risk taker Lovely, you take risk every day in this business, why can't you take a risk with your love life. All I'm asking for right now, today, this very moment is one date. We will go from there; I won't harbor any feelings if it doesn't work out. I'll still be your business partner and friend."

Lovely thought about his words for a few seconds and then made her decision. "Today, this very moment, right now, I will accept your invitation for one date." Desmond looked at her intensely before a smile crept onto his beautiful face. He bent down and his lips hovered over her. He stared at her hypnotic eyes before looking at her full plump lickable lips. "You won't regret it." He said before he closed the gap and gave her small quick peck to her lips.

He got up to walk out of her office before she could respond to the chaste kiss that he had just given. Lovely started to gather her belonging so she could be on her way to hit the street of Manhattan in search for her father's gift. She let out a sigh hoping she was doing the right thing by accepting Desmond's date.

She really didn't want it to jeopardize anything, her thoughts went back to when he was given her a massage. How her body yearned for the caress of his fingers, hell right about now in her life she yearned for any male fingers to caress her. She shook her head to get the thoughts out of her mind. She walked out of her office and advised Sasha that she will be back by three for her conference call. She hopped on the elevator to get to the lobby of the building. As she approached the lobby and stepped off she spotted a woman whose frame looked all too familiar to her. Her body tensed when she realized who it was. She tried to walk quickly out of the back-lobby doors to the garage to get to her car.

"Lovely Daniels, well it's nice seeing you, what are you doing in this building." Stated the lady

"Hello Heather, nice to see you also." Said Lovely as she tried to maneuver pass Heather.

"I had seen Michael not too long ago, have you spoken to him recently," she asked with a smirk on her face. Lovely's back went rod straight at the name and whose mouth it was coming from.

"Last time I checked Heather you were fucking my then boyfriend, so why would I need to speak with him."

"Lovely are you still harping over that whole thing that was college, I did you a favor, besides everyone knew you weren't giving up the goods."

"Is that what you and Michael's pillow talk consisted of, me? Damn even when you had the man in your bed he still thought about me. You must have not been doing what you were supposed to if he was thinking about his girlfriend." Heather's face became beet red you could tell she was angry it looked like smoke was coming from her ears. Lovely smirked at her reaction, again Lovely tried to move pass Heather but she was blocked again by her.

"Darling the only thing Michael and I ever discussed concerning you was how you were lacking in certain intimate areas."

"Please Heather I'm not going to continue to entertain your shenanigans, please move willingly before I move you forcefully."

"Oh did I strike a nerve, any who I'll be sure to tell Michael we saw each other and we caught up." she laughed.

Lovely walked passed her and headed inside the parking garage to her money green Range Rover. She unlocked the doors and got in. She let out a frustrated scream after finally settling into the car. As she was putting her truck in reverse her phone rang. She looked down to see the caller id stated her best friend Marisol. She activated the hands-free device in her car and answered Marisol's call.

"Hey Boo." Marisol yelled into the car. This brought a slight smile onto her face. Marisol was so outgoing and spontaneous there was never a dull moment with her.

"Hey sis. How are you and what are you doing?" She asked

"I'm good, swamped in work you know the deal, how are you? Did you remember Pops retirement party tonight Miss work-a-holic?" Marisol chuckled

"Ha ha ha I did forget but my 'oh so darling' mother called to remind me in a not so nice way. And along with that reminder came another lecture about slowing down and enjoying the fruits of my labor. But anyways I'm on my way to try and find my dad something for tonight, do you have any suggestions?"

"Girl anything you get for your dad he is going to love because it's from you and you are a daddy's girl."

"Yeah I know all of that but I want to make it special, but not cliché and I don't have a lot of time to make it personable. I feel so incompetent right now I couldn't even remember to get my only father a gift for all his hard work, because I'm too busy." Lovely said in a sad tone

"Aww Love bug don't worry you'll get him a great gift I'm sure, you have great taste when it comes to things like that. What else is going on besides that?"

"I just ran into Heather Sidora on my way out, the bitch had the audacity to ask me if I spoke to Michael's ass."

"No, she didn't, do I need to get ratchet on that silicone Barbie?" Marisol asked

"No, we don't need you to go off on her, she's just doing her normal hating she saw me leaving my building and asked in a sarcastic manner what was I doing there; like I didn't have a right to be in that particular office building. I swear that girl eats a bowl of hater flakes for breakfast or something." Lovely chuckled

"Girl you are crazy, hater flakes for real. Well besides that I was calling you to see if you wanted to go out tonight, after Pops party."

"No not tonight I have too many things to catch up on after dad's party."

"Girl you need to live a little, well not a little but a lot, you need to go out have some drinks, find a man and just let him eat the box, knowing you I know you ain't about to give up the whole hot pocket." Marisol laughed

"Shut up, for your info I have a date planned with a man."

"Bitch who?" Marisol asked

"I'm not about to tell you."

"Lovely Marie Daniels, I will cut you, who is it? Do I know him? How did you two meet? Bitch I need the details. As a matter of fact, I'm about to head to lunch meet me at the bistro in fifteen minutes. I need to talk face to face about this." Marisol rambled all at once.

Lovely laughed at her friend "Alright chica I'll see you in fifteen minutes and don't be late I have things to do."

"I'll see you soon." Lovely continued onto her destination anxiously ready to talk to her best friend and confidant. She needed to make sure she was making the right decision in going on a date with Desmond. She contemplated in her thoughts and just drove to the Bistro.

CHAPTER TWO

The ringing of his cellphone caught his attention and could be heard over the slurps and moans of the broad who was topping him off. Shannon reached for his cell phone and glanced down to see who it was before he swiped the green accept button. Shannon looked down to see the woman's head steadily bobbing up and down trying to take his ten-inch dick all to the way back to her throat. Shannon hissed as the woman was accomplishing her mission of exerting pleasure on him.

"Nigga slide up out the pussy" said his best friend Sincere.

"Nigga I'm not even in no pussy yet just getting top." stated Shannon. Sincere laughed and shook his head he knew without a doubt his friend would be fuckin the broad by the time he got off the phone. If he needed Rico to be at a meeting he would give him an earlier time then the meeting would actually start, the nigga was always late for one reason and one reason only pussy. But if he knew money needed to be made he would make sure that he was on time he would stop the bitch in mid stroke and put her out. "What up though B." Rico's New York accent rang in Sincere's ear.

"I need you to meet me at the dealership in about an hour and a half. We got to discuss this next fleet of cars that are supposed to be coming in and we need to make sure that all of the distributors are ready to receive their cars." Sincere was trying to speak in as much code as it allowed just in case the feds were listening. He really did own a dealership that was expecting a shipment of new cars but that part of his business had nothing to do with Rico. Both men were successful in their joint business ventures as well as their personal.

Shannon owned a nightclub as well as a gentlemen's club and a restaurant. When he first entered the drug game he knew he wanted to make moves and big moves at that. Everyone knows the lifespan of a drug pusher on the streets was maybe three to five years before death or prison. Shannon wasn't going that route and neither was Sincere. Best friends since elementary school and partners in crime they've been through it all together. Like the saying goes blood make you related but loyalty makes you family. And that's what Sincere and Shannon were; they were family not by blood but by their loyalty to one another.

"Aight fam I'll be up there soon- damn ma, shit." His breathing started to become choppy.

"Bruh don't be late and why you answering the damn phone if you getting top, I swear you do that type of shit on purpose." Said Sincere

"Nigga you sound mad, I know you ain't have no pussy in a minute" he laughed.

"Yea Aight B don't try to play me with that shit, you know how I get down."

"B I'm 'a see you in a few I'll hit ya up when I'm almost there."

"Nigga do not be late I'm telling you now this is important."

"Aight B one." Rico hung up the phone and dropped his head on the back of the couch. The female who he picked up last night was doing her thing with the little mid-day head. Rico felt the bitch gag on his thick long dick trying to swallow his entire manhood. He grabbed the woman's hair deciding to help her achieve the goal, after all team work makes the dream work and began to fuck her mouth.

"Damn ma swallow that shit." The woman proceeded to use her hands for the remaining parts that she couldn't fit into the mouth she tried to wrap as much of his thick penis around both her hands and it still didn't come together all the way. She bobbed her head up and down as Shannon gripped her hair. She pulled back and licked him from the base of his dick all the way to the top, inserting her tongue in his tip trying to lick and dig the pre-cum that was oozing of his tip. Shannon hissed and grunted while he watched her. She made eye contact with him and put her pouty full lips on his head and sucked it like she was a hoover vacuum.

"Damn ma fuck, spit on it." She gave him a sensual smile and obliged his request she spat on his long thick pole then motioned her head to go back at it. She worked his dick and could see the satisfaction on his face as he looked down at her and her brown round ass was slightly tooted up in the air. He could tell she was playing with her pussy which only aroused him even more. He pushed her head up and lifted her up off her knees and placed her on his lap to straddle him. He grabbed the condom from the night stand. He slipped it on as she positioned herself over his dick and slid down, they both hissed at the contact.

"Mmmmm daddy, you feel so good" she moaned as she bounced up and down on his dick. Shannon was trying to push all 11 inches of his dick in until he hit bottom he thrusted up with every down motion. She began rotating her hips trying to get that g spot friction. Rico slid down the couch and moved his dick until he felt the spongy button he was looking for. He began pounding the fuck out of it

"Mmmmm fuck daddy yes, right there rig-go-t-t THERE"

"This dick hittin the spot huh"

"Y-y-yes fuck!!" she screamed she put her hands on his knees trying to lift up to remove a few inches

"Naw don't do that, take all this of this dick" he knew she was trying to ease up some of the pressure on her g spot. He wasn't letting up he continued to hammer at it and shove his entire dick up in her. He knew he was on a time limit and that he needed to bust one soon cause he had to go meet up with Sin. He grabbed her hands and put them behind her back like he was arresting her and began to drill his dick in her channel.

"O-oh -oh my G-G-GOD!! I'm about to cum, fuck I'm about to." She screamed. She came on him and her juices flowed from between her thighs onto his rod. He stood both of them up and turned her around.

"Bend over and grab them ankles" he stated as he slapped her ass and watched it jiggle. He positioned himself behind her and slowly stroked her with the head first, he teased her with a few more strokes before she started begging for him to put it all the way in. soon her pussy started to drool on his dick. Her moans were all the incentive he needed to push deeper. He sped up his pace and winding his hips trying to reach that spot again. He started jack hammering her trying to knock the bottom out of her pussy. He sped up as he looked down and watched her ass bounce off his dick. She started popping back on him trying to initiate his release. He gripped her hips tightly "ahh fuck, shit move that ass just like that" he lifted his head back and pulled out his dick snatched the condom off and busted all on her ass. He stroked his rod in a jerking motion pushing out the rest of his semen onto her ass and back.

"Get up and go take a shower I need to be somewhere" he slapped her bottom as she stood and turned around and tried to kiss him. He turned his head "I ain't for all that so just do what I asked and be out" She smacked her lips and turned to walk to the guest bathroom to shower.

He walked into his room to and pulled out his drawer to pull out a pair of black boxers and black wife beater. He moved to the enormous bathroom and turned on the control for the six shower heads. He hopped in and let the soft shower heads relax his muscle. He knew he had to be hasty since he had to meet Sincere all the way across town.

~

Lovely gathered her purse and phone and locked her vehicle. As she entered the quaint space she looked around to see if she would spot her friend. Lovely walked up to the hostess table to ask if by chance her friend was already there.

"Hello welcome to D'Noir Bistro how many will be in your party?" The blonde-haired hostess asked sizing Lovely up.

"Well actually I was trying to see if you had already seated a young woman. Her name is Marisol and I was trying to see if she left her name at the hostess station." Lovely asked. The petite hostess stared for a brief moment before she looked at her list to see if Marisol's name would register. When she spotted Marisol's name she smirked and nodded her head.

"Yes the beautiful Latina woman." The Hostess' snicker came off as snobby. The Hostess smirked and gestured for Lovely to follow her.

"Your friend walked in here with those traffic stopping curves." the Hostess laughed. Lovely didn't see the humor and her expressionless faced showed it. The Hostess elaborated, "She literally stopped traffic when she walked in, some drivers were gawking so hard at her, and even a few got out of their cars to approach her." Lovely just shook her head and smirked because she believed every word the blonde said. She could also hear the jealousy in her tone. Lovely just chuckled, her best friend was fuckin' bad and she knew it.

Lovely was just as gorgeous as her best friend, her looks complimented her personality she was beautiful inside and out. Lovely received attention from men and women, her honey colored almond shaped eyes sparkled on their own. Lovely had full plump lips that required no fillers. Her slim frame was packaged perfectly, she had full perky breast, a toned flat stomach, full round hips and a plump round ass to match.

But, Marisol she was an entirely different story. Her body was crazy; women paid thousands of dollars to have a body like hers. Her full D cup breast that accentuated down to her taunt waist and tight abs, her full hips and that ass of hers was just as ridiculous. When people finally finished gawking at her body and worked their way to her face they were equally pleased. She had full plump lips, a straight Anglo-Saxon nose and exotic light green eyes that almost looked clear. Men wanted her with heated passion, while women's pores seeped green with envy when she was around.

As the hostess directed her to patio table, Marisol stood up when she saw her friend approach. She smiled and greeted her with a hug and kiss on the cheek. "Thank you miss." Lovely directed to the hostess who looked at Marisol with a jealous glare. Marisol took notice of the hostess' face and gave a scowl in return. Lovely saw this and looked back at her friend.

The hostess cleared her throat "You are welcome, you ladies enjoy your meal" The hostess replied with sarcasm dripping with every word. The friends hugged each other and took a seat; as they sat down they looked at each other and then began to laugh. They were used to the jealous looks and remarks from women so they just brushed it off.

"She mad or nah?" Lovely laughed out.

"What did you do Mari?" Marisol laughed and shrugged her shoulders and replied "I didn't do shit but be me, I can't control who's gawking or flirting with me. I guess she mad that I had someone's attention but who cares. Anyways don't be coy spill the tea"

Lovely was slightly nervous to tell her friend about accepting her date with Desmond; she knew she wouldn't be judgmental in the least, she knew her friend was going to keep it real on so many levels. Lovely picked up her menu and scanned the specials, she already knew what she wanted to order but she just browsed to see if anything caught her eye. Lovely looked up to see Marisol glaring at her. "Bitch you already know what you want to order so put the menu down and talk." Marisol demanded.

The waiter shortly approached their table more than ready to take their order. The handsome man looked like he was still in college but had a nice physique. He looked like he spent some time in the gym and he had a perfect smile. "Hello Ladies, I see your friend has arrived." He stated to Marisol with a wink. Marisol just sexily licked her lips and shrugged her shoulders. She crossed her legs and her dress slightly moved up her toned olive skin thighs. The young waiter's eyes casually followed the hem of Marisol's dress, taking in her thick thighs. He turned his eyes on her for the briefest moment and his smile got wider. Lovely cleared her throat before giving a pointed look at her friend that registered as stop flirting. Marisol blushed and went back to stare at the young man.

" Ladies I'm Tyrell, it is a pleasure to serve you. What can I get you ladies to drink?" He asked.

"Well I'm actually ready to order I'll have the Dijon chicken with asparagus and pilaf rice, with a glass of Merlot." Lovely advised the waiter

"I'll have the filet mignon medium rare with grilled shrimp and steamed vegetables. And I'll have a glass of D 'sati Moscato." Marisol stated.

"I'll put those orders in right away ladies and will be out with your salads and bread. And if there is absolutely anything you need please let me know." Tyrell walked away to go put in their orders. Marisol leaned over to watch him walk away, she thought he had a nice firm ass and his walk made her think about what she could do with him. She arched her eyebrow in a naughty way before pulling her gaze to her friend.

"You are too much" Lovely commented. "Could you get the look of lust out of your eyes for just one moment?"

"Hey don't be made at me because I like what I see. I just might take him up on his offer to serve me." Marisol said.

Lovely just shook her head she knew her friend had a healthy sex life so it was no surprise at her remark. They had been friends ever since Lovely moved to New York for school. They both went to NYU for school with Lovely majoring in accounting and Marisol in marketing. They were roommates Lovely's freshman year and from that point on they were best friends. The fact that Marisol was older by two years made Lovely feel like she had a big sister and a best friend.

"So, bitch spill the tea who are you going out with?" Marisol asked. Their drinks and salads arrived by another waiter other than Tyrell.

"Well I need your advice first before I tell you and I need you to be real honest with me don't hold back, ok."

"Of course, Love when do I ever hold back with you, hell with anybody unless its work related." She responded,

"What are your feelings on mixing business and pleasure? Would you ever date a fellow colleague?" Lovely asked.

"My honest opinion is that I don't think it mixes at all, someone is bound to get hurt and that will mess with the business part of your relationship. Now if the two-people involved know for certain that it's just sex and no strings attached then I say go for it, have an office fuck or two. Get it in on your lunch break, on the conference room table, be adventurous but know the boundaries. Why what happened?"

"Well that's why I wanted your opinion. Desmond and I were in my office today and we were talking and one minute he is giving me a neck and back massage and it was turning me on like I never would have imagined."

"Wait Desmond your business partner Desmond?"

"Yes Des, Desmond Bryans, my business partner Marisol."

"NO! Do not do it, I repeat don't do it. Forget what I just said. I always suspected that he wanted more than a business relationship with you. This would ruin your friendship and business relationship Lovely, only because I don't think you are ready to settle with anyone yet. You're too career driven for a relationship, but anyway continue I know there's more."

Their entrees were presented by Tyrell, he placed the dishes down for each of them. "Is there anything else I can get you ladies?" They both shook their heads no and Marisol winked at him.

"As I was saying before I was rudely interrupted and slightly lectured, Desmond was giving me a massage and soon his hands started to lower and I became flushed and hot. I wanted him to continue his path I could feel my flesh starting to burn by his touch. We were interrupted by Sasha when she entered the room and we jumped back like we were caught doing something. But the entire time his fingers were touching my skin I was imagining his hands going to other places and I'm pretty sure I moaned out loud." She looked at Marisol to grasp her expression which was one of shock.

"After Sasha entered and left we began talking about business then somehow it drifted to him telling me he has had feelings for me for a while. He asked me out on a date and after continuous persuasion I finally said yes. As he was about to leave he bent down and kissed me. I mean it wasn't a tongue battling toe curling kiss it was just a 'caught me off guard' type of kiss." She stopped to take a sip of her wine. "Now that you've heard do you think I should still go out with him?"

"I'm shocked that you allowed him to get that close to your body." Marisol laughed "I feel that it's not wise to start an intimate relationship with him. I say go out to dinner just because you've already accepted and just let him know that it would be the one and only because you don't mix business and pleasure and that you only want a platonic and outstanding business relationship with him." She sipped her wine and took a bite out of her chicken. As she finished chewing she told Lovely, "What you were feeling when he was touching you is desire, you and I both know why that is and if that's what you are needing from someone you need to go out and find that person. But not Desmond it would fail on many ends. I don't understand how you have gone this long without it but hey everyone is different."

Lovely looked out at the hustle and bustle of the corner and pondered on everything that her friend stated. She knew she was right and that she needed to go out and mingle. Lovely felt that the timing was just not right. They finished up their meals and were idly talking. "Do you have an idea of what you are getting Pops?" Marisol asked referring to Lovely's father who in a way was like a father figure to her as well.

"No that's why the majority of my day will be spent looking for, I might do something crazy and go and buy him a real fast car like a Maserati or something, my mom would have a cow if I did that." Marisol laughed at her best friend. Lovely was never a last-minute person so Marisol knew she had no clue what to get her own father.

"You should do it I would like to see the look on Mom's face. I'll even go in on it with you." Lovely pondered on the gift for her father. Tyrell approached their table and asked if they wanted dessert. They both declined the offer. Tyrell walked back with their check, he placed the check on the table, he turned to Marisol with a smile and said "It's been a real pleasure to serve you I hope you would allow me to do it again in a more private setting" Marisol looked at the lustful gaze he was giving off. It made her shift in her seat as her panties became a little damp at the thought of what he could do to her body. She blushed and cleared her throat before speaking.

 "Well I'd be more than happy to seek your services in a more private setting."

~

Lovely walked into the dealership browsing the selection of designer automobiles. The colors, sleek selection and designs were going to make the decision hard. She looked at the price tags on some of the models. Now she had to convince herself to drop two hundred or more stacks on the luxury automobile. Lovely was focused on the cars, she didn't hear the person approaching her. The exotic fragrance that wafted her senses had her intoxicated. She could feel him standing behind her the heat emanating from his body.

"Excuse me miss is there anything I can help you with?" The sexy baritone voice made the hair on the back of her neck stand. She turned around hoping the sexy voice shared an even sexier face. Lovely turned around and gasped at the sight before her. There stood the sexiest man she had ever seen. Her eyes stared into the most beautiful bedroom eyes, she looked deeper trying to figure out what color they were. They looked blue with purple irises and looked like they could see through a person's soul. They slowly started to change colors and Lovely had to pry her eyes away from his. She looked at the straight nose that led down to the set of perfect pink lips. Her panties were getting moist just looking at them, when she saw the pink tongue dart out to caress the beautiful set of lips it was in that moment she wished she could be that tongue. The strong powerful structure of his jawline with the goatee neatly lined up. Her eyes traveled over his physique and she could tell he was built. The biceps that outlined his suit jacket, the lean tight torso to the firm thighs. She could see an outlined print of what look like a monster waiting to be unleashed, she gasped and looked back up at the handsome man and said "Fuck me."

CHAPTER THREE

I was sitting there talking to Rico about the newest shipment that was coming in from South America. I felt comfortable speaking in my office since I always have it swept for any recording devices anytime I leave. I was actually surprised that Rico showed up on time, but I kind of figured he would. Anytime it's money involved he gone be here, but if it's just to meet up just because, he gone be later that late. He would be late for his own funeral if he could. I sat there listening to him tell me about his latest broad, I had to shake my head back and forth about how he basically kicked the girl out his crib after he got his shit off. I swear this boy is straight wild when it comes to the females. Not saying I'm not but I tend to have a little more class with them then he does, and some of my other niggas that I get up with. Make no mistake I treat a hoe like a hoe, if you gone act like a hoe I'm going to treat you as such. But I do have respect for the ones that are independent and loyal.

"Nigga you know mixing business with a thot ain't nothing but trouble. I thought you had a strict no fucking the staff policy?"

"Shit, nigga I do, but shorty must have been on her pill Cosby shit." He stated. I had to laugh at his remark. We both knew that he was just making an excuse as to why he slept with one of his workers, but the shit was funny.

"Son you straight wildin'. You know shorty ain't slip you shit. She probably said some fly shit and you was feelin it."

"Man get the fuck on with that, I just needed to get my shit off and the bitch was there and more than willing. I thought for sure shorty was gone die if she didn't get a chance to taste my dick, straight thirstin'." Rico had zero filter, he said what he wanted whenever he wanted. I was used to it, I respected him more for it. I had to get the meeting back on track, we had important business to tend to.

"We need to set up a meeting with all the main distributors to make sure that they set on getting the product and they have our money ready no questions asked." I said to Rico.

"Are we going to supply that down south nigga and his peoples?" He asked.

I wasn't too sure if I wanted to bring in any new customers to the operation, I'm trying to fall back from this shit in a few years and I don't need to get caught up because I let some snakes in the garden. I let out a slight sigh, I was unsure, but I knew one thing all business ain't good business. Now I just had figure out if these niggas business would be profitable.

"Man how much we know about these niggas? How we know they gone have our money, shit we working with pure and last time I checked fish scale ain't cheap. Shit, where these niggas come from anyway and how they know to connect with us?"

See these were things I was skeptical of. I only deal with certain people; you have to be able to buy no less than ten bricks at twenty-five stacks a piece. And depending on if you buy more than ten I'll work with you on lowering the price. I supply wholesale, none of that a kilo here and there; my enterprise is kingpin status fuck around and catch a rico charge. That nickel and diming corner boy was never really my style but we had to start somewhere. We built this empire from the ground up, Rico and I had to start from the bottom; even though my father was already the connect. We was still in the kitchen cooking up that shit.

My father would always tell us we needed to start off at the bottom. We needed to know how it felt to have to grind on the streets from sun up to sun down. He said we needed to know how desperate fiends were to get that rock, they would so much as sell their child and their fuckin soul for a hit. His lessons of starting from the bottom, showed us who were loyal to the code and it helped weed out the snakes. The grind revealed how grimey a nigga could be, your street corner competitors had no problem dropping information to the jakes just to obtain your corners. I've been in this shit for so long, far longer than its intentional life span. I've collected my stripes of the streets and dope game in more ways than one. I'm a fucking General in this game and my product and business reflects as such. I can't be out here giving buying weight 101 lessons.

"Man, King trying to get them on, he says they on the up and up and they just trying to get they work up. They trying to take the shit back to where they lay their heads." Rico explained.

"I'm saying tho, I'm sure we should have somebody near them that can supply them. I don't understand why they had to come out here for work?"

"What part of the south they from?" I asked, we had territories all over the U.S. Our hands reached from here to several countries overseas.

"Atlanta, Alabama some shit like that" Rico absently stated.

"Well how do you feel about it?" I continuously had my eyes locked on the security monitors that were leveled at the showroom floor.

Rico is my partner and right hand so his opinion mattered; we were equals in the operation; no man bigger than the other. I think that's why we've been friends for so long. We always have each other's back from day one. Me and this nigga been friends since elementary and it ain't gone stop until we both in the dirt.

"Let's go ahead and set up the meeting with King and then go from there. Put that lick on them see how them niggas react to that shit. Plus, I want to know why they trying to link up with us instead of where they at."

"You right, you right, let's do that th-" I was unable to finish when I looked at the monitor. Somehow, I was transfixed at the beautiful woman. The way she walked into the dealership damn near demanded my attention. Shit I was actually stuck. Her walk was so sensual; her legs looked a mile long and were perfect for wrapping around my waist. She was eyeing some of the Maserati's that were on the showroom floor.

"Bruh, Bruh... Sincere!!" Rico yelled. I turned my head to focus back on him but through my peripherals I checked to make sure she was still there.

"What nigga?" I asked

"What done snatch your attention fam?"

I turned the monitor on to the 55-inch television that was hanging up on the wall. I focused on the camera that she was near. I zoomed in on her, while I tried to take everything in. She was beautiful from what the camera allowed me to see, I had to get downstairs to the showroom floor and get a better view.

"Damn shorty bad" I heard Rico say.

"You ain't never lied. I think I need to make my way downstairs to show some phenomenal customer service" I said turning on the charm.

"Oh, so now meeting adjourned huh." He said sarcastically.

"What day and time you want to set up the meeting with King and these out of town niggas, Mr. Casanova?" He asked.

"Man, whenever it's convenient but not too soon I might be pre-occupied for a few days." I said as I nodded my head towards the monitor.

"Man, that girl ain't bout to give you no play. She doesn't look like a fuck on a first, second or third date bruh. You got a better chance with the hoes at my spot then with her. She looks like the three-month rule to me." Rico assessed the beautiful woman on the monitor.

"Nigga we'll see; from what I can tell right now she don't look like a hoe but you know they got them suit wearing briefcase toting hoes now a day, hell look at Olivia Pope." Rico started laughing really hard. He knew I watched Scandal and he always tried to call me out on it, saying it was a show for bitches. I just shrugged my shoulders at him. Fuck that Kerry Washington is fine as hell.

"Man get the fuck outta here with that pussy show you talking about. Real niggas don't watch that shit. Real niggas watch Power, I'm going to revoke your hood status for real." He said. I stood up to walk out the door. I grabbed my suit jacket and checked myself in the mirror just for good measure.

"What you bout to get into?" I asked him.

"I'm about to head to the restaurant to check upon shit, light paperwork shit like that, I'll set that meeting up with them niggas when I get to club this evening."

"Aight let me know the play and I'll probably stop by the club tonight anyway, shit a nigga need some ass shaking, titties bouncing all up on him tonight."

"You giving up on shorty already, I know you know I'm right about her. But let me know what happens."

"Aight one"

CHAPTER FOUR

She couldn't believe those words came out of her mouth. From the slight smirk on his handsome face she knew without a doubt that he heard her loud and clear. Lovely looked around to see if anyone else had heard her also. There was a sexy milk chocolate man walking by them that had a mischievous glint in his slanted grey eyes. She knew he must have heard her as well. She was mortified to say the least. She didn't understand how her reaction to one man could make her act out of character. But she looked back at him then realized this man was sexy beyond dreams and not only were her soaking panties evidence enough but her outburst sure did give it away as well.

"As much as I would like to take immense pleasure on your offer, how about I show you what I have to offer first, I mean car wise of course." Sincere said with a wink. He was astounded by her beauty. Her beautiful doll eyes drew you in. Her full pouty lips made him want to know what she tastes like and if she knew what to do with those full lips. He shook the thoughts away and tried to get back to business. His eyes roamed her body from head to toe and he was pleased with what he saw. The camera didn't do her body or beauty the justice as being front and center. Her mouth formed into a circle as she began to speak.

"I'm so sorry please excuse me. I - I've never said" she glanced down at the ground trying to collect her thoughts and actually form complete sentences.

Sincere tried to hold in a chuckle at how flustered and embarrassed she was. Her face was red from her neck to the top of her face. "Look its ok, you don't have to explain. I understand how sexy I am, I would have said the same thing if I were looking at me for the first time too." He plastered on a big smile. He was trying to lighten the tension both sexual and physical. She looked back up at him with her eyebrow arched. "Well aren't you mister confident?" She said, he shrugged his shoulders.

"I'm in the presence of a beautiful woman, confident is the only thing I know how to be. But on a lighter note how may I assist you miss..."

"Lovely, I'm Lovely Daniels."

"Beautiful name for an even more beautiful woman it fits you."

"Ummm thanks, I'm looking to buy a car"

"Well what other reason would you be here for?" he stated, she glared at him for stating the obvious. She was a mess she couldn't think straight and look at him at the same time. She needed to gain her confidence back.

"I saw you looking at the Maserati, is that what you're interested in?"

"This is actually a gift that I'm looking for."

"For a man or woman?"

"It's for a very special guy in my life."

"Damn he must be well worth it, this is a hell of a gift if you ask me, and shouldn't your man be buying you the car, not the other way around." Sincere inquired. Lovely whipped her head up at the comment and smirked *so he thinks it's for my man, well I'll just let him assume, no need to correct him.*

Sincere zeroed in on her lips as she moistened them with the tip of her pink tongue. "Yes I was eyeing the Maserati but the Aston Martin looks appealing as well. The person I'm purchasing this for needs some power behind the wheel it needs to caress the curves and knows how to throttle in the right gears" She smirked at the last remark. She knew the image she was painting and couldn't help but feel hot and bothered on the inside. That's what he gets for assuming. She mentally rolled her eyes. "I could show you a few more of our other cars we do have some Ferrari's, Maybachs and Mercedes. I don't have it here but I do have a few Rolls Royce" He extended his arm out to have her follow him to a different part of the showroom. She listened as he explained the different cars and the horse power and all that jazz. Lovely was too busy staring back and forth from his lips, face and his ass. Sincere could feel her eyes on him as he was turned around trying to get the information off the car that she said she was interested in. She was going to purchase the Aston Martin but she wanted the color customized. "So beautiful what color were you looking at?"

"It's Lovely, mister..." she paused because she realized this entire time she didn't ask for his name. Her raised perfectly arched eyebrow indicated that she was waiting on a response. Sincere smiled he knew what he wanted her to call him. But telling her daddy might just piss off the gorgeous woman. Before he could give her the answer he was interrupted by his receptionist. "Excuse me but you have a call on line three it's your father." Sincere tore his eyes away from Lovely to look at his receptionist her face was twisted like she just got done sucking on a lemon. He tilted his head trying to figure out what her problem was. He knew he shouldn't have fucked her that one time now she sprung off the dick.

He turned and smiled at Lovely. He looked around to find his best salesman he wanted to pass the commission onto him and have him finish assisting her. Sincere called over Manny and explained to him what Lovely was wanting to purchase.

"By the way what color and when did you need it by?" He asked with a smile.

"It's going to be candy apple red and by 7 pm tonight." She said as she put on her sweetest smile and batted her long thick eye lashes. From the look on his and the salesman's faces it didn't look like that was possible.

"Tonight as in today?" Manny asked. She nodded her head and plastered on another brilliant smile. Sincere smiled back and shook his head.

"Damn baby that's not only short time its damn near impossible last minute." The way he said baby didn't get past Lovely, she imagined it being said during sex and a blush crept onto her face. She darted her eyes to hide her passionate thoughts. The look or blush didn't miss Sincere he was too observant he had to be. He told Manny to make some calls to other dealerships to see if they had the car she wanted to purchase. He also instructed him to waive the customization fees and apply a discount for her.

"There's no need for any discount I'm aware this is last minute request. I'm willing to pay the cost for all the features and add-ons."

"150,000 is a lot for a lady like yourself to pay, I would take the discounts that are being offered." At that moment everyone turned to look at the receptionist Monica who stood there with her hand resting on her hips in her 'round the way' girl stance. Both Sincere and Lovely went to speak at the same time but Lovely words beat him to it.

"Excuse you first off my monthly salary alone is four times more than what you make in a year and by looking at those knock off Louboutin's you're wearing I'm sure you earn around twenty-five to twenty-eight thousand. Secondly if I wanted to I could buy you this damn car, that damn car, and that one over there today and still be financially stable. Don't assume every female needs a hand out from a man or a "discount" I can pay for my own. Now if you don't mind

I'd like to purchase my car full price and be on my way. Don't you have phones to answer, papers to staple and smiles to give out?" Manny looked on with an open mouth at Lovely's response.

Sincere's stood with his jaw tight he was grinding the back of his teeth from holding in his temper. He was ready to curse out Monica for being rude to a customer. Lovely turned towards Manny and asked if he was ready to get everything finalized. Sincere grabbed Monica's arm and practically dragged her towards the stairs to his office. Forgetting that his dad had called and probably hung up by now if he didn't call his cell he knew it wasn't too important. He swiped his thumb over the fingerprint recognition the doors automatically opened. He nudged Monica in the room before closing the door. He waited thirty more seconds to give his bug sweeping software its full time to work. Plus he needed to calm down. Monica went to sit down on the couch but before she could Sincere cold even tone broke her motion.

"Did I fuckin tell you to sit down? Let me know something Monica what reason did you have to insult the customer like that? Do you know you could have cost me money?" Monica just stood there with her arms folded and a mug on her face. She proceeded to look at her manicure nails like she was bored.

"ANSWER ME!!" he yelled causing her to jump back.

"Why are you yelling, so I was a little rude to her did you not hear the way she spoke to me like I'm some low budget classless bitch. Shit with the way you were smiling and flirting with her. I'm sure you were probably too busy staring at her ass." Sincere tried to count to ten in his head but he only made it to three.

"Yo what the fuck is yo problem. Why you so worried about what I'm doing? Yo ass is supposed to be doing your job which is picking up a fucking phone directing calls and greeting customers, not worrin about me. Seeing as how I'm a grown ass man and I ain't never needed a bitch to worry about my shit. That whole jealous shit you just pulled out there is for the birds and bums I ain't with that. We need to be very clear you and I are not together; one fuck and a nut later don't make you my bitch hell not even my side piece. It was a one-time deal so that shit you just did ain't do nothing to change my mind."

Monica's face was scrunched up. She stared at him for a minute or two and was turned on by his aggression she was ready to put mouth, hands, and ass to work. She stalked towards him and they stood face to face she had to tilt her heard up slightly as she was on only several inches shorter to his six- foot three height. She put her hands on his chest and slide them up and down admiring the feel of his toned body beneath her finger tips. Her hands inched further down towards his dick. It was long and thick but she knew he wasn't hard because its full length wasn't present. She started to unzip his pants and slip her hand deep inside to pull out his blessed package. She looked down and admires him, she stroked him to a semi hard arousal, she got down on her knees wetting her mouth preparing to slip his oversized mushroom dick head into her mouth. Planting kisses on and around his head she stroked and kissed until she was ready to taste. She opened her mouth as wide as she could and slipped him in. Using her tongue, she licked him from his base all the way back to the top. She repeated the action again and twirled her tongue around his head. As she prepared to deep throat him his hands grabbed her hair and pulled her mouth away from his still semi aroused python. He stared down at her and pulled her hair back. Her eyes connected with his, while lust shined in hers his had a mischievous glint.

"Were you enjoying yourself?" Monica tried to nod but he still had her hair in a tight grip, so she just smiled.

"I'm glad you were because that's the last time you'll ever get to taste my dick again" with that said he released her hair and zipped himself up. He walked around towards his restroom.

"Now go back out there and do what you're paid to do." He stated as he glared at her from over his shoulders. Monica stood dumfounded her hair was a mess and her pride was on the floor. She walked towards the door and exited the office. Sincere stepped out of the restroom after cleaning himself off. He shook his head and thought about what took place, he wasn't even fully aroused when she was attempting to get him off. That alone should have told her he wasn't feeling her. But some broads need step by step instructions to fully comprehend shit. He sat down and checked his monitor to see if Lovely was still in the building. When he didn't see her on the cameras he assumed she had taken care of everything. He dialed Manny's extension. It rang twice before he greeted him.

"Sup Sin" He answered.

"Did she get everything that she wanted?"

"Yes and no," Sincere was silent as he waited for him to elaborate.

"None of the other dealerships had the color she wanted so she opted to just have it delivered when it was ready to her father's house and she took the pamphlet with a mock key and the key chain to present to him as her gift." Manny informed. Sincere's ears perked up when he heard her the gift was for her father and not her man.

"What was the final price she paid?"

"Man Sin with the upgrades, extended warranties and the customization she paid $190,000." Manny braved himself for the backlash he was about to receive he knew once Sincere heard the amount without the discount he was probably going to be pissed.

"Manny you can't fuckin add or subtract; I said give her a discount. It shouldn't have been that much with the fees waived!" He slightly shouted.

"I tried we debated for ten minutes on it and she wouldn't budge. It was either lose the sale or give her what she wanted and what she wanted was to pay full price bruh." Manny explained.

"Man, alright I see she stubborn." He smirked. Damn baby paid full price for a car that wasn't for her.

"Aye how you know ole girl anyway. I ain't never seen you offer discounts to anybody male, female, celebrity or the mayor." he chuckled out.

"I don't know her I just met her today." Manny pulled the phone away from his ear and stared at it. That gesture was not Sin.

"Nigga why you look like that? You do know I can see yo ass."

"You just caught me off guard with that response. You must be feeling shorty."

"Man dead that. I'll holla at you later and make sure you have all her info in the computer. I'm bout to head up out."

"I got you Boss."

Sincere hung up the phone and sighed. He shook his head back and forth. He collected he things and locked up his safe before departing. As he walked out of the building he thought back to his conversation with Lovely. Damn Ma got my head all fucked up. He got in his all blacked out Tesla Model S and drove off to his parents' estate.

CHAPTER FIVE

As she sat in her walk in closet trying to figure out what to wear for her date with Desmond she looked at all of the clothes and outfits she could wear for tonight. Even with the abundance of clothes she couldn't figure out how to approach the dress code for tonight's dinner. She pondered as she didn't want to send off the wrong message.

Her house phone rang as she walked to retrieve it, she glanced at the delivery receipt to her dad's brand customized Aston Martin. She was happy that everything was in top condition when it arrived. She thought back to the expression on her parent's face when she presented her gift to him. She glanced at the phone's screen and smiled when she seen it was her best friend Marisol. Lovely had not spoken to her since their lunch date last week.

"Hey Boo" Lovely shouted into the phone

"Hola Chica, what are you up to?"

"I'm sitting booty butt naked in my closet trying to figure out what I'm going to wear for tonight."

"Oooh is tonight the night. And booty butt naked huh, well sounds like someone is preparing for a dick down." Marisol laughed into the phone.

"Please that's not going to be the case at all. Now I feel like I need to wear something less revealing. I'm not trying to give him any mixed signals."

"Well then I suggest you wear a moo-moo because anything else you wear tonight is probably going to be tight and right for penetration." Marisol giggled into the phone.

Lovely laughed into the phone, "You're right. Anyways what's up why didn't I see you at dad's party?" Lovely asked while picking up an Alexander McQueen red silk colored mid-thigh dress.

"Girl I had to tend to something." Marisol said without details.

"Uh huh who was he and did he tend to your needs." Lovely said with her lips pursed.

"He was ok."

"Just ok Puchi." Lovely called her by her family given nickname.

"Yeah, I mean I had to give him a few instructions on how to eat the box, he could have used a few more pointers on his stroke game. But myself, I was fuckin fabulous as usual, I put it on him so damn good, he wanted me to stay and cuddle. I was like, pause, I don't cuddle." Lovely shook her head at her friend.

"Well that's what you get for ditching dad's party to sleep with. Wait, who did you sleep with?" Lovely inquired.

"Girl he talked such a good game I had to give him a taste." Marisol explained

"Who Puchi?" Lovely laughed out into the room

"The waiter from the Bistro." Lovely gasped, "Marisol you fucked the waiter!"

After hanging up with Marisol she had about an hour to get dressed. She hopped into her shower and proceeded to clean every inch of her body. After twenty minutes, she decided to get out. Patting herself dry, she placed the wet towel in the hamper. Lovely moved towards her red granite top sink and picked up her moisturizing cream and began to lotion her entire body. Her hair was already done in big flowy curls. She sat at her huge vanity with the dressing room lights surrounding the entire mirror, she couldn't decide if she wanted to do a full face of highlight and contouring or just keep it simple with a light foundation. She lightly brushed her perfectly full natural eyebrows and filled them in a little. She checked for the time, and as if in on queue the doorbell rang.

"Shit, he's already here and I'm not even finished." She said to herself. She proceeded to pick up her dress for the evening and carefully pulled it on. The doorbell chimed again as she headed towards the stairs. "Coming" she called out. She paused and looked at self on the mirror just to make sure nothing was out of place. Her long tresses bounced as she rushed towards the door. She reached for the door knob and pasted a smile on her face. She was indeed nervous, opening the door she exhaled a deep breath. Desmond stood there in tailored black trousers and a royal blue shirt and black blazer. His bright blue eyes took her in and his perfect white smile was shining bright. He looked sexy. She cocked her head to the side a little bit just to take him all in from head to toe. The twinkle in his bedroom eyes was infectious.

"Hello beautiful" He said in his deep baritone voice. He bent down to kiss her cheek.

"Hello Desmond, please come in. I apologize I'm not completely ready. I got distracted and the time flew by before I knew it. I'll only be a few more minutes." She explained

Desmond let out a small chuckle. "I can't believe Miss punctual is actually not ready. You look amazing by the way" He said his smile never faltering.

"Thank you. You look very handsome as well. I'm going to go finish getting ready, ok."

"Yeah, take your time." Desmomd drawled out.

She turned around to head back up the stairs to put the finishing touches on her face and slip on her shoes. As she walked she felt like he was staring at her. She turned her head while walking up the stairs only to see his eyes skillfully focused on the sway of her hips. His eyes trailed up to her face and he winked and threw on his dazzling smile. She smirked and put an extra twist in her hips since he was watching.

Parking his Maybach in front of valet, Desmond tossed the keys to the valet driver. He jogged over to Lovely's side of the car and carefully opened and extended his hand to let her out. She stared up at him with a smile on her face and accepted his hand. She read the name of the restaurant. Lovely had read reviews on the restaurant and knew there was a six-month waiting list just to dine at the five star establishment. She was impressed that Desmond could get a reservation on such short notice. She wanted to ask who he had to ask a favor for in order to pull this off. As they entered they walked up to the Maître D station.

"Hello and welcome to SJs what is the name of your reservation?" The Maître D asked the couple. Lovely looked to Desmond to give the answer.

"Bryans. Desmond Bryans." He gave the Maître D.

The Maître D looked down at the list and spotted the name. He smiled back at them and gestured his hand to follow the hostess. Lovely admired the decor and ambiance of the restaurant the Roman columns and fixtures brought out elegance. The colors were vibrant with sunburst oranges and Moroccan reds that mingled in with blues so deep they looked like the seas of the Greek Isles and purples so royal they were fit for kings and queens. Lovely thought whoever chose the colors had immaculate taste. They were seated and the Maître D asked if they would like to hear the wine selections. Desmond shook his head and ordered a vintage wine that was two hundred and fifty dollars a bottle. Lovely looked at him like he was crazy and just shook her head on the inside. If he wanted to blow his money on a bottle she knew they weren't going to finish, then so be it.

"Des, to be a financial manager you sure know how to spend frivolously." she stated to him.

He smiled at her and stated, "Well I'm hoping for more than one date and I consider it an investment if things progress between us in more than a business partner relationship. I already told you how I feel about you, now I just figure I'd show you as well." His eyes bore into hers.

He was entrapped at how the lighting almost made her eyes seem to glow. She was beyond beautiful to him. He could honestly say that he was nervous. He finally gotten a date with Lovely, and he was going to make the most of it since he kind of knew her apprehensions on dating. "Well I guess I'll drink to that." she laughed out. Their bottle of wine was brought to their table and glasses were poured. They clinked their glasses and drank the crisp distinctive long finish wine. The waiter informed them of the chef specials. Roasted Quail in a wine sauce with Cous Cous, Braised Lamb Steaks with Pesto over rice pilaf. The waiter allowed them a moment to mull over their selection.

"Did you have an idea of what you'd like to eat?" Desmond asked Lovely.

"I was thinking about going with the lamb steaks. They sound good. But I must ask, how did you get reservations for this place at such a short notice?" Lovely inquired.

He chuckled and wonder if he should tell her the truth. He briefly thought it over and figured why the hell not.

"Well I actually had my name on the waiting list for some time now. But when you agreed to go on a date with me I called in a favor to the owner. We went to college together so he got my name moved up on the list." He explained.

"Who were you planning on taking once your name did come up?"

"This amazing, beautiful woman that caught my eye a few years back. I've just been waiting on the opportunity to ask her on a date." Lovely could feel her face heat up.

"Well I'm glad you asked and I'm happy to be here." Lovely stated

"Oh, I-I wasn't talking about you. There was another woman I was waiting to take here." He said. Lovely looked at him waiting for the punch line, when he didn't crack a smile she felt embarrassed.

"Oh...Um well..." she had no words. Desmond laughed out loud, "I'm kidding Lovely. You should have seen your face."

Lovely smacked her lips and threw a piece of bread at him. Before she could respond the waiter showed up to take their orders. After giving their food selection there was an awkward silence. Lovely wasn't sure if she should bring up her feelings about dating him. She didn't want to ruin the night and it had already begun. As if reading her mind Desmond spoke of it.

"You're still not sure of this, us... If there is going to be us huh?" he asked

"To be quite honest, no I'm not. I don't want to ruin the relationship we have now. Des, I know me and I know I'm a workaholic. I'm trying to figure out where a relationship would fit into my life. Then the fact that it's you and not just some random guy. I can only think about what if it doesn't work out then how would we interact around the office with each other."

"I understand but how would you know what it could be like if you don't take the risk? Relationships are a gamble and we both know about those in the business that we are in. If it doesn't work out then it doesn't. I'll move on and I'm sure you will and everything will stay the same, we'll still be business partners. I wouldn't do anything to jeopardize our friendship. All I'm asking you for is to take the risk with me." Their food arrived and they ate and talked. They shared stories of their childhood and their years in undergrad.

"So, you mean to tell me that you Miss prim and proper had to spend the night in jail for indecent exposure. I don't believe it I need to see proof." He laughed out.

"Yes it's true I was so pissed off at Marisol for accepting that damn dare from the other sorority. Our entire line had to do it and somehow, she and I were the only ones caught! My mom found out because she had a cousin of mine supposedly keeping an eye on me. I was so scared when I spoke to her I knew she was just going to fly out to whoop my ass." They both laughed at the story. Desmond started to tell her one of his embarrassing stories that got him into trouble with his parents. Lovely was focused on what he was saying until someone caught her attention. She saw him walking toward the back of the restaurant. Her eyes followed him to where the Maître D was seating him and his guest. As if he sensed someone staring at him, he turned around. His eyes searched the restaurant until they landed on hers they stared at each other and he smiled. Lovely wasn't sure why she didn't stop staring at him when he turned around it was like she was drawn to him, like a moth to a flame. Her line of vision was blocked from being able to see him. Someone had approached their table. Lovely looked up to see who was in her way.

"Well this is interesting seeing you here Lovely." Heather said.

"Heather." was all Lovely said before for going back to her meal. Lovely hoped the gesture wasn't lost on Heather, she wanted her to leave just as fast as she had appeared. Heather took slight to Lovely trying to dismiss her. Heather looked over at Lovely's dinner guest. A taunting smirk appeared on her thin lips

"Hello handsome. Nice to meet you I'm Heather Sidora." She introduced herself to Desmond.

"Nice to meet you I'm Desmond Bryans."

"Oh you're her business partner. For a moment there I actually thought she was on a date." Heather chuckled. Lovely was about to respond with some uncouth words but Desmond had spoken before she could.

"Actually, we are on a date that you are interrupting, so if you'd be kind and leave us to it. My beautiful date and I would appreciate it" He explained to Heather in his baritone voice. Heather was dumbstruck by his response.

"Wow. I'm surprised at you Lovely, dating and then dating outside of your race at that. I guess since you couldn't handle all that chocolate with Michael you decided to give vanilla a try. Desmond is it don't put all your eggs in one basket with this one. Why I'd bet she's sti--" Lovely interrupted her before she could say to much more.

"Listen, Heather you know that you and I aren't friends. The fact that you're over here in my space is frankly making me and my date uncomfortable. So again, if you'd please leave us to finish our meal in peace. I know a person like you wouldn't understand that two's a company and three's a crowd. I'll just say it in a way that you will, bitch leave."

Heather huffed out her distaste for the words that were used, "There is no need to be uncouth Lovely. Desmond is it? When you realize what a waste of time this is please give me a call. I know a few things that I can do with a handsome man like you." Heather said as she tried to hand him her card. Lovely stood abruptly out of her chair.

"Bitch didn't I just say..." Before Lovely could react Desmond gently pulled her back down. Lovely could see people staring at the commotion at her table. At this point she could care less. Heather was being disrespectful. Lovely looked around and saw him looking at her. It was then she started to feel a little bit embarrassed by her reaction. She was about to speak but the Maître D walked over and politely asked Heather to leave the table. Lovely was surprised that she and Desmond weren't asked to leave as well. She looked at Desmond and apologized for her outburst. He told her he understood and asked if she wanted to finish dinner and dessert.

"I'm going to head to the ladies' room. I'll be right back." Lovely stood and walked towards the restrooms.

As she entered she pulled out her cell phone to call Marisol. Her friend's line just rang and rang. She decided to not leave a voicemail. She texted her to call back when she got in. Lovely washed her hands and re-applied her lipstick before heading back out. As she walked out she bumped into something solid and almost unmovable like a wall. Before she flew to the ground, hands outstretched and caught her by the waist. She looked up to see who or what she bumped into. Her breath was lodged in her throat. Suddenly heat arose where he was holding her. She couldn't breathe or speak.

"You need to exhale before you pass out. You're turning a deep red ma." He said in that sexy voice.

Lovely blinked a few times. The pressure in her lungs started to ache then she remembered that she needed to breathe she just forgot how. Sincere was afraid that she was actually going to pass out from holding her breath. He inched closer and suddenly his lips were a pinch away from hers.

"Breathe baby." He whispered on her lips.

All of a sudden it was like he breathed life back into her with those two simple words. Lovely exhaled her breathe onto his lips. Sincere looked down at her lips and wanted to taste them so bad. Lovely's eyes also darted down to his lips without conscious thought Lovely licked her lips, with that motion because they were so close her tongue lightly swiped his. Sincere let out a small groan and bent his head to go in and bring their lips together. Suddenly they heard someone clear their throat and the haze that they were in cleared up quickly. Sincere looked behind him, his hands still attached to Lovely's waist. He saw it was one of the waitress.

"Ummm excuse me Mr. Riz, but I'm in need of the lady's room." She gestured at the entrance.

Realizing that they were in fact blocking the ladies room entrance they pulled apart. Lovely eyes darted everywhere but at him. Sincere saw this and thought it was funny. Ten minutes ago, she was ready to throw down on some female now she couldn't even look at him.

"You are an interesting woman Lovely." He said to her.

"Why do you say that?" She asked him.

"One moment you do or say something off the wall. Then the next you turn shy and bashful. It's interesting ma."

"Oh." Was her only response. She seemed to be at a loss for words again around him.

"If you would excuse me I need to get back to my date." Lovely went to walk around him he caught her by the waist and said,

"She's right you know. He doesn't seem like your type at all."

"How would you know what my type is? You've spoken to me less than thirty minutes in one day. Now you think you know what my type is."

"I'm usually a great judge of character. And yes, from speaking to you for thirty minutes I can tell you ole boy ain't for you."

"Well it's none of your business anyway. Now if you would please let me go so I can go back to enjoying my evening."

"Yeah alright ma, but let me ask you this when you leave here tonight who's going to invade your dreams. Because since the day that we met I can't stop dreaming about you allowing me to, how did you say it that day to 'fuck you.' And every dream ends up the same you riding on top of my dick effortlessly while biting that sexy ass bottom lip, rotating those hips while I'm thrusting in you every time you come down. My dick is hitting on your spot and right before you cum I seem to wake up. I guess I need to feel it in its real form, how beautiful you will look when I'm making you cum."

Lovely couldn't breathe properly, instead of responding to him she just walked back towards her table. She could feel her desire rise between her thighs. She saw Desmond stand as she was about to sit down. She looked at him and moved towards him. She looked up at him with those deep blue eyes and decided what the hell why not.

Her arms wrapped around his neck he bent down kind of confused by the sudden change but didn't say anything. Lovely kissed his lips as he kissed back she slightly opened her mouth and allowed his tongue to graze against hers. Out of her peripherals she saw him walking back to his table. Her adrenaline started pumping and she put more passion into the kiss with Des. Her tongue searched for his and they began to tongue wrestled. After hearing about his dreams, she could only think about her dreams of him. Them kissing passionately, her sucking on his tongue like she was doing to Desmond. Him taking her bottom lip into his mouth and nibbling on it. His hands squeezing her ass and lifting her up to wrap her legs around his waist. She had to pull back to breathe. Desmond was panting just as heavy. She saw the lust in his eyes. She could feel eyes on her and as true to her thoughts she saw him looking at her with a knowing look like he could read her thoughts and know she was thinking about him with that kiss. Desmond cleared his throat and asked,

"Umm are you ready for desert?" Desmond asked her.

"No I'm ready to go if you are?" She said

"Yeah let me settle the check." Desmond got up to find the waiter to pay for their meal.

Lovely sat down and started to try to put some sense in what she was doing or going to do. The hairs on the back of neck stood up. She felt his body heat. Next to her neck. She felt his breath on her ear, "Nice show you put on there. Now I know you will be dreaming about me tonight, freaky dreams ma." He placed a kiss on the back of her neck before walking towards the exit.

Lovely was flustered. She was thinking about this man and still didn't know who he was. She was daydreaming when Desmond walked back to the table. He smiled at her and asked if she was ready. She got up with her clutch purse in hand, ready for whatever. They walked outside and waited on valet to bring the vehicle around. As she was looking to her right she saw him just about to get into his car.

"Mr. Riz, Mr. Riz." She saw a waitress yelling for his attention. He looked up spotted Lovely and winked.

"Mr. Riz you forgot your phone." She said.

"Thanks Melanie." He reached into his pocket to tip her. He handed her the two crisp one hundred-dollar bills.

"Oh thanks Mr. Riz." She said beaming at the quick tip she just received.

"Please call me Sincere." Lovely watched the quick exchange and finally heard his name. Sincere Riz she thought. She now knew the name of the handsome man who had captivated her dreams for the last few nights. Lovely saw his car speed off into the night as Desmond's approached. He opened the car door for her waiting for her to get in. He jogged to the driver side. He turned to her and asked,

"Your place or mine?" He asked.

"My place, definitely mine." She responded.

As they left the restaurant Lovely phone buzzed. She looked down to see a text from Marisol.

Mami Marisol: Hey just saw your missed call. How did it go? I hope you let him down easy. Call me bitch!!!

Lovely laughed at the end of Marisol's text. Her friend was crazy. She was glad that Marisol texted her back. She forgot the reason for tonight's dinner was to explain to Desmond that she couldn't date him. She sighed and figured she might as well tell him at her house over a night cap.

CHAPTER SIX

"Simple Simon mu'fuckas, I swear. How you not get up to make money, B?" Rico said to no one in particular while in his office. He got up to head down stairs to assist at the main bar. One bartender called out for tonight knowing that tonight was one of his busiest nights at the club. His Assistant Manager was out also since his Fiancée gave birth earlier this morning. Now Rico had to take himself down to the bar to help until his Manager Q got in. Opening the door to his office he walked out towards the private elevator. As the elevator descended he could hear the bass bumping inside the club. The two-story club housed three dance floors. There were two and a half bars with the biggest bar on the first level. The VIP rooms held plush loungers and couches and had its own separate mini bar. As he exited the elevator he went and dapped up his head of security and friend Kam. Kam would always seem to be right by Rico's side when he never noticed, he would come up out of nowhere and was always posted close by Rico.

"My nigga, you are creepy as fuck bruh. How you always seem to know when I'm coming down to the floor?" Rico asked.

Kam which was short for Kameron was a six foot seven, solid dude, he used to be real skinny in his youth but after a few years in the penitentiary he was pumping all those weights and bulked up. He was another person Rico considered a best friend. He'd known Kam since he was a youngin. When Rico's mother moved to the states from the islands Rico knew no one. He went to school at P.S. 39 where he met Sincere. One day while he and Sincere were walking home they saw a few other young boys trying to beat up on this smaller kid. It was about five boys versus the one. The little boy was trying his best to fight them off. When Rico saw this, he ran over and helped him. Soon Rico, Sincere and Kameron were giving the bullies a beat down, after several minutes the boys figured the bullies had enough and decided to let up. The other boys walked, stumbled and crawled away from the scene.

"Yo son I 'preciate the help fam." said Kameron

"No prawblem, mi hate whack ass niggas mon." Rico stated.

"Yo, so like where you from B?" Kameron asked hearing his accent "Mi and mi family jus moved hea from da islands bout tree or fo' weeks ago." Rico explained

"Oh that's a wassup, so you always talk like that. I mean I know a few people from Jamaica and what not but ya'll hard to understand." Kameron said.

Sincere standing to the side laughed at the remark. Even though he had just met Rico about three weeks ago he knew the reason why he was speaking in his native tongue. Kameron looked to his right and saw Sincere.

"My fault fam, thanks for the help too." Kameron went to dap up Sincere. "You straight B. But umm I was about to kick ya ass, you over here thanking this nigga and shit and ignoring me like I wasn't in the fight throwing fists and kicks too." Sincere chuckled

"Whud ya name boi." Rico asked.

"Oh yeah, it's Kameron but my peoples call me Bear."

"Nigga why they call you that?" Sincere asked with a scrunched up face.

"Shit ion even know. My moms gave me that name from birth and it just stuck, and my ass too damn skinny to be called bear." Kameron stated

"Dats di same ting me was tinking." Rico said.

"On the real tho, I ain't about to call you Bear, it don't fit you, Kam tho that's you." Kameron waived off his remark and asked

"Who ya'll niggas though?" Kameron asked.

"I'm Rico and this here is my manz Sin." Rico said in perfect English dialect.

"Nigga you speak regular too!?" Kameron asked with a shocked expression.

"Yeah nigga I can speak regular English I ain't stupid." Rico said

"That nigga calm now his accent only comes out when he hype and shit." Sincere explained. Kameron just nodded his head he understood.

"Yo you niggas want to come to my house to play Sega?" And from that day they've been friends ever since.

"You bout to head the bar?" Kam asked ignoring Rico's comment about being near every time he was in the club. He felt that he owed Rico a lot. Since day one he and Rico been cool and Rico always seemed to look out for him, even when he got locked up on drug and gun charges, Rico and Sincere looked out for him and his family.

"Yeah nigga, these mu'fuckas act like they don't want their jobs so they sure as fuck ain't about to have one. Ya feel me?" Rico stated as he looked around his club and saw that it was packed everywhere you turned. That excited and made him nervous at the same time, he didn't do well with crowded places, but he knew niggas weren't stupid enough to pop off in his spot.

Not if they wanted to make it home of course. But he knew that one day somebody would try it, so he stayed prepared, he had enough security near the entrance and exit, by the bars, posted in the VIP section and even had some posted near the dance floor and DJ booth. He looked to his right and spotted DJ Envy on the turntables. He was his preferred DJ for 'Ladies Night' he always kept the place turned up and had people staying on the dance floors until closing. DJ Envy spotted Rico and decided to shout him out.

"Yo we got my nigga Rico in the building, which one of you thots trying to take the boss man home tonight." The DJ shouted out into the mic. The music started blaring Jay-Z's 'Fuck with me know I got it' through the speakers. Rico and Kam laughed at the DJ's antics while getting looks from a few females that were near.

"Aight B let me make my way to the bar and see how much help I'm really gone need 'fore the nights out." He said shaking his head; Rico stepped into the crowd, Kameron was traveling not too far behind him. As they approached the bar a few females tried to stop Rico and hold a conversation, he declined their advances he was too focused on seeing how he was going to manage the bar until Q came through.

"Sup Boss, are you here to help lil ole me out tonight?" The petite bartender Nikki asked.

"Yeah I'm going to be down here for a few to help out until Q comes in. This manual labor, this ain't for the kid though." He said with a serious expression.

"Aww boss man it'll be okay, I'll show you the ropes." Nikki stated. Rico scuffed and started assisting Nikki in mixing Blue Motherfuckers and Leg spreaders. Nikki was impressed her boss actually knew what to do.

"You thought I didn't know what I was doing huh? I'm the Boss remember I need to know every aspect about the business I run, down to mixing drinks to what kind of shit paper these broads like to use." Rico stated. Nikki just chuckled at her boss' last remark. Nikki turned to the bar to get the patron's drink order.

"What can I get you honey?" Nikki asked.

"Ummm let me get an orgasm and a shot of Patrón" The female stated.

"Boss man I need an orgasm." Nikki shouted out. Rico snapped his head to the side and looked at Nikki with a scowl on his face.

"It's a drink, it's called an Orgasm and it's for the lady in the black romper." Nikki laughed at Rico's facial expression. Rico looked the drink up on the mixer database and started to mix the drink and was getting ready to hand it to Nikki but he saw that she was down at the end of the bar taking an order. He turned to look for the person she had stated the drink was for, he saw about three women in black and he damn sure didn't remember what Nikki said she was wearing. He stopped in front of two women and a male standing at the bar.

"Whose orgasm do I have in my hand?" he asked slyly. The females chuckled and he heard a few side comments *"I wish it was you giving me an orgasm" "yes daddy you can give me an orgasm anytime with those hands."* Rico ignored the comments waiting for the patron to speak up. "It's my drink" he heard a female voice say. Rico went to hand her the drink and return to finish mixing and pouring the rest of the orders but he stopped dead in his tracks when he looked at her. It was like a one two punch straight to the gut when he saw her. He blinked twice just to make sure it wasn't the lighting in the club making this woman appear so damn gorgeous. He stood for a moment and the two-held eye contact, neither moving nor listening to the sounds around them. They were captured in each other's gazes. Seeing who would look away first. His mystery lady smiled and spoke, "Excuse me Papí can I have my orgasm, please." In the velvetiest seductive voice he had ever heard on a woman.

Thrown out of his trance he handed the drink to the exotic beauty. An electric current shot between their fingers as the woman reached for the glass; they both stared at each other again as if time stood still.

"Boss man, boss man." Rico turned to see Nikki handing him a shot of Patrón.

"This is for the lady who you just handed the drink too." Nikki advised.

Rico took the shot glass out of her hand and handed it to the exotic beauty. The lady raised the glass to gesture her thanks and pulled out her money and placed it on the counter to pay for her drinks. Rico cleared his throat and said, "Nah ma it's on the house."

"Are you sure I wouldn't want you to get in any trouble with your boss." the lady responded flirtatiously . Rico laughed, and leaned in towards the woman.

"I think it would be worth getting into trouble for you, ma." He winked at her.

He watched her as she ran her fingers through her long silky tresses. Her eyes sparkled with mischief. She was about to say something when she seen a tall gentleman appear by his side. Rico turned to see that his Manager Q had finally arrived.

"Nigga what took you so damn long? I called ya ass damn near two hours ago" he spoke loud over the music, he questioned.

"Man boss, some straight bullshit with my baby momma and stuff, but I'm here. I got the bar on this level now. How many people we short?" Q asked Rico. Rico leaned in so they could hear each other better over the bass pumping sound system.

"That lazy ass Justice didn't show up and Vince out with his shorty. Bridget said she'll be in but I ain't seen her pale looking as yet. We got the VIP covered and the second floor is straight right now for bout another hour or so until the late people start coming in." Rico explained to Q.

"Aight Boss I got this covered. I'll station Bridget when she gets in and call a few more to see if they can cover Justice's shift" Q said.

"See that's why I pay you to manage. Aight let me head back to the office and finish this paperwork up and shit." He dapped up Q again he turned around to see if the beautiful woman was still at the bar, he looked around and didn't see her. He shrugged his shoulders and headed to the private elevator. He walked and stopped to talk to one of the security guards. He was speaking to Rondo as best as he could over the loud music about making sure the dance floor stayed cleared of drinks, he didn't want or need any one cutting themselves on broken glass. As he was surveying the area he suddenly felt a tap on his shoulder. He turned to see who was vying for his attention. He turned and faced the woman from the bar, she was smiling at him, and her exotic features were on display. He stared at her taking in her face, smile and body. He looked her up from head to toe and smiled to himself. Shorty is bad ass fuck he thought. He could definitely do something with her. He looked back up at her face and notice she was equally checking him out.

"Can I help you, beautiful." Rico asked while leaning into her.

"Yes, actually I think I need another orgasm." She said in her velvety voice. Rico lifted his eyebrow trying to decipher if she was being serious or if she was really talking about the drink. From her approach, he pretty much figured she was serious as she had sought him out.

"I can definitely help you with that," he stated. He grabbed her hand and led her to the VIP section of the club, he guided her to one of the plush couches near the back

"What's your name ma?" he asked the beauty. She giggled and told him Marisol with a sexy Spanish accent. Damn even the way she said her name sounds sexy thought Rico

"What's your name handsome?" She asked as she stared into his eyes, she licked her lips. His build was just something she knew she could work with, his lips were full and sexy as hell. His chocolate skin made her want to lick him from head to toe to see if he tasted as delicious as he looked.

"It's Rico" he stated as he looked at her sitting next to him on the couch.

"Mm...hmm Rico okay, so what do you do here at this fine establishment. I know you aren't a bartender." Marisol asked.

"What makes you think that I'm not? I'm a good ass bartender; you liked your drink didn't you." He said sarcastically.

"Don't flatter yourself; I've had a better orgasm than that." She said with a serious expression. Rico thought about her statement as he looked at her, he leaned over to her and whispered in her ear.

"You're right that wasn't my best work; allow me to show you what I can really do." Marisol shivered at the words and warmth of his breath on her ear, he was playing with fire. Her ear was her hot spot, and him just being near it made her pussy throb. She cut her eyes at him as she was about to speak, but she heard the intro to one of her favorite songs.

As the beat dropped and the bass bumped through the speakers Marisol grabbed Rico's hand and gracefully stood up from the couch. She leaned in and placed her hands on his chest and pushed him back towards the couch. Her hands trailed up and down his hard pecks, she unbuttoned his shirt slowly opening the first three buttons. She peeked at his chocolate skin and licked her lips. Her eyes wandered up to his and she could see the lust in them. His eyes were focused on her lips. Rico was thinking about how her lips would soon be wrapped around his long thick shaft. He leaned forward only an inch from her lips, his tongue snaked out and licked her bottom lip. His actions had him slightly perplexed and his thoughts of actually wanting to kiss her.

He didn't do the whole kissing thing and he definitely didn't to the cunnilingus, Rico didn't care how good a female's pussy felt around his dick he wasn't into eating pussy. Marisol smiled at the gesture. She began to sway her hips back and forth; she turned around seductively and showed him her ample back side. She heard him curse underneath his breath. She could see some of the others in VIP watching what they were doing, she smiled on the inside guess I have to put on a good show she thought to herself. She winded her body up and down and started to do a slow twerk, she looked behind her to make sure she had all of his attention, Rico's eyes were focused on her ass so hard it was funny. She brought it back up and straddled his lap her hips grinded to the beat in his lap and she could feel his hard dick resting on his thigh GOD damn, PLEASE let him know what to do with this big ole thang! she internally screamed.

His hands rested on her thick thighs inching its way up to her round derrière, her eyes darted up to his, she licked her lips and leaned in and started to nip at his neck, she twirled her hips into his erection even more, she worked her way up to his ear "I want your body right here, daddy, I want you, right now, can't keep your eyes off my fatty Daddy, I want you" she seductively sang in Rico's ear, before she licked his earlobe and tugged on it. She could feel his body heat radiating off of him. She turned her head to face him and they both stared at each other; one declaring the offer and the other accepting, Marisol on instinct licked her lips which drew his eyes towards them. Rico moved in and captured his lips with hers, he felt hypnotized, she tasted like pineapples and coconut, the sweet taste made him deepen the kiss.

Her body felt like it was on fire with the connection of his lips. She moved closer wanting to get more if that was even possible from the kiss, Rico trailed his tongue against her mouth; she allowed him entrance and let out a moan when their tongues collided. Marisol wrapped her arms around his neck and turned her head to the side trying to get more. Rico's tongue caressed the roof of her mouth, grazed against teeth. Marisol was so turned on by the sexy chocolate man; his hands were on her hips grinding them into his hard shaft up and down. Marisol captured his tongue and began to suck on it; the action caused him to groan in her mouth.

They were so caught up in the moment they forgot they were still in the VIP section with and small audience. Rico pulled away and left Marisol gasping for air. Rico picked her up off his lap and placed her on the ground. He looked down at her making sure that you were in agreement about what was about to happen between them. He saw that mischievous gaze in her eyes, the same look that caught him at the bar. He grabbed her hand and led her away from the VIP section towards the elevator to his office. Marisol was confused about where they were going all she could see were walls, there were no doors that led to anything. Rico placed his hand on a wall, a laser light scanned his hand and opened the wall up to reveal an elevator. Rico looked up to see Kam standing not too far from them. He gestured for Marisol to enter the elevator first. He punched in the code for the office floor. Rico stood against the wall and just admired Marisol's beauty in the light, he thought she was gorgeous when he first laid eyes on her but the club lighting wasn't doing her justice. She turned to see him staring at her.

"What do I have something on my face?" she asked. He smiled but didn't respond, the elevator came to a stop. Rico grabbed her hand and walked to his office. He inputted the code to his office door, "Who are you James Bond or somebody with all these damn codes and secret walls" she remarked.

"I just like my privacy and I don't need anyone in my shit that's all, but enough about that ma" he replied. Marisol looked around the huge lavish office, she like the espresso colored walls with the red and creamed themed accents. His office had pictures along the wall of a tall beauty with rich ebony skin and the same full lips and almond shaped eyes. There were others of him and a man who was as equally handsome. She saw a small platform near the corner of the room, intrigued she walked near it and stepped up. There was a hole in the center she looked up and asked him. "What's this area for?" Marisol inquired.

He walked towards his desk and grabbed a remote tablet. Soon the lights dimmed in the room, a red spotlight hit the platform and a pole emerged through the ground until it was secured through the roof of the room. R. Kelly's *Seems like Your Ready* crooned through the Bose speakers strategically placed throughout the room. She was impressed with the setup but wonder why he needed a stripper pole in his office. Marisol walked over toward where he was at; she admired his six-foot two frame leaning up against the corner of his desk. They were slightly eye leveled, "Are you trying to tell me something with all of this?" She questioned. He grabbed her by her hips and pulled her closer to him. His hands running up and down her exposed skin in her romper and up towards her rounded hips.

"I'm trying to see what that ass do." He chuckled.

"Ha, I see you are a comedian as well as a bartender." She stated sarcastically.

"Nah ma, I'm just messing with you, but I wouldn't mind seeing you do your thang up there." Rico expressed.

"Is that a request?" She asked.

Marisol placed her hands on his chest rubbing up and down on the fabric. She decided they had had clothes on for too long. She began to unbutton the remaining buttons on his dress shirt. She finally gotten to the last button and a surge of excitement ran through her body. It was like unwrapping a gift in the teal colored box that every woman had to experience at least once. She opened the shirt and exposed the eight pack abs, hard and chiseled body; the v cut was on display. She ran her finger tips over his hard abs, her mouth began to salivate she had to taste him and she couldn't wait. She zoned in on his pectorals and licked her top lip. Her body was hot as well as his. She could feel her arousal soaking her thong. She began at his pecks, licking her way up to his neck. Her hands slid down towards his shaft and started to rub him through his pants. His hands were firmly planted on her ass squeezing with a vengeance.

Marisol stepped out of his hold and reached for the zipper on the back of her romper. Marisol stripped out of her romper, as it fell to the floor she stepped out of the garment and walked back towards the platform. Her hips swayed left and right, she was clad in a lace crimson colored bra and thong and five-inch designer stilettos. She stepped onto the platform and grasped the pole as she seductively walked around it until she faced him. She had his full attention; he was still leaning against the edge of his desk with his hands palms down for support. The song playing in the background gave her all the incentive to seduce (*I ain't trying to think about it, no yeah I said it, boy get up inside it. I want you to homicide it going slow and I want you to pop it).* Her hands traveled from her neck in a tantalizing pace as she grazed her throat, she slowly winded her body down the pole as her hands followed a path against her body.

Men were visual creatures, they wanted to see everything. She reached her belly button and paused before traveling further, she was crouched down standing on her heels to support her weight. Her fingers rubbed the edge of her panty inching slowly inside, his eyes were on her every move; he was transfixed on her movements. *(Boy I always like to show. Get a little bit, come a little close, no take it home on your camera phone. Get a little bad, nigga, watch me blow it down)* She removed her hand from inside her panty deciding to tease him some more. She leaned forward on all fours and backed up against the pole. Putting the deep arch in her back she started grinding and slow twerking against the pole with her ass on display. She allowed the beat and the lyrics of the song to persuade the movement of her hips. She fixed her eyes on him and bit her bottom lip; she swung her hair to the side and pushed back up onto her heels. She twerked against the pole working her way back up. She grabbed the pole and started climbing up to the middle, she spread eagle and spun back down towards the ground, as she landed she seductively bounced her ass cheeks, right, left, right left to the beat.

Rico was mesmerized at her seductive moves. Him being an owner of a strip club he had seen plenty women work a pole. The way Marisol worked she was simply a seductress, it aroused him and made him ready to knock the bottom out. He couldn't take her teasing and seductive gyrating any longer he started walking towards her.

He stood on the platform so close to her the tips of their nose were touching. Marisol stood biting her lips and her hands wrapped around his neck. Her back was up against the cold metal pole but the change in temperature only briefly cooled down her body. Rico teased her neck with his tongue as his hands were making its way towards her breast. He grabbed her breast through her bra and gently squeezed. All the while sucking on her neck, Marisol moaned at the gesture and tightened her fingers around the back of his neck. He

unclasped the bra from the front and slid it off her shoulders.
Looking down, he could see her harden caramel nipples. After
placing one last kiss on her neck he bent his head and took the
harden pebble into his mouth. Her back arched off the steel pole.
"Mmmmm that feels good" she moaned.

The sound turned him on; he caressed the other breast while
sucking on her nipple. He twirled his tongue and placed the nipple
back in his mouth before pulling back and tugging it between his
teeth. Marisol breathing was erratic. Her pulse was beating so fast
she didn't know why she hadn't gone into cardiac arrest. Rico
switched from one breast to the next giving the same attention.

Marisol grinded her pelvis against his and realized he still had
his pants on. She reached for the belt and got it out of the loop.
Rico grabbed her hands with one of his. She looked up at him to
gauge why he stopped her from unbuckling his pants. He took his
free hand and trailed it down her belly button to the top of her
panty. He continued his journey building her anticipation just as
she was doing to him a few minutes ago. He slid her panty to the
side as his finger grazed her clitoral hood. It sent a shiver down
her spine and caused her to thrust her pelvis against his again. His
fingers traveled down to her pussy lips. He rubbed up and down
teasing her but not actually plunging his fingers in her hot core.
Marisol felt that she should have been embarrassed at how wet
she was, but she didn't the man that she had her legs wrapped
around was sex on legs. She knew the attraction was mutual the
moment they looked at each other at the bar "Mmmmm don't
tease me, just fuck me please" she moaned out as he inserted one
finger inside of her he motioned in and out before adding another
finger in.

Marisol began to gyrate up and down on his fingers, he took
her breast again trying to suck the entire breast into his mouth,
and he twirled his tongue over her nipple as he twirled his fingers.
He was in search for her spongy g spot as he curved his fingers
inside her, once he felt it, Marisol moaned out "Mmmmm oh my
right there" she was panting heavily, he continues to tease and

poke her g spot until he felt her legs tighten and shake around him.

"Fuuck Papí I'm bout to - ahhhhhh" she screamed out as her juices flowed freely from her body onto his fingers and hand.

Her body jerked as she tried still the aftershocks. She removed her legs from around his waist; she tugged her panty down her hips ankles and stepped out of them. She reached for his belt buckle again while licking her lips. He pulled back and turned towards his desk. He went inside the smallest drawer and took out a condom. Marisol smirked and took the golden foil from his hands. She went back to work on his belt buckle. Tugging his slacks down with his black silk boxers was like unwrapping a gift to her. Her body was on fire and she couldn't wait to get hosed down with his package. After finally getting his pants off she looked down at his impressive shaft and took a slight step back. Looking back up at him he had a smug look on his face.

Marisol looked back down and knew she wasn't going to be walking properly when they were finished. She stroked his member up and down as best as she could with one hand while applying pressure, his shaft began to swell even more in her tiny hands. Marisol lowered herself to the floor while pushing Rico towards the desk so he could lean against it. She continued to stroke him while feathering kisses on and around the top of his dick head. Rico was biting his bottom lip trying to hold in the groan that was bound to escape. She proceeded to lick him from the bottom of his shaft all the way to the top, before covering him with her hot moist mouth.

"Ahh…. sssss, damn" he groaned through clenched teeth.

Marisol continued to bob up and down on his dick keeping her mouth nice and wet; she licked and twirled her tongue around his dick.

"Mmmmm" she moaned as she placed both her hands on her knees she inserted his dick even further into her mouth.

"GOTDAMN!" He yelled his head hung back in pure pleasure as his hands tangled and groped her hair as he penetrated deeper into her mouth. Marisol closed her throat around his head breathing through her nose.

"Mmm. Fuck ma" he moaned his knees slightly bent like they were about to give out but he quickly recovered as he pumped his shaft in and out of her mouth. He was in the zone as he continued to stroke inside her mouth, this time Marisol closed her throat around his shaft holding it before making her esophagus pulse. Rico held her still and slid out of her mouth with a popping sound. He couldn't take any more he had good head before but Marisol was on some next level shit. Marisol looked up at him in confusion because she sure wasn't done tasting him.

"You trying to make a nigga bust all up in that mouth I see" he pulled her up and placed her on the desk, Marisol stroked his impressive length up and down before rolling the latex onto his member; she guided him towards her entrance. Rico lifted one leg onto his shoulder as Marisol lay back on the desk; he slipped the head inside her tight snatch. He stroked in and out teasing her with his tip. Marisol's pelvis pushed forward trying to get him to plunge deeper. He smirked at her attempts. Her eyes were closed tight and a look of agonizing pleasure played across her face. Rico bent down and sucked her nipples again, to him her breast tasted sweet as hell, he felt her hands grab his ass trying to get him to go all the way in. He pulled out his tip rubbed it up and down on her click.

"Fu-uck Papí, stop playing and fuck me please." She requested from him, her hands rose up towards her breast as she began to squeeze and tug on her nipples.

Marisol slightly rose up and caressed her breast before bending her head down and licking and inserting her own nipple into her mouth. This turned Rico on and he thrusted deep inside her. "OOOOOHHHH, fuck!" Marisol moaned out. He groaned at her tightness, he paused so she could adjust to his size, she was too tight and he was very large so he knew she was going to be sore when they finished. Marisol started moving her hips slowly, so he took that as his queue to start moving. He started giving her long strokes as he found a rhythm they both could move to. Her hips were winding underneath him as his pelvis caressed her clit causing even more friction.

"Don't stop mmm right there , y-y-yes" she stuttered as he picked up the pace, his dick head pulled back and he found her g spot and started fucking it

"Ahhhh, yes! yes! Yes....Oh my god." She panted out

"Right there baby? Fuck I feel it." He continued to stroke her g spot. Her legs started shaking and her pussy muscles tighten around him as he pulsed. He sped up the pace and angled her so that his dick was going to give her a g spot climax. "ahhhhh, wait wait" She pleaded trying to push him back. Rico didn't budge he continued to pound on her.

"Nah ma don't run from it... fuck this pussy's good and tight" sweat dripped from his body onto hers. The pressure built up inside her and she knew she was going to cum hard. He continued to stroke her and she fucked him back. The pleasure started at her toes giving off a tingling sensation it shot up to her legs that were already shaking, the pleasurable sensation moved inside, Rico felt her pussy spasm and clamped down on his dick. He groaned and told her "Don't hold it back cum on this dick" with that Marisol released a drenching amount of juices onto his shaft. "Ahhhh... mmmm....slow down, mmm fuck Papí" Rico pulled out and looked at his dick that was covered in her cream he looked back up at her hot core and it was still jerking, he slapped her on her round thick ass. "We not done yet, turn around" Marisol gave him a sloppy kiss before turning around an assumed the position. Face down ass up. She felt him move behind her before he plunged in deep trying to hit bottom. She moaned out and started moving her ass and hips back into his thrust. Little did he know this was her favorite position she could dominate in this position and that what she planned to do.

"That's right ma throw that ass back onto this dick." His hands were planted firmly onto her hips as he watched her move along with him.

"Mmmm you like that Papí... hmmm my pussy feels good huh?!"

"Fuck yeah it do" he panted he dug into her as she lifted one leg up on the desk for a deeper penetration. He let a moan slip out he tried to cover it up by biting on his bottom lip but Marisol had already heard him. It was time to show him what her ass and pussy could really do. Her ass started popping on his dick as she tightens her pussy around his shaft. Her daily Kegels regimen and ben wan balls allowed her total control over her pussy muscles. Rico's mind was gone as he thought about how her tight wet pussy gripped him like a glove. You could hear the slapping of his balls on her pelvis the splatting sounds of her wetness every time he gave her short strokes. He felt his climax approaching as he pulsed inside of her.

"I feel you Papí...mmm I feel you."

"Oh Yea, what you feel baby" Marisol was fucking with his mind he was doing and saying things out of character first kissing now terms of endearment during sex. Yeah he was mind fucked.

"I -I ahhh I feel that big long dick in my stomach". He was pounding in her like he was trying to rearrange organs. He bent over her and pulled her neck toward him and started giving her a sloppy kiss. He picked up the pace as his balls became heavy. Marisol tore away from the kiss screaming and moaning.

"Fuck I'm bout to bust" Rico stated. Marisol hopped off the desk and pulled the condom off. She placed her mouth on his dick and sucked on it like it was the biggest blow pop ever and stroked him.

"Fuck girl, suck on that, ahhhh I'm bout to…. Sssss fuuck" he continued to pump as he climaxed inside her mouth, he slowed his strokes as his euphoric high depleted. He looked down at her and smirked and thought to himself she a straight freak. Had me moaning like a bitch. He collapsed into the chair and she sat in his lap. They both were breathing hard. Marisol leaned in and pulled at his bottom lip before gently nibbling on it. She looked up at him and said, "Are you ready for round two?"

CHAPTER SEVEN

S he jolted out of her sleep looking from left to right trying to figure out where she was and how she got in the bed. As things came into focus, she saw light coming from the crack in the door, as she wrapped herself in the sheet from the bed and headed towards the door. Marisol's legs felt weak and her thighs were sore. The memory gate flooded to a few hours ago when she and Rico were fucking each other up and down this office. She peeked out the crack and stared, he looked so serious concentrating on whatever was on his computer. The door creaked as she opened it some; he cut his eyes up towards her and gave a half smile briefly before turning his focus back to the computer. From that lack of response Marisol didn't know if she should have just gotten her clothes and left or stayed and try to hold a conversation. Looking at her wrist to see the time and it was 3:30 in the morning. She wondered why he was up and how long he had been up. Clearing her throat, she prepared to speak. He was so warped in his work she felt that he would not have noticed if she were just to leave. Maybe he was the type of guy that needed no further conversation after the deed had been done. She couldn't be mad at that since she was the same way. What reason was needed to linger when the obligation had been fulfilled.

"Have you seen my clothes?" Marisol asked him. He pointed to the couch where the romper was neatly placed along with a bra on top and the five-inch heels where next to them. He still didn't speak or look up too much and it was starting to irritate her. Marisol stood a little longer, waiting for some kind of acknowledgment of their tryst.

"Is it ok if I use your shower, before I leave?"

"Yeah go ahead ma knock yourself out" He stated.

Finally, words, actual words she thought to herself, as she turned back towards the door and went inside. The room was pretty spacious for it to be inside an office. The colors matched the office and the bed was nice queen which she thought was kind of small for him since he was so tall. Marisol headed towards the bathroom and turned on the shower. She looked to see if there were any toiletries inside the cabinet and surprisingly there were feminine wash and body wash, Oh this is something he does on a regular I see she thought to herself. So maybe his rude nonchalant attitude is his way of saying thank you for the fuck goodbye. "Well fuck it let me wash my ass and get on up out his space. I'm not one to linger so, oh well it is what it is." She said in the empty bathroom. She stepped into the hot shower and the water relaxed her sore muscles. That man worked her over like straight overtime. She had to lightly pat between her legs; I know I'm going to need to soak in my jet Jacuzzi when I get home. Marisol finished about fifteen minutes later, she wrapped in one of the towels and went to the vanity sink to see if there were any extra unused toothbrushes. She brushed her teeth with the spare toothbrush she found; her tresses were now extremely curly due to the hot shower. As she continued to get dressed she realized that she was missing her thong panties. I walked back out to the office and he was standing looking out at the windows to the inside of the club. I went over towards the couch and bent down looking under it, I was in search of my panty and I was not leaving without them. I walked towards the desk and looked around and under it as well. I saw him turn around and stare at me.

"What are you looking for?" He asked.

"I'm in search for my underwear they weren't with the rest of my things." Marisol said and stood to face him. His bulging biceps was on display, he had slipped on a white tank shirt, his slacks hung off his narrow hips in the sexiest way, becoming distracted and Marisol looked further down to see if her new best friend was lurking.

"Did you check the back room for them?" She heard him ask.

"They weren't removed in the bedroom last time I checked. They were taken off in this area and they could have been shuffled when we moved from the platform, to the desk, to the couch or the windows" she expressed with a raised eyebrow.

"Do you really need them?" He asked

"Yes I need them I don't leave any man's space without my underwear, so yes I need to find them" she explained.

"So, you do this often is what you're telling me?" Tilting her head to the side she replayed his words. Oh no, I know this nigga not saying what I think he saying.

"What are you implying, that I get around or something?"

"No. But that's how you're going to take it" He stated

"There's no other way to take it and please don't try to explain. I don't like to leave without my things. And seeing how this, 'office fucking' might not be a new thing for you, I wouldn't want you to get in any trouble with the misses." She stated with a smirk on her face.

"What makes you think I have a woman?"

"So you're saying that you like to have Summers Eve fresh balls and vanilla bean body wash." His face scrunched up and his jaws tighten.

"Nah that ain't something that I particularly wash with, but that don't mean they belong to somebody I'm fucking or fucked" he explained.

"It's whatever; I'll just be on my way. If you find them, just trash them please" She instructed him. As she started gathering her clutch and walked to the couch to sit down and put on her heels. She didn't feel like walking in them but she remembered she parked her vehicle across the street from the club. Rico moved about his office and started to gather his shirt and put it on. "Where did you park?" He asked Marisol. It caught her off guard that he was actually going to walk her out she felt that he had been her the iceberg shoulder since she awoken.

"Across the street, but you don't have to walk me out, I'm sure you have more important things to tend to." I told him

"Yeah alright ma, what I look like not seeing you to your car at this time of night." He stated

"I'm thrown off right now actually, you were just being an asshole to me a few minutes ago, I wouldn't have pegged you as the walking the girl to her car man." He looked down at me and rubbed the back of his head and down his face.

"My fault I have a lot on my mind. And…. Just my bad ma aight" she shrugged off his attempt of an apology and stood up to head to the door, he went back to his desk and grabbed his keys and walked back and stopped in front of her. The two just stood there looking at each other, the attraction that she felt for him was strong, like a semi-truck in a head on collision type of attraction. It was intense and she could remember the last time she felt that way about a man. That turned out to be just a heart break that took her years to heal from. She realized that she probably wouldn't see Rico again unless she came back to the club, she had no plans on returning. Staring into his eyes she thought they were the most seductive shade of grey she had ever seen on a man especially a man with such rich mahogany skin.

"You have beautiful eyes" she told him

"Funny I was just thinking the same about yours." He said.

There was a baby's breath of a pause and then he lowered his head towards her. He lightly pecked Marisol's lips before adding another one. Tilting her head back she pushed herself closer to his body, and kissed him back. The feeling of his arms wrapping around her waist as he applied more pressure to her lips. She tugged on his bottom lip with her teeth, before he slid his tongue back into her warm mouth. The electricity that flowed through her body from his touch left Marisol not wanting to let go, but at the same time needing to push away. The couple were both panting as he placed several small pecks to those swollen kissed lips.

He was trailing behind her and as they exited. Rico grabbed Marisol's hand and led her to the elevator. The two stood in the elevator her back to his front with his hand still entwined with hers. The club was empty minus the cleanup crew and a few employees. As they exited the elevator, Marisol spotted someone standing off to her left. Rico stopped to speak to his Manager and then they proceeded to walk out of the club. She looked back and the man was only a few steps behind them.

"Why do you need a body guard" Marisol inquired. He looked down at her, then over his shoulder and shook his head.

"I don't need a damn body guard, he just seemed to appoint himself as one." He stated in a nonchalant manner. She looked back over her shoulder at the guy and gave him a small smile. He winked at her, Marisol giggled at him, and she was tempted to wink back for what reason she was unsure. She thought he was cute in a bad boy type of way. Rico looked at her with a scowl then turned and mugged Kameron. They crossed the street, there were only a few other cars in the parking lot. Marisol led him towards her car.

"Which one is yours?" He asked. She retrieved her keys from her clutch and chirped the alarm to the Porsche Panamera indicating that the car belonged to her. "Do I need to follow you to make sure you make it home?" he asked.

"Is this your way of trying to apologize for being jerk in your office? First walking me to the car now you want to make sure I get home ok?" He shrugged his shoulders leaving the question in the air but the look on his face made it seem like he was battling something.

"I did enjoy myself tonight and no I don't need you to follow me home, but thanks for asking" She said.

"No problem beautiful and I enjoyed myself as well, so how do I get in contact with you?" He asked

"Why do you need to get in contact with me?" Marisol asked

"Just in case I find your panties I want to at least return them to you" he had slight smirk on his face. She bit the corner of my bottom lip, thinking back to the things that happened in his office.

"I thought I already told you what to do in regards to those"

"Aight I got you, now how do I get in contact with you?" He asked again.

She pondered on it briefly as she looked out to the street. Kam was still near, he was posted next to the light pole about fifteen feet away.

"Let me see your phone" she said to him.

He searched his pockets to hand her the phone, "Damn I left it inside." He said.

Her phone's battery was dead and she had no charger in the car. She opened her car door and reached in. She lifted the center console and pulled out a pen and a small piece of paper, she wrote down her cell phone number and handed it to him. Rico pulled her in for a brief hug and his sexy male scent assaulted her nostrils. Marisol took in a deep breath trying to commence his scent to memory, they pulled away from each other as Marisol slid inside of the car. She went to close the door but was stopped by Rico's hand.

"Oh yeah by the way, I think I'll just keep these as a parting gift for a hell of a night." He winked, she looked up and saw him dangling the crimson colored thong in his fingers.

"RICO!! Give me my panties." She yelled at him, Rico had the panties the entire time and was going to keep them. Marisol reached for them but he snatched his hand back and dug his hands back into his pockets.

"Nah ma, I got'em. Get home safe and we'll be talking soon."
He then closed the door to the vehicle. Marisol pushed the start
button to the car and the engine purred to life.

CHAPTER EIGHT

"Who said you can't find love in a club? Cause I wanna tell them they wrong come on, baby, just try a new thing and let's spark a new flame. You gon' be my baby love me, love you crazy tell me if you with it baby, come and get it maybe try a new thing and let's spark a new flame" Marisol crooned her heart out to the song. I looked over at her and the crazy heffa had the nerve to have her eyes closed while driving.

"Hoe I don't care how good you can sing or who you singing it for but if you don't open your eyes while you're driving before you and I be up in flames." I expressed to her.

She just laughed, I hope she didn't think I was playing. Who sings with their eyes closed knowing they are driving. "My bad best friend I was caught up in the moment." She said

"So I see, so tell me hooker who you were you just singing your heart out to now!" I asked her, secretly I lived vicariously through Marisol her sexcapades were very interesting and jaw dropping.

I looked over and saw her blushing. Now I really was interested on who this mystery guy is.

"Where do I start?" Marisol gushed out.

"How about his name, what he looks like and where did you meet him."

"We met at that hot new night club *Treacherous* I was there for ladies' night solo since somebody had a date, which by the way I need to know what happen, but back to the matter at hand. I was at the bar when he served me my drink."

"The bartender, Marisol really, first the waiter now the bartender what are you equal opportunity." I said laughing.

"No bitch, and if you are going to throw shade let me know so I remember not to tell you another story."

"No shade, no shade, but I'm going to sit over here and enjoy this tea though." I couldn't help but laugh.

"Whatever, Lovely." Marisol stated. She began to tell me about her rendezvous, and as I figured my jaw dropped, this girl was so spontaneous it was ridiculous. I had to stop her in the middle of the story, just to get clarification "So wait you were up in the office. I thought he was the bartender, how did you two get into inspector gadgets office?"

"Lovely, do you really think he was the bartender?" I shrugged my shoulders.

"Girl bye. He is not a bartender he was assisting, he is the owner of the damn club. To be so smart girl you sure can be naïve." Marisol said.

"So are you going to see him again or was this just a one night stand" I asked, since she over here singing like she got a new boo.

"I would like to see him again, but I probably won't. I mean if I'm interested in someone then I usually don't sleep with them on the first night, I just sexed this man like a porn star in the office of his club. Do you think he is going to want to get to know me on a personal level?" She asked.

"Well did you guys exchange numbers or anything?" I asked.

She sighed before responding, "Yeah I gave him mine, now that I think about it, and I shouldn't have."

"Why not." I inquired; she cut her eyes at me. "I gave him my number like on some hey if you want to hook up again, call me type of shit, he didn't give me his." Oh I thought.

"Enough about me and my thotting coochie, tell me how your date with Desmond was? Did you set the boundaries of your friendship?" She asked.

I thought back to that night, dinner was interesting I had fun talking with Des, getting to know him better than what I already did. It didn't help that his baby blue eyes would stare into mine keeping eye contact while I was telling him about my undergrad years and crazy things Marisol and I did.

"Dinner was fine; we talked and got to know each other on a personal level. But I'm currently avoiding him at this moment."

"How and why are you avoiding him, you both work in the same office so how is that even working?" She asked.

"Well I've been working from home for the past week, but I'm avoiding him because things didn't exactly go according to plans that night we went out."

"Spill it bitch, I hate when you do that you wait until I ask you for the details instead of picking up the phone and calling me. My feelings are hurt as your best friend you should be able to tell me everything, instead of me having to pull molars for you to tell me." She expressed with a scowl on her face. I sighed because I knew what she meant by this.

"I'm sorry Puchi, I'll be more mindful of it; I swear I don't do it on purpose you know how I keep shit closed up." Marisol smacked her lips and nodded for me to continue.

"We had a great time just enjoying each other's company he told me things about his parents and his other siblings and I shared with him stories about my childhood, you of course and my parents. He was very attentive and a gentleman. Somewhere between talking and getting the check to end the date I never actually got around to setting up boundaries. I mean, I don't think it would have been a good idea to say hey we just need to be business partners and oh yeah just forget the fact that I just shoved my tongue down your throat." The car swerved to the left as Marisol try to gain control of the wheel.

"Hold up you kissed him!?"

~

We sat in awkward silence as he drove to my place. I still don't know what came over me. How could I let someone have control over my emotions like that? I sat back and thought about him, how he looked tonight, how he felt as he brushed up against me. My body started to heat up, I could feel the throbbing in between my legs. These feelings were unbearable to deal with. I looked over at Desmond's profile and at the moment he looked delicious, then out of nowhere his profile changed into his. I blinked and shook my head. We were almost at the turnabout to my house. We paused at the gate and I greeted the security guy Javier. As we got closer to my home I was trying to prepare my speech, what stance I should take. The car stopped and he cut the engine off, I stared out the window trying to disappear. I didn't want to have this conversation but I knew it needed to be done I acted out of character and I'm sure I've led him on.

"Would you like to come in for some coffee?" No stupid I thought to myself I should have just said what I needed to say instead of inviting him in.

"Yeah coffee would be nice, hold on let me get your door."

He is such a gentleman this would be easier if he was an asshole or if we didn't work together. He came around and opened my door, his hand was outstretched to assist me out of the car. I took his hand in mine, mine felt slightly moist his were hot.

"Thanks" I stated as I looked up at him, those baby blue eyes were bright in the night's light.

"You are more than welcome beautiful." I sighed and I knew this was going to be hard. I slide my key into my door and was greeted by a brush of cold air, turning on the foyer light I walked inside as Desmond trailed behind me.

"Have a seat, I'll be right out with the coffee." I entered the spacious kitchen and gathered the items for the coffee. As I was getting everything together I was trying to figure out how to approach the subject with Des, I wanted to break it down easy about why he and I couldn't date and to apologize for kissing him earlier. I was so deep in my thoughts I didn't hear him come up behind me. He cleared his throat which made me turn around abruptly.

"Oh I didn't hear you come in, did you need something?"

He just stood there, arms crossed leaning against the frame of the kitchen. I felt slightly nervous that he was just standing there not saying anything, well at least not verbally, the look on his eyes were telling it all. I cleared my throat nervously before I spoke, "Listen Desmond, I actually wanted to talk to you about us." He pushed himself off the door frame and started approaching me near the center island. I could feel the perspiration start to form near my temples, my palms were starting to sweat a little. A few steps and he was standing directly in front of me. We were a breath away from breathing in sync.

"We can talk later." He said and then the atmosphere changed.

He leaned in and his hesitation heightened my arousal. My breathing was choppy, my heart was beating fast. I soon felt his lips on my neck Desmond's, lips were soft, his cool breath did nothing to bring down my body temperature. His hands caressed my neck as I leaned back. I grabbed onto his shoulders for balance as well as strength. I felt his hands underneath my thighs. He lifted me up and I wrapped my legs around his torso as he carried me over towards the couch. I was placed on the edge with the bottom of my dress pushed up to my hips. My legs were gapped open slightly. He leaned forward and grabbed a hold of my face with both hands. The kiss was sensual but I felt it was missing something. I retreated back and looked up at his face that had changed right before my eyes. His eyes were no longer an ocean blue but a mixture of indigo, his skin was now a golden color as if it was kissed by the sun.

His lips were fuller; he was taller in a way. My body reacted to this person I was seeing; my panties were soaked, I could feel the moisture on my thighs. I reached for him and kissed him, he tasted of peppermint and chocolate and I was yearning for more. We broke apart and I gasped for air to enter my lungs. His eyes were ablaze with lust and I could only imagine what he saw in mine. I closed my eyes as I felt him feel me up, one of his strong hands were under my dress and the other was placed on my breast. The nibbling on my collar bone towards the strap of my dress where he pulled it down with his teeth. My breast was exposed the cool air harden my caramel nipples.

"Damn, baby," he said.

His tongued appeared and he licked at the tip of my perky nipple. "Mmmm" I heard myself moan. He licked around my areola and teased me before trying to suck my entire breast in his mouth.

"Oh my... mmmm...yes," my head had fallen back as his hand reached my panties. His finger caressed my panty line, and he began rubbing my clit through them. I whimpered and tried to close my thighs together to stop the sensation that I felt coming on. Between the attention that he was giving my breast and the feeling between my legs I felt that I was going to combust. He lifted his head from my chest and smirked, gripping my thighs he pulled me closer to the edge on the arm of the sofa. I felt him tug at my panties as he looked up at me for that additional help to remove them. I lifted my hips up to assist. He lowered his tall frame eye level with my pussy, he spread my thighs and placed one of my legs in the crook of his arm. He licked his lips as those beautiful eyes were trained on my throbbing clit. I knew he could see what my reaction to him and what he was doing to me. My anticipation was on high my breathing was deep and erratic. I was waiting for him to hose down this fire that he had created. I felt the first lick on my clit and then the twirl of his tongue.

"Mmm, yes" I moaned

I arched my back and placed my hand on his head. I needed his tongue to touch other places. He dipped his head lower——

I was abruptly jolted out of my flashback by the car horns and the swerving of Marisol's vehicle.

"Oh my god, are you ok?" I asked Marisol.

"Yeah girl I'm good. Are you ok?" She asked

"Yeah, what happened?" I asked looking around to see if any cars had been damaged.

"Girl I was so into you telling me the story I took my eyes of the road for like maybe two minutes," she explained.

"Damn so what happened next, did you sleep with him? If you did and you didn't sneak out the room to call me after or at least the next day, we officially are no longer best friends."

"No, we didn't sleep with each other. But that's not the real issue, at first when Desmond kissed me it felt like there was something missing. Then all of sudden I was imagining this man that I barely know while Des was licking on my clit." I explained

"So did you at least get an orgasm out if it?"

"Yes, I was so damn wet and I came so damn hard. I was embarrassed when he got up off his knees."

The laugh Marisol let out made me laugh as well. I thought about the possible look on my face when Desmond got up, I'm sure the look of regret was plastered on my face. After tugging down my dress, I rushed into the powder room and locked the door. I explained to her.

"Do you see why I've been avoiding him, how can I face him now, what do I say?" I turned and saw the amused look on her face like she was holding in her laugh.

"Do you want to get slapped, I see you over there."

"Listen Love you need to stop being so apprehensive about sex, I think it's time for you to get out there and either date and find someone you feel you can give that part of you to or just say fuck it I'm tired of being a twenty-seven-year-old virgin, who likes to get her boxed ate out but nothing more. Maybe Desmond can be that person or maybe you can connect with this guy who obviously got your pussy thumping."

I just stared at the side of her head. I knew she had a slight point but I didn't want to complicate myself with a relationship and other emotions that come with it. Marisol's phone rang on her Bluetooth in the car as I was about to express my thoughts.

"Marisol Montega speaking." Marisol greeted into the car.

"Wassup Ma?" the caller's voice vibrated through the car speakers. From the corner of my eye I saw Marisol shift uncomfortably in her seat, I looked at her and mouthed who is that?

"Well hello to you too Papí, what do I owe the pleasure of this call Rico?"

I gasped once she stated the mystery caller's name, I looked at Marisol who was trying to hold in her smile, why I wasn't sure it's not like he can see her.

He chuckled before replying, "The pleasure huh, well I was seeing if you were available this Wednesday to go out."

"Such short notice, but I'm sure you are used to women dropping everything to adhere to your requests?" Marisol replied.

"It's a simple yes or no, I understand its short notice but that's my only real free evening. So, what you tryin to do?"

"You sir need to work on your manners, but can I call you back, is this the best number to reach you at?" Marisol asked him.

"Aight ma go head, hit me up when you get free." He responded. Marisol pressed the end button the steering wheel.

"Are you going to go out with him?" I asked her.

"Girl, no did you hear the way he spoke to me, this nigga act like he doing me a favor, he doesn't know I'm da baddest puta."

CHAPTER NINE

S tanding at the floor to ceiling window looking out at the view of the city. The hustle and bustle on the streets always got my adrenaline for the day going. As my thoughts were interrupted by the opening of my door, I turned to see who had intruded without my permission.

"I didn't take you as a woman who ran from things Lovely." Desmond said.

"I'm not running from anything, I was working at home for the past week, just trying to get caught up."

"Yeah, and you're also a horrible liar as well. Listen, I thought we were on the same page that night, if I would have known that you would have went into hiding, then maybe, no, I know I would have not taken things as far as they did." Desmond explained.

My tried to keep my attention on the words that were coming out if his mouth. I found myself giving him a slight appraisal, I couldn't even lie to myself, Desmond looked nice. He always made sure his appearance was up to par. I wasn't sure what it was exactly. Maybe it was the blue tie making his baby blue eyes that much more striking. Maybe there is an underlying attraction that I have for him but my conscience isn't allowing it to surface, and probably for good reason.

"I wasn't my normal self and I got caught got up in the moment. I apologize for--" I was cut off by the voice of my assistant telling me that my ten o' clock appointment had arrived. The day was already getting ahead of me, as I walked toward my desk to retrieve the file sheet that my assistant typed out. The potential client had made smart investments. His portfolio was very lucrative. I was definitely curious as to why he would possibly be seeking new financial management for his investments. Not that I'm turning down a client. I'm great at what I do so I'm just wondering how he came onto my firm.

"Go ahead and send in the client Sasha." I told my assistant.

"Can we talk later?" I asked Desmond, he nodded his head yes in response.

"I'll have my assistant make lunch reservations at the Thai restaurant." He said. The small glint of hope that fluttered in his eyes, made me realize I needed to make myself clear to him that he and I couldn't pursue anything outside of a business relationship.

"That sounds good. I'll see you then." I simply replied.

I was tiding up my desk a bit when the door slowly opened; the cologne that wafted into the room made my senses tingle. The pungent scent of wood and spice reminded me of the Dolce and Gabbana Anthology L'Amoureux fragrance. Looking up I seen him enter the room. Somehow my large office seemed small, I wasn't sure if I had suddenly become claustrophobic. His six-foot three stature and broad shoulders almost filled the door frame. He looked like supremacy that commanded attention in his tailored Tom Ford Martini charcoal colored suit.

The gleam from his diamond earring reflected off the sun that was shining throughout the office. As he came towards the desk to shake my hand with a slight smug look on his face. I assumed that my facial expression was very noticeable since I was in astonishment that the man that just walked into my office was the man I have been having dreams about, the man I woke up in a cold sweat and had a throbbing clit for. I looked back down at the client folder and schemed through it briefly. His last name was familiar but this is New York there are plenty of people with the last name Riz. I knew I should have done my usual extensive research instead of leaving it to my assistants.

Usually I have a picture of my client, background checks, and the whole shebang. I need to know who I'm potentially working with should I accept to take them on. You can't trust everybody these days for there is always a Bernie Madoff trying to get richer. He outstretched his hand and his olive skin just seemed to glow. I didn't know men could glow. I looked up at those eyes that were his personal mood ring. They were bright with amusement and a piercing sky blue with brown around the orbs. His eyes make you squirm a bit with the odd colors that they changed.

"Good Morning Ms. Daniels. Thank you for allowing me to meet with you today." He said shaking my hand.

That tingle sensation ran through my body, up and down my spine. I quickly shook his hand and pulled away. He smiled and those pearly white teeth and those deep depressions appeared of the side of his face. I continued to stare until I was pulled out of my stupor by my assistant Sasha clearing her throat. Blinking a few times, I put my poker face on to try to hide the emotions I was going through, lust, anger and bliss. More lust than the others.

"Mr. Riz it's a pleasure to see you again." *Why did I say 'pleasure', now he's going to think that I actually wanted to see him, uh stupid Lovely.*

"Believe me the pleasure is all mine Ms. Daniels." His sexy baritone voice stated.

"Ms. Davis could you please bring in refreshments for Mr. Riz and I."

"Sure Ms. Daniels, I'll be just a moment." She says

"Please have a seat Mr. Riz." I motioned to the taupe leather guest chair. The brief walk to the chair allowed me to see his firm ass and the arrogance in his walk. Sasha came back in the office with a tray of assortments from croissants to bagels and teas, coffee and juice. He stood to help Sasha place the tray down on the coffee table. As we sat across from each other the light reflected off his gold Rolex that was accentuated by diamonds. It was simple and classy. He reached for the coffee pot and began to make his concoction.

"Mr. Riz what brings you here searching for a new financial advisor? Your portfolio clearly shows that your current financial managers has been lucrative on your behalf."

"Well I am here for more than one reason. Yes William & Cross Investments has been very successful in gaining lots of profit on my behalf. But I want to make some changes on how and where I invest my money. I have stock in a plethora of companies' some from my own start up and others in those that were suggested to me by W&C. I want to take more risk and W&C just aren't really feeling that." He chuckled.

"I understand, you have been playing it safe with your dealings and I feel that if you are willing to take risk with your money who am I or anyone else to stop you. You should have representation that support and back you in everything that you do in your business." I stated.

He just stared at me as if he wanted me to continue. I briefly got caught in his eyes they weren't the same color from when he walked in. *He should learn to wear contacts his eyes change to often and any observant person can tell that when his mood changes and so does his eyes, dead giveaway not a good poker face.* I thought to myself

"I have been told that on many occasions, I'm starting to think my eyes are transparent." He says with laughter in his voice. My eyes slightly bulge out of my head and my mouth is agape. I swallowed hard

"My apologies Mr. Riz, I didn't mean to say that out loud. I'm sorry if I offend you in anyway."

He laughs "No worries, my delicate sensibilities were not offended this time, unlike our first encounter, Ms. Daniels." he winked at me making me slightly lower in my chair, remembering our first encounter with each other, I blatantly asked him to fuck me in those exact words.

"Again I am sorry about that, that day was not my norm and I seriously am not the way I came off. I hope that doesn't affect any future business dealings Mr. Riz."

"Please call me Sincere, Mr. Riz is so formal and you and I have met on two separate encounters; so we are practically friends." He smirks. I really began to blush then.

Mr. Riz I hope this new business venture meets your expectations. I'll have my assistant contact yours for another meeting with my business partner and so we can go over your investments. How does that sound?" She asked him

"How about dinner tomorrow night?" Sincere asked with a determined look on his face.

"Mr. Riz un--"

"Sincere, please call me Sincere" he stated

"As I was going to say, I like to keep things strictly professional. If any dinners should transpire between us it would be regarding business, meeting investors, going over investments. That would be the only time we should share a meal. As far as calling you by your first name I think that it's sort of tactless in the business setting. I am your financial advisor and we should keep it that way." Lovely explained to him. He stood tall buttoning his suit jacket as he peered over at Lovely.

"Do you always speak so strongly to clients? Are you always this direct? If so, I'm highly surprised you have clients who aren't walking away."

"Mr. Riz I'm very prominent at what I do, that speaks for its self as one of the fastest growing and lucrative brokerage in the state. I like to set boundaries and high expectations for my clients, you being no different. You aren't the first client to try and pursue something more than business and I'm sure you won't be the last. With that said I hope we are clear on our standings for business, yes?"

"Ms. Daniels, you are right about a few things. Your business is thriving, you are impeccable at what you do and I can't wait to gain from that beautiful mind of yours, but I will say this. I might not be the last client to pursue you outside of business, but I guarantee that I will be the only one who will get the opportunity to see what makes you, how can I put it delicately, climax in and out that business attire."

"Mr. Riz you are out of line."

"No, what I am is honest and you denying the attraction between us is only going to make me even more persistent, and trust me I have more than enough stamina in and out of the bedroom to pursue you."

Lovely back stood straight, with her hands at her side she slowly approached him and stood face to face. She teasingly licked her lips as his eyes zoned in on her plump moist nude painted mouth. The knocking on her door stopped her from using some choice words to the sexy man standing in front of her. Sincere turned to walk towards the door, as the door opened, Desmond stood in the frame. Looking from Desmond back to Lovely, Sincere chuckled winked his eyes and said, "See you soon Lovely." As he walked past Desmond without so much as a hand shake of acknowledgement.

Lovely nerves were a wreck, she needed a drink and fresh panties. She stood there for what felt like forever until Desmond's voice filled the room. "New client of ours?" He asked. "Yes" was all she could say.

"Sorry to interrupt, but Sasha said this would be the only free time you would have today, if I would have known you were still with a client I would have rescheduled." He said with an apologetic look on his face.

"No, it's ok, perfect timing we were finished. Let me just use the restroom and then we can go." Lovely said as she headed into the in-suite bathroom.

"Hey the new client looks kind of familiar, I think I've seen him before." Desmond mentioned, Lovely took pause towards the bathroom. *Oh shit did he see me and Sincere at the restaurant* she thought to herself.

"Really! How so?"

He shrugged his shoulders "I'm not sure he just seems familiar. I'm sure it will come to me once I meet him properly since he is a new client. He was rude though."

"Yeah and stubborn as far as I can tell." Lovely responded.

A few minutes passed as Lovely came back from the restroom. "I'm ready." They headed out of the office towards the parking garage.

~

"Is everything ready?" Sincere asked as he spoke into the phone to Rico, while sitting in his car.

"Yeah we all set, those niggas confirmed the time." Rico stated into the phone.

"Aight son, let's see what these niggas talking about, even though I still think they fraud. But we'll see tonight." Sincere responded while watching the few people that were in the parking garage going to their vehicles. He always made

"Aight fam, I'm at the restaurant, I'll be here for a min- well look who we have here." Rico stated

"Who?" Sincere asked wanting to know what had caught his friend's attention.

"Aye Sin I'll hit you up when I'm on my way to the spot." Rico said

"Nigga don't be late, I'm serious mufucka. I'm already skeptical about these niggas so no late bullshit Shannon."

"Yeah yeah nigga, I got you. And don't be calling me by my government the fuck wrong with you? I don't even let my bitches call me that." Rico stated with seriousness.

"Don't be so sensitive, besides ya momma gave me permission last night."

"Fuck you nigga don't get--" Sincere hung up the line while Rico was in the middle of his rant.

He was always entertained knowing he could get under Rico's skin. He knew what would make his best friend pop off. Sincere was putting his Bentley Coupe in gear to leave the garage. He spotted Lovely walking out alongside the same man that was in her office and at the restaurant. "This nigga just doesn't know he's about to be knocked out the race." Sincere pulled out with his tires screeching. Both Lovely and Desmond look to the side to see the car racing out of the garage along with another black escalade following suit.

CHAPTER TEN

Marisol sat poised explaining to her clients the benefits of advertising through social media. The vintage business owners were trying to gain more profits but they had notice that business was declining in the more recent months. At first, they figured it was due to the economy, but as researched showed people were still buying into the products they were selling. Sure, fine jewelry or custom jewelry was for more of the elite. The family owned business had been established for decades, always turning with the tide. But the Social Media age was just something that they were geared for. The waiter sat down the bottle and began pouring into the flutes.

"Oh I'm sorry, we didn't order this bottle of champagne." Marisol said.

"It is on the house, compliments of the owner, please enjoy." The young waiter explained.

"Well please express my gratitude to the owner, better yet how about you let them know I would like to thank them in person." She said.

"Yes Ma'am, I'll see if the owner is available to speak." The waiter said as he walked off.

Marisol looked around the restaurant again soaking in the ambiance and its elegance; she'd only frequent the restaurant twice.

"Well I guess we should enjoy. As I was saying Mr. Braxtly social media is the way to get business out there. I understand your apprehension about losing your loyal customers if you were to mix things up a bit. But I encourage you to think about the profits you'll make with new clientele." Marisol said before sipping the champagne.

"I hear what you're saying Ms. Montega and my wife and I will look over your proposal more thorough. It's like you said earlier more people are gathering to social media for shopping and what's new. And as a prominent business of fine custom jewelry we want to stay in the loop and continue to profit." Mr. Braxtly stated.

"Pardon me Miss but the owner stated they were available to speak with you when you were finished with your dinner and guest." The waiter informed; as Marisol was about to respond Mr. Braxtly said to her, "Go ahead Ms. Montega, we're just about finished and it is getting late. And old bird like me has a scheduled bedtime."

"Thank you for your time Mr. Braxtly, please call me if you have any questions about the proposal or the numbers."

"I will do that if I have any questions. Our next meeting is already scheduled but I might not be in attendance. I'll send one of the children to go over any thing I need clarification on. If not, I'll just have them sign contracts so we can begin."

Mr. Braxtly stood up to leave as did Marisol. She reached over and shook his hand and thanked him. The waiter stood off to the side waiting for Marisol to finish her conversation before leading her to the upstairs to the office.

"Right this way Miss." The waiter instructed. As they entered the elevator the waiter pushed in the code to start the elevator. Marisol chuckled lightly while thinking of the last time she had seen a code needing to be entered just to ride the elevator. The young waiter looked over at her wanting to ask her about the laugh but decided not to. The elevator chimed signaling their arrival. The waiter held the door open as Marisol stepped out.

"It's the second door on the right ma'am I'm sure he is waiting on you." He said.

"Wait, he?" Marisol asked as the elevator doors were already shut. She walked down the beautiful hall and stood in front of the door. Raising her hand to knock there was a buzzing sound then a click. She placed her hand on the handle and cautiously opened the door.

He sat there in a relaxed pose waiting for her to enter. Their eyes connected, his roamed her body in the fitted but professional dress. Her heels added to her height and toned legs accentuating them. She stood by the door watching him. His crisp tailored shirt fitted his muscles that she had embedded to memory. The color against his dark smooth skin made her want to rip open the fabric and touch those amazing abs, his grey eyes were sharp, staring at her. She cleared her throat to begin to speak.

"Thank you for the champagne my guest and I enjoyed it." He continued to stare and said nothing, his eyes still focused on her. She felt like she was being inspected, she suddenly felt nervous and slightly intimidated; something that never happened with her whether it was a man or a woman in her presence. Reaching up to push her overgrown bangs out of her eyes, she licked her lips in the process.

"Are you going to stare the entire time or are you going to say something?" She asked him; the corner of his mouth turned up, still nothing just the scrutinizing of his stare.

"Ok so you're going to stare." She stopped and paused "Well thanks again."

Turning to walk back out the door, she grabbed the handle to exit but the door wouldn't budge. Turning around she glared at him.

"Unlock the door Rico." She demanded.

"Are you asking me or telling me?" he questioned, "Imagine my surprise, seeing you downstairs, once again in one of my establishment."

"You have a beautiful and in demand restaurant. I come here for business meetings for potential clients when I can get on the list. Which is very hard by the way?"

"I know the wait list is several months out. How are you able to dine here on short notice?"

"That's for me to know and for you to not find out. I'm not trying to see anyone unemployed because they're doing me a favor." He laughed and nodded his head up and down. His smile was contagious, it made Marisol smile as well.

"What type of client were you entertaining? I mean what is it that you do?" She rolled her eyes at his initial question.

"I own my own marketing company. I've been in business almost five years now. The fact that I've nearly made it to the five-year mark is no easy feat." She explained.

"Advertising huh I could use some good marketing for my clubs." Marisol walked towards him and handed him a business card.

"Oh a nigga gets a business card, now if I call the business line would you actually return the phone call?" Marisol laughed at the comment. Knowing he was referring to her not calling him back last week after his so-called dinner proposal.

"What, were you waiting by the phone waiting on my call?"

"That's not my style ma I don't wait on pussy, besides isn't it too late to be doing that?"

"Doing what exactly?" She inquired.

"Playing hard to get, trying to make a nigga chase. I've already got the pussy so what more would I need from you?" He said with a straight face.

"At first, I thought it was kind of cute, you know, you not knowing what to say so you stick your foot in your mouth. But now I believe you truly are an asshole and if that's real, I don't need to be bothered." Marisol said.

"I just call it like I see it ma, if that's me being an asshole then I guess I am." He stated back. Retreating back to the door Marisol paused her stride and turned around to see Rico closing the distance between them.

"Well thank you for showing the real you before I did something I regret."

"Oh so you don't regret fucking me? That's good to know."

Rico took steps towards her, backing her up against the wall. With both hands placed on the wall he had her cornered. Rico could see the uncertainty in Marisol's eyes, the vein on the side of her neck was pulsing fast as she tried to keep controlled breaths.

"You Papí-" she said as her hands roamed up and down his chest, she trailed them up towards his neck caressing him. Looking into his eyes one of her hands slid down slightly skimming his manhood that was semi hard lying against his thigh. Biting her lip, she moved closer towards him. She took his hand in hers and placed it underneath her dress, his fingers began slowly stalking up towards her center. As the tips of his fingers began to feel the lining of her panties, he could feel the heat coming from her core. As she led his hands closer to her center, her lips fell onto his. Giving a light nibble, she pulled back and said "Nunca volverás el interior de este coño."

"You should do something about that down there." She said as she looked down at his bulging erection; Marisol pushed him slightly out of her way as she exited the door. Rico stood in the open-door frame with his hands balled up; he was hard as a brick. He counted slowly to ten and watched her wait for the elevator. Stepping out of the office he walked towards her with her back facing him she refused to turn around. Punching in the code to the elevator Rico watched as she lightly fidgeted.

The dinging sound announced the arrival of Marisol's temporary safe haven. As she was about to step inside the cabin he grabbed her arm; not bothering to look at him it only made him smirk at her stubbornness. "Ma never say never that pussy will be on this dick sooner than you think." With that he let her arm go. She walked into the elevator and turned around to glare at him. Unable to resist the urge she stuck the middle finger up as the doors were closing. She could hear him laughing. As the elevator descended Rico's phone began to ring, he looked at the caller id and seen it was a broad he met up with a few nights ago. Sending the call to voicemail he walked back towards his office to grab his keys and lock up. He knew he had to be on time to the meeting. Picking up his keys, jacket and his business cell phone and Marisol's card he headed towards the door. The business line rang he answered it without even looking. He knew who it was so there was really no need to screen the call.

"Nigga I'm leaving now." He said to Sincere.

"Change of plans, we about to have some unexpected visitors."

"Who nigga?" Rico asked.

"I just got a call from the Dons. They want to meet up tonight no questions asked."

"Damn, did they say about what?"

"Nah son. I'll know when you know. Meet me at the club so we can roll together. I know that nigga Kam is near so hit him up and let him know what the deal is."

"Aight fam I'll see ya in minute B."

"Send a text to King and tell him that shit postponed."

"Yo am I ya fucking secretary? Do this, do that. What happen to please, nigga?" Rico joked.

"Oh you on some funny shit, huh. What's that all about shorty finally hit you up?"

Rico laughed thinking about Marisol and her attitude. If he had time he would have fucked her up against the door, but he was going to let her think she had the upper hand for now.

"Something like that, I'll tell you on the way to the meeting." He said

"Aight son" Sincere replied

"One" Rico stated as he ended the call.

CHAPTER ELEVEN

A few weeks later......

Nigga turn that shit down. Mayne, niggas always thinking they gangsta, but when shit bout ta go down ya niggas straight pussies." DeMarcus said while taking a pull on the blunt being passed around.

"Yo, why are we meeting these niggas at this spot?" Marcos inquired.

"This da address that nigga King gave, told us to be there at nine. I didn't know it was a residential area. I know these niggas not holding weight in the suburbs?" TK responded with his own question.

"I guess we'll find out soon enough, King gon' be here right?" Marcos asked no one in particular, he just wanted an answer. He already didn't feel like dealing with Sin and Rico.

He heard how ruthless they were when they were on the streets but now as suppliers they didn't give a damn; you could be dying in front of them, they wanted their money when it was time to collect.

DeMarcus wanted to see if they could get weight on consignment. Their prices were high, but they had the best quality product. So in a way it was worth it if you knew how to step on the kilos a couple times.

"Dats what dat nigga said over the burner" TK mumbled in a low ton

"What!? Nigga speak up. I told you about that mumbling shit. Don't be doing that shit in there with them niggas." DeMarcus yelled.

"I know how to speak mayne." TK had a mug on his face as he looked at DeMarcus through the rear view mirror.

"Shit barely, matta of fact don't say shit mayne. I don't need these dudes thinking I'm runnin with slow mu'fuckas" DeMarcus expressed.

"Shit this the place right here. Call that nigga King and see if he in there or something, got us looking all out of place out this bitch." said DeMarcus

"Yo King we here. What you want us to do mayne, wait? Wait on what." Demarcus mouthed to Marcos to put him on speaker phone. As Marcos did what was requested of him, the men in the car listened as King gave instructions.

"Yeah nigga wait, I'm almost there." King stated

"Say mayne how you gone tell us to be here at a certain time and you not even here. That's some hoe shit." DeMarcus complained

"What? Look just keep ya black ass there I'm not far." King told them

"Yeah aight." Demarcus said as he sucked his teeth. Marcos disconnected the call.

They continued to smoke while waiting for King. The car was silent as they all were trying to figure out what was about to go down.

Demarcus was low key pissed off that he was actually waiting around on a dude. Soon headlights appeared on the street. They all turned and saw a white van approaching. All the men tensed and reached for their guns. Marcos pulled out his Beretta and prepared to cock it back. The van parked in front of their truck. Seeing King come out of the passenger door he slowly put away the weapon. DeMarcus exited the car first, pulling up his jeans and wiping off imaginary lent.

"It's about time nigga, thought I was going to have to put an APB out on ya ass, what's with the van?" He asked King.

"This here you niggas ride to the spot?" King said with a straight face

"Whatcha mean mayne, we got to ride in the back of the van, like on some kidnapping shit?" DeMarcus said with a slight attitude.

"Aye son, boss man orders. This how we do things, get with it or get gone, your choice." King said.

DeMarcus didn't like the way he was being spoken to by King. First being told to wait on him, now he was being told that he and his crew would have to ride in the back of the pedophile looking van and ride to the destination.

"What about my car?" he asked King. King looked back at the driver door and nodded his head. The van doors opened up and out came a big burly looking dude stepped out. He walked to where King was standing waiting for orders.

"Smoke gon' tail behind the van with ya'll as extra security. So your car will be with him.

"Mayne alright. All this extra shit, homie." Demarcus signaled to the men in the SUV and they began to pile out.

"What up King." Laz spoke, King nodded his head as a response. Laz looked around at the other men then back at King, not sure the reason for the nonchalant attitude he shrugged it off

"What's with the Scooby Doo van." Marcos asked

"This here our ride to the location." DeMarcus responded to his crew

"What?!" the men responded in unison

"Same thing I told him, I'm going to tell the rest of you niggas. This ya ride take it or leave it, this how moves are made with us. The bosses don't know ya'll and don't trust ya'll so get with it or beat ya muthafuckin feet." King states while looking at each one of them.

"Man look we ain't got no real choice, shit we trying to cop some of the finest drugs, so it is what it is. Let's do this. "Laz said. King looked around and began nodding his head in agreement.

"Load up niggas!" yelled King.

"So what the fuck happened?" Sincere asked looking at the men inside the warehouse "Don't leave out any details." Rico said, his stance showed he was not in the mood for the current issue, his mind was elsewhere, but he knew this part of the business was important and he had to make sure that anyone that they did business with knew they weren't going to get over on them. Everyone looked at each other trying to figure out who should speak first. The warehouse was quiet no sound coming from any of the men standing before Sincere and Rico. The damp cold air smelled of mold and the dripping sound of water became a melody in the abandoned space.

"Please, I don't want to hear all you niggas at once." Sin said with an angry glare. You could feel the tension and fear in the room.

"They mighty quiet for niggas who just got fifty keys lifted off them." said Rico

Laz stepped up and began to speak "Once we arrived to the spot, we got out the van, King let us know the amount of keys we were coping and that the work was on consignment like we all agreed on. Once the shit was loaded and secured we also loaded up to follow the product. Now ya'll got us niggas in the back of a van with no windows so we can't see shit. Out of nowhere the van stopped then we heard some shots ring out. We reaching for our hammers and then the van door is snatched open. Some niggas got AKs and choppas on us and shit yellin for us to get the fuck out the van." He explained

"Who was in the van with the driver?" Rico asked

"Shit none of us went with the driver. That's yo people so we figured he was straight." Marcos said

Rico and Sin looked at each other and no words were said between them, Sin gestured for Laz to continue. "I see two of them pull ya peoples out the van and get in. They had us down with them hammas all around us. I guess they knew which van had the product in it, they barely searched the van we were in." Laz explained

"Did ya'll see any faces or anything." Sin asked Laz. He began to wonder why DeMarcus wasn't the one explaining everything that happened.

"Naw Sin they had ski masks on." Laz said. Sin and Rico shook their heads and began to ponder. Sin began pacing back and forth, making the men even more nervous than they already were. Watching Sin angry was like watching a trained killing pit-bull. Sincere stopped in front of DeMarcus before he began to speak.

"So that's fifty keys of pure and on top of that, ya'll had the work on consignment. So what I need to know is how are ya'll going to get us our money or product. And I don't want to sound arrogant but our shit ain't cheap or smashed down." Rico said with a slight smirk.

"Fuck!" was all Marcos yelled. He knew the shit was too good to be true. Sin and Rico actually allowing the product to go off of on consignment alone, he knew that was too good of a deal. Now they had to figure out a way to get fifty keys of pure cocaine to appear out of thin air with the money they already had. Owing these two is exactly what he didn't want to happen.

"You know what I find kind of suspicious, how is it that no bodies dropped during this whole thing? None of you niggas thought to shoot first, bleed later? Ya niggas wasn't on ya bully to bust once them doors opened. Makes me think ya'll might be in on this take down." Rico said staring at the men in the room. Kameron moved closer towards Rico and Sin, he was standing in the back, but once Rico made his accusations he knew something could pop off, calling niggas thieves and liars was one way for shit to go down.

"What? naw nigga my team ain't have shit to do with this here. We trying to come up big but not on no sheisty shit. Leave that too them corner boy stick up kid niggas. Dats not us fam." Marcos explained.

"Yeah, well all I know is I'm out of almost a million in product and I want my muthafuckin money." Sincere barked out

DeMarcus finally spoke up, holding his hands up he started to approach Sincere. "Nigga what you got yo hands up fo' like you on some 'don't shoot' type of shit. Do I look like the fuckin police?" Sin snarled

"Nawl, nawl Sin, it ain't like that, we'll find a way to get ya'll ya paper or product back." Demarcus said

"How nigga? You already wasn't working with the type of prices we charge, so explain to me how a bunch of niggas with broke pockets gone get me back a fuckin mil?" Sincere looked at Kam and nodded. Kameron passed Sincere the pistol. Sin stance looked tense and ready to kill a man. The men looked on; nervous eyes darting back and forth between Sincere and Demarcus.

"You niggas got a week to get me my shit; either my money or my product." Sincere stated, DeMarcus held in a sigh, he was trying to think of how he was going to get something he only had for nearly twenty minutes back and on top of that back in a city that he wasn't even from. Laz shook his head, he had no idea what they were getting into doing business with Sin and Rico but now he knew why their names rang so much power.

"We got it Sin." was the only thing DeMarcus could say. The men looking somber started to walk towards the door to the warehouse.

"Oh and just to make sure ya'll niggas know I'm serious-" The men turned around just as Sincere raised the pistol up and shot off a round. The bullet hit DeMarcus in the shoulder. DeMarcus grunted and grabbed his shoulder in pain.

"What the fuck was that for?" Marcos questioned, looking at his twin brother hunching over holding on to his shoulder.

"Just to let ya'll know, that was a warning shot the next ones will end lives if I don't get my money." Sin explained. The men shook their heads in acknowledgement of the threat, well the warning. Marcos applied pressure onto DeMarcus' wound as they helped him out the building to the car. Watching them exit, Kameron went to the door to make sure everything was secured and locked. He didn't need the niggas gaining any kind of courage and coming in blasting. Kameron gave the all clear sign, Rico looked at Sin and shook his head before laughing.

"Them niggas shook B. Did you see their faces when you raised the gun? And why that nigga Laz doing all the explaining and shit if its DeMarcus' crew." He asked to no one in particular. King who was in the back laughed along with Rico and the rest of them. Sin on the other hand stayed in the zone, he was curious as to why Laz was doing all the talking, when King brought up this crew he made it seem like DeMarcus was the leader. Today he sure didn't make a stance like one, that's why he shot him in the shoulder. Not only to intimidate the men but to show them that the men in their crew were weak. No real man would have allowed himself to be shot without causing some type of immediate retaliation. "So you're giving them a week?" Rico asked

"That's what I said, didn't I." Rico looked at Sincere like he lost his damn mind speaking to him like a subordinate. Sincere let out a sigh; he was in an all-around bad mood. First The Dons coming in a few days ago with an impromptu meeting, then telling them that they need to push more product into some different states. That's one of the only reasons Sincere took King up on these southern dudes. But once they heard the prices they asked for the shit on consignment, they didn't have the type of cash upfront for the type of product he and Rico were pushing. Then there was Lovely she wanted to schedule a meeting to go over the recent investment loss that he just had taken. She didn't disclose the amount but he knew it had to be big since she actually called instead of her assistants.

"What you think their reaction gone be when they find out we set the whole thing up. " King asked

"It's a surprise test, if they true hustlers they gone make a way to get me my money or product. One week will tell what they can do when the pressure is on."

"That nigga DeMarcus gone be pissed that he just took a bullet for a hoax take down." Kameron said

"Shit he better be happy that it was his shoulder and not his fuckin heart." Sincere replied.

~

The next day Sincere met with Lovely to discuss the investment loss. They sat next to each other in her plush office going over the schematics on whether to sell the remaining stock that Sincere had acquired or stick through with the company once their board devised a plan to their investors. Lovely was going over the documents when she heard Sincere's pestering question. As she tried to ignore the question, curiosity got the best of her.

"Why do you keep asking me out on a date? I'm sure there are plenty of women that would want to date you Sincere. "Lovely asked him

"I'll continue to ask because you look like you need to be fucked." He responded

"So that's it, the reason you want to take me out is so you can fuck me. You just want my body. You know what, this conversation is over. Anything else we need to discuss I'll give the information to my business partner." She started to pack up folders, she was ready to be out of his presence.

"You misunderstand me Lovely. Yes, I do want to fuck you, but what I want to fuck no one else has ever done. I want to fuck your mind, make it understand how much I desire you. I want to make it submissive to your man. I want to hit every single spot and not leave any part of it wanting. And when I'm done fuckin your mind, then I want to fuck this beautiful body of yours. I want it calling and yearning for me when I'm in your presence or if I'm hundreds of miles away. Baby when I'm done fucking you; the men before me won't even be remembered."

"You want to control me. That's it, you want to control me? And what about the men after you." He shook his head at her stubbornness.

"Ma there won't be any man after me; and a submissive woman is not a controlled woman, a submissive woman to her man is the sexiest woman in the world."

"God your persistence is really starting to get annoying." She stated.

"It's my persistence that has gotten me where I am now in this world." He said.

"Oh yeah and what is that?" She asked

"A rich muthafucka, simple as that." Was his reply with a devilish smile.

"You're so crass." She said as she tried not to roll her eyes at his response.

"Call me what you want, but you know at least that much is true. Which is why I think you owe me dinner for my substantial loss."

"You think dinner with me is worth two and a half million dollars?" she asked him

"No," he responded, she looked on a little shocked but quickly erased the expression from her face.

"But I'd still like to have dinner with you." Sincere said, Lovely stood and just thought about his request, finally making her decision she figured what harm could come of it. He was finally wearing her thin with asking her out. Plus she did feel kind of responsible for the investment loss. Sure this was a typical type of occurrence in this business, but Sincere was originally against the investment on the newly acquired company. Lovely had convinced him that the company would profit well in the third quarter. What they weren't expecting was the CEO to be doing some inside trading and the company took a hit, as did Sincere and a few other clients. Lovely had been working overtime to assure her clients that the entire scandal would blow over and profits would turn.

"Fine I'll go out to dinner with you, only because I do feel guilty about the investment. You didn't want to take it on at first and I convinced you otherwise. I would normally never do this only because if I did I would be going out all the time with clients. This is a risky business and my clients know what they are getting into. I'll do this dinner as a sign of faith that you'll continue to stay on as a client, but I get to pick the place, agreed." She stated.

"No." Lovely blinked not expecting that same answer again. Shifting from one foot to the other she crossed her arms around her chest and looked at him with one eyebrow raised. Sincere took in her stance and laughed to himself, and though she's cute when she doesn't get her way.

"You owe me, this is my dinner. I choose the time, and place. Since you already agreed to have dinner with me what's one more agreement." He shrugged; he waited for her response, he could see in her beautiful honey eyes the wheels turning. After a brief pause, she reluctantly nodded her head in agreement.

"Good, see that wasn't so bad. I'll pick you up at six sharp Ms. Daniels." He said.

"Tonight? I figured later on this week, umm tonight isn't good. I really have some work to finish and get some more calls made and. Tonight is just no good." She tried to explain. Sincere wanted Lovely in a bad way, he knew he had to get her on this date tonight before she changed her mind and reneged.

"Tonight is the only night I'm available I have some travels this week."

"Ok see, that's why we should try another time. You're busy, I'm obviously busy." She said, Sincere shook his head already shutting down her way out. Lovely thought to herself how sexy he was sitting there looking at her with those eyes. "Fine, what should I wear?" After Lovely said it she knew the mistake she made. She saw the smirk on his face and before he could even allow words to come from his sexy lips lovely raised her hand halting his response.

"I mean how should I dress for the dinner, what's the dress code."

"Well something," he paused and thought about his response, he didn't want her to think the only reason he wanted her was to just have sex. "Anything you want to wear, beautiful, just dress comfortable." Lovely gave a slight nod to show her understanding.

"Well then I guess I'll see you tonight Mr. Riz." She stood up to walk him out of the office, it was barely noon and she was already trying to figure out how she was going to get a hair appointment in at her favorite hair salon. Watching him walk out of her office she bit her bottom lip, he had a sexy, powerful walk and his broad shoulders sat up straight, he filled out his suit impeccably and with ease. She opened the door as she did so he turned around and leaned in towards her ear and whispered, "Don't even think about cancelling due to work, I've already had your assistant clear your appointments for the day, after noon of course." She looked up at him with blazing eyes.

"You have no right to do that Mr. Riz, I have a business to run, now tell me why I shouldn't cancel on you after what you did." He looked at her and saw the seriousness of his actions, his apology came off as sincere, "Listen, yes I was wrong, I can admit that and to be honest I didn't want you to use work as an excuse. I apologize for overstepping and I can admit that I did bribe your assistant with a nice fee and a 'win them over smile'. I hope I didn't get her fired." Lovely laughed at the last part, she could see Sasha giving into a handsome dimpled smile and sexy eyes. She couldn't let him think he could do that in her own office.

"Look don't worry about my assistant I'm her employer so I have to deal with it accordingly." He nodded his head in understanding.

"Take it easy on her, I'll see you tonight. Six, ok?" He asked it as a question because he knew she was still upset with what he had done.

"Yeah, six." Was all she said. She watched him walk out as she headed to Sasha's desk. Sasha could hear the tapping of her boss's heels but she dared not look up. She knew what she had done and she knew Lovely was going to be mad, Sasha was well aware of the chemistry between Lovely and Sincere.

"So, should I call you Madam Sasha?" Her assistant looked up bracing herself for Lovely's wrath.

"Umm, what are you talking about boss?" Sasha faked not knowing what her boss was referring to.

"Boss? Boss, oh now I'm the boss. Seems like earlier I was the high-priced escort that you were pimping out to a John."

"Lovely I get you're upset." Lovely's eyebrows arched.

"Okay you're very upset. But in my defense, that man is smart, sexy, and rich and did I say sexy. I know I shouldn't have taken the bribe, let alone listen to him or cleared your schedule but you need to get out and date. And girlfriend, if you're going to date someone, please date that fine ass man that just walked out of here." Lovely just shook her head as she turned to walk back into her office. Her thoughts were everywhere, she wasn't sure about the date this evening, she was tempted to call him and cancel. Letting out a small sigh, she headed towards her desk and began to pack up.

"Well let me call and see if I can get a hair appointment this afternoon." She grabbed her cell phone, keys and headed out the door.

CHAPTER TWELVE

The doorbell rang as she was placing her clutch purse on the coffee table. Lovely walked towards the door but stopped to do a double check of her makeup and attire. She exhaled deeply, as the doorbell rang again. Opening the door, she saw a tall older man standing waiting for the door to be opened. With a puzzled look on her face she stepped out and looked left and right of the driveway for Sincere.

"Good Evening Ms. Daniels, I'm Bennie, Mr. Riz's chauffeur and I will be driving you to your destination." He stated.

"Mr. Bennie, is Mr. Riz in the car?"

"No, ma'am he is not, I was instructed to drive you to your destination."

"Mr. Bennie can you do me a favor, can you call your boss for me?" Lovely asked.

He looked at her with bewilderment as he pulled his cellphone out of his pocket and began to dial. As he waited for Sincere to answer he took in Lovely's features, she was beautiful he thought to himself, over the years as the driver for Sincere he has seen him with many women, but as he looked at Lovely he could sense that she might not be like all the others. For one she had him calling his boss, for god knows what reason.

"Good Evening Mr. Riz---no I think everything's okay, but Ms. Daniels wanted me to contact you." He paused and looked at Lovely while Sincere spoke "Yes Sir, I understand." He passed the phone to Lovely, "Here you go Ms. Daniels."

Lovely took the phone and placed it up to her ear, "Is there a reason why you had my driver call me instead of yourself?" Sincere asked through the phone.

"Yes, I wanted to make sure he was your driver, I thought you were picking me up personally, not a driver," she told him.

"Well now that you know he works for me are you going to get in the car so you won't be late for dinner?" He asked with a chuckle.

"Yes I guess I'll see you soon. By the way what restaurant are we dining at?"

"You'll see when you get here beautiful." He disconnected the call. She stared at the phone for a moment before handing it back to Bennie.

"Everything ok ma'am?" Bennie asked her.

"Yes Mr. Bennie, sorry about that I just wasn't informed I was being picked up by a driver."

"It's okay Miss, and call me Bennie, shall we." He said as he gestured towards the car. Lovely walked towards the car as Bennie held the door open. She lifted the bottom of her flowy Givenchy sundress careful not to get it stuck in the door. As Bennie closed the door with a head nod, Lovely looked at the interior of the vehicle. It reminded her to contact her dad and see how he was enjoying his retirement gift. As they started off towards the highway Lovely's mind started to wonder about the evening ahead, her thoughts were interrupted by Bennie asking her a question.

"Ms. Daniels what is that you do if you don't mind me asking?"

"Not at all Bennie, I'm co-owner of an investment firm."

"That's good, how is business going in this economy?"

"Actually, with the Obama administration business is going smooth, when I was interning during Bush's second administration of course it was a strain, it made me question if this is something that I wanted to do for the rest of my life. But life has its ups and downs, you just have to know when to fight harder, be stronger and when to ask for a helping hand."

"Sounds like you're a smart woman Ms. Daniels."

"I try to make smart decisions that will affect me in the future as well as the present." The car got quiet briefly, before Bennie could ask another question Lovely had one of her own, "Do you normally drive Mr. Riz's dates to him?"

"No Ma'am I can't say that I do."

"Interesting." Was Lovely's only response, she looked out the window and saw that they were exiting the freeway.

"Where are we going?"

"Were heading over to the East 34th street heliport." He responded.

"The heliport, why? Where is he taking me?"

"Ms. Daniels, please stay calm, he only told me where to drive you, that's all I know, and the pilot will have the flight plan to the destination."

Lovely was fuming inside, first he sends someone to her home to pick her up without being notified, then he plans on flying her to an unknown destination, well unknown to her. She had half a thought to have Bennie take her back home, she knew he was only following orders from his arrogant boss. She sat back and huffed and waited until they reached the heliport. The car stopped and Bennie got out to open the door for Lovely.

"Enjoy your dinner Ms. Daniels." Bennies stated politely as he got out to open her door.

"I will try, thank you for the car ride Bennie."

"You're most welcome ma'am I hope to see you again soon." He said with a wink.

Lovely walked towards the heliport where a pilot had her name on a piece a paper holding it up. She looked around and saw no one else in the vicinity. She was unsure why the pilot had a piece of paper bearing her name as if he were picking her up at overcrowded airport.

"I'm Lovely Daniels." She said as she walked up to the pilot.

"Right this way Ms. Daniels, we're slightly behind schedule."

"Can you tell me where we are going?"

"Yes, our destination is The Hamptons. After you Miss." He gestured toward the sleek air transportation.

Arriving after the forty-five minute helicopter ride and another twenty minute drive Lovely finally pulled up to the nice size beach house. The driver stepped out of the car to open her door. As she stepped out and grabbed the bottom of her dress she saw the front door opening to the house. She looked up and saw Sincere standing there wearing off white slacks and a Ralph Lauren Polo she felt better about her attire, she was glad she wasn't overdressed. Sincere came down the steps toward her and she too started walking his way. He gave a head nod to the driver as he was getting back into the car.

"You look beautiful, glad you could make it." He said sarcastically.

"Thank you Sincere, you're lucky I came at all. With your little stunt earlier, I had half a mind to stay at home." He laughed a little at Lovely's response.

"I know baby but I wanted a change of scenery for our first date. Forgive me for not informing you." Lovely stared into his eyes with a resting bitch face for a few moments before smiling and shaking her head back and forth.

"Let's see how this dinner goes first before I do any forgiving." Sincere showed off his perfect smile and dimples and replied,

"Alright Ma lets go inside and enjoy dinner."

They both walked into the home. Lovely looked around the enormous entry way. The colors were a rich cream and brown. Sincere gently grabbed her hand and led her on a short tour of the house. Their tour ended in the beautiful chef inspired kitchen where two chefs were preparing their dinner.

"These are my private chefs James and Fiona they of course will be preparing our meal." Lovely greeted both Chefs with handshakes and a smile.

"It smells good in here." She said

"Thank you I hope you enjoy the meal we are preparing for you tonight." James said.

"Do you have any food allergies or particular food you don't eat?" Fiona inquired.

"Oh no I enjoy everything, but I am allergic to strawberries." Lovely informed the chefs, both James and Fiona looked at each other and nodded, "Well in that case we will accommodate dessert for you ma'am."

"I'm sorry did the dessert have strawberries in them?"

"We had incorporated the fruit but it's not something we can't change we will ensure it is still a wonderful dessert." Lovely felt a little bummed out that her food allergies were going to cause the chefs to re-make the dessert. Sincere came by her as the Chefs went back to preparing the meal.

"Let's go in the sitting room and talk while they finish up." He suggested.

"Sure, lead the way." The two sat and talked getting to know each other. Thirty minutes later Chef James came into the sitting room to announce that dinner was ready to be served. Sincere took Lovely towards the back of the house out to the private patio that lead to the private beach.

"We're eating outside on the patio?" She asked him

"No, I thought we could enjoy dinner on the beach, I had them set out our table towards the beach. Is that okay, I can always get them to move it inside."

"No, no the beach is perfectly fine, I've never dined on a beach before. And the weather is real nice right now."

"Well Ma, I hope I can be a first for many other things as well. Do you want me to hold your heels?"

Lovely looked down and forgot she had on heels and knew she couldn't walk in the sand with them on. She took one heel off at a time and held them by the strap and began to walk towards the table that was set up for them. Sincere followed behind her getting a view of her ass moving in her sun dress. They reached the candle lit table for two. Silver trays were already on the table along with a bottle of fine imported wine. The pair began to enjoy the prepared food and wine. After two glasses of the imported wine Lovely started to get more comfortable in Sincere's presence. Chef Fiona came and cleared the table from their dinner. Chef James came and placed a dessert plate with a silver covering. He lifted the cover and on the plate was a big ball made of white chocolate. James poured melted dark chocolate over the white chocolate ball as Lovely watched on; the white chocolate dissolved and underneath was the delicious dessert. Lovely smiled on as she took a bite into the moist cake garnished with raspberries and blueberries. A moan escaped her lips as she ate the decadent dessert and sipped on the dessert wine that was exchanged out as well. The more relaxed Lovely became the more she opened up to Sincere.

"Tell me how did you get your start in life? I can tell you are doing really well, but how did you get that kick start?" Lovely asked. Sincere sat quietly thinking about how he entered the drug game, how his father had passed it onto him when he retired and how he hoped to be able to do the same one day with his future son. He looked Lovely in the eyes and knew he couldn't reveal that part of him to her yet.

"My father actually instilled the business man that I am today. He showed me how to profit from a dollar and how to keep my money making money. After I graduated college I bought my first investment property and flipped the house. From there I just continued to invest in property residential and commercial. I always had a love for cars, nice luxury cars so when I had the opportunity to buy the dealership I took it." Lovely listened as he continued to speak on. His next question caught her off guard "Tell me something you wouldn't normally tell me." He said.

"What do you mean? Like a goal or a dream?"

"Nah something you would be too bashful to tell me on a first date." Lovely shook her head and giggled.

"Now why would I tell you something like that?" She asked him.

"Because I want to get to know you on another level than just business." Lovely thought about it and started to speak but shook her head.

"Naw tell me what you were going to say. Tomorrow isn't guaranteed you should always get your feelings out when the opportunity is present."

"I'll only tell you if promise not to laugh or judge me,"

"I could never laugh at you, you're too beautiful to laugh at."

"Are you always like this on dates?"

"I'll answer that as soon as you stop deviating from the original topic. What were you going to say?" Lovely nibbled on her bottom lip in a nervous action contemplating if she should tell him what was really on her mind or make up something. She went gusto and decided to give into her original thoughts.

"I was going to say that; I have been having dreams about you. These dreams seem so real, even though I know they aren't; because you haven't touched me the way you touch me in my dreams. Your lips haven't touched mine with this unexplainable passion like it is in my dreams. And the lust in your eyes as you hold me is nothing like the way you're looking at me now." Wait maybe it is the same way she thought to herself. Lovely looked down after the words left her mouth. She glanced at her watch and looked around the beach as the waves splashed against each other and the night. Sincere didn't respond to what she had said. He just looked on at her, wanting her to continue.

"Listen it's getting late and I think it's time for me to go."

"You're right it is getting late, and driving to the city would be at least two hours if the traffic is good. Just stay the night."

"I can't I have important meetings in the morning and on top of that I have no clothes, wait driving, what happen to the helicopter?"

"I didn't have a return flight plan for the helicopter, so we would have to drive back to the city. Lovely I give you my word I won't come anywhere near you the rest of the evening. As for the clothes I have an entire closet one that has women's clothes."

"Oh you do huh, so is that what you do, get the women here by helicopter and the no way to get back so you can fuck them. Would I be wearing the clothes your last conquest left behind?"

He touched the bridge of his nose and shook his head. A slight chuckle escaped his lips.

"Ma you have got to stop with the overthinking. Yes, a woman did leave behind the clothes, no they have never been worn, and no I don't bring women to this house you're the first actually. I'm rarely here during this time of year. Mostly my younger siblings use the place during the summer." She looked at him skeptical, she did get a tour of the house and knew any room she chose would be furthest from the master bedroom.

"I'll just take the drive back to the city. Having dinner with you was one thing, but staying the night, this is just not something I feel is acceptable between us." Sincere nodded his head with her decision.

"Let me call you a car service."

"You're not going to ride back with me?" She asked.

"No, I'm going to stay here, I have a flight to catch in the morning, so I will be leaving from here." He explained.

"Right you did say that you had to travel." Sincere stood up to walk back towards the deck to retrieve his phone, he called the car service he used when he frequented the Hamptons. Lovely watched the waves of the ocean as Sincere spoke on the phone. She kept telling herself she was doing the right thing, making sure there were boundaries between the two of them. She didn't hear him approach as he informed her the car service would be there shortly. Lovely nodded her head in response. She turned her head to look back at the ocean, when she felt Sincere's finger come in contact with her chin. He turned her towards him as they stared into each other's eyes. He ran his fingers down her face, towards her neck. Lovely didn't realize she closed her eyes until she heard him ask her to walk alongside the beach with her. She shook her head in agreement as he held out his hand for her to take. Lovely removed her shoes and grabbed the end of her dress as they began to walk along the water. They walked in silence for a few minutes both in their own thoughts. Sincere was the one to break the silence.

"Do you swim?" He asked her she looked up at him and smiled.

"Like a fish, I think I should have been born in the water. I love the water, its relaxing, powerful and peaceful. If that makes any sense." Was her response.

"Really, well when you come back we will definitely have to take a dip in the ocean or the pool if you prefer." Lovely stopped mid stride, seeing her stop Sincere did as well. They turned to face each other.

"There won't be a next time Sincere. I don't know how else to tell you why there won't be us in a setting like this again." He looked away back out to the ocean as his cell phone vibrated in his pocket, he looked at the caller ID before answering.

"Hello? Yes, we'll be ready, thank you" Lovely listened to the one-sided conversation.

"We should start walking back. That was the car service letting me know they were fifteen minutes away." Lovely shook her head and turned to start walking back to the house. They walked in silence, allowing themselves to think. As they approached the beautiful home, Sincere stopped by the table where they were eating and picked up his and Lovely's shoes. As she continued to walk towards the deck steps Lovely felt Sincere heat from his hand on her forearm. He turned her towards him, "Lovely I want to thank you for coming out and having dinner with me tonight, I enjoyed your company, your laughter and smile. I also enjoyed the silence between us it gave me time to admire your beauty." The blush crept up to her cheeks as she listened to him speak. She admitted to herself that she enjoyed his company as well and getting to know him. "I uhm," She cleared her throat "I enjoyed your company as well Sincere, you are an interesting man." She said as she stepped upon the steps.

Sincere followed suit as they were still facing each other. Sincere continued to look into Lovely's golden eyes, he saw a calmness that she didn't have when she first arrived. As he continued to stare, his hands started making its way towards her shoulders. He stepped closer to her eliminating the space that was between them. His hands traveled to her face cupping her cheeks, neither was unsure who leaned into who but they were a breath away from each other, tilting her head up slightly, her eyes darted towards his lips, she looked back up into his eyes. Lovely closed the mini gap between their faces as her lips landed onto his. The crashing of their lips felt like tingling sensation flowing through their bodies. Sincere deepen the kiss as he took hold of her face, his hands eased down towards her neck trying to get her closer than close would allow. Their tongues started searching for the others wanted to absorb each other's taste. Lovely moaned, her hands worked towards the collar of his shirt. The kiss was as sensual and seductive as any first kiss could be, their tongues were taking its time learning the plumpness of each other's lips, the taste, the feel, the warmth.

The vibrating cell phone in Sincere's pocket put their kiss to a stop. The two were at the front door waiting for the driver to pull up. Sincere turned towards Lovely as she looked out the window.

"Are you sure you don't want to stay the night? Like I said I won't be near you the rest of the night"

"I find that hard to believe with the kiss we just shared Sin." Sincere smiled at her shorting his name.

"Did you not enjoy it?" He asked he wanted to see if she was going to lie to him. Her words could say she didn't enjoy it but her body told him something different.

"It doesn't matter if I enjoyed it, I already told you we can't conflict our business relationship."

"We can't or we shouldn't because I believe we can do anything we want to ma. The only person stopping us is you." She sighed and said nothing. The driver pulled up to the beach house. Lovely walked to the door as Sincere opened it.

"Thank you again for dinner." He nodded his head in acknowledgment. Lovely walked out the door and headed to the car. She heard Sincere call her name as he walked down the stairs. "I just had one last question, did the kiss feel anything like it did in your dreams?" The driver pulled open the door for Lovely to get in, she stood at the car door before responding "Goodnight Sincere, thank you for dinner again." Lovely ducked inside the car to allow the driver to close the door. The car soon backed up from the driveway. Lovely had to refrain herself from looking out the back window to see if Sincere was still standing there.

As the car pulled out of the estate and onto the road Lovely sat back a reflected on the man she just left. She could admit to herself that she had a good time getting to know him, there was definite chemistry flowing between the two of them. She felt herself being comfortable in his presence which for her these days were normally far-fetched. She sighed in the back seat as the car continued to move through the traffic. *What am I doing* she thought to herself but before she could stop herself she made the request "Driver can you take me back please" she said as the partition was rolled half way down. The driver looked through the rear-view mirror, "Ma'am; Back to the Estate?" He asked, she nodded her head yes, the driver made a quick dash between the lanes as he need to exit to turn back around. Car horns blared their annoyance at the quick sharp move that was made.

Lovely walked up to the big wooden doors and used the door knocker to sound her unexpected arrival. No immediate answer so she looked in the windows to see if anyone was still there. The lights were dimmed in the entry way. She decided to use the doorbell as she waited. No response again, she took out her cell phone and was about to dial, when the door burst open. Sincere stood in a plush white towel wrapped around his taunt lower body. Water was dripping down making its way from the top of his neck down to his hard abdominal into the valley of unimaginable pleasure.

"Is everything ok, did the driver do something?" He questioned as he started to step down toward the driveway. Lovely shook her head out of her reverie as her eyes trailed up to his face.

"I was wondering if the offer to stay the night was still on the table." He looked at her and stepped to the side to allow her entrance into the house.

"Yeah let me show you to the room."

They climbed the stairs with Sincere trailing behind her taking in the view of her round peach shaped ass. He was so transfixed on her hips swaying and body movement he didn't notice she stopped and was looking back at him. She was at the top of the stairs.

"Are you going to show me which room or are you going to continue to stare at my ass?" She asked.

He walked past her and opened the door to the room closest to the master bedroom. They walked into a soft grey colored bedroom.

"Everything you need should be in here, the towels are in the cabinet in the bathroom as well as toiletries. The closet and drawers should have night attire, if not just let me know and I'll show you to the other closet in the other room."

He prepared to walk out of the room when she looked at him "I know you said you wouldn't bother me the rest of the night if I chose to stay"

"Yeah that's what I said." He replied.

She took a step closer to him and looked back down at the towel still wrapped around his waist, her eyes traveled up to his tight abs that showed he worked out religiously, up to his biceps which she wanted to grab on at the moment.

"What if I told you that I didn't want that?" He held onto his towel with one hand as he rubbed his goatee, "I would say you need to be more specific with what you want exactly." She cleared her throat and replied, "I want to spend the night with you in your bed, lying next to you and whatever happens I wouldn't stop it."

"Listen Ma that's not what tonight was about, I really wanted to get to know the woman that you are. I already know the businesswoman. I didn't bring you out here to fuck, on some real shit." Lovely shook her head up and down feeling rejected, the look in her eyes said so as well, she turned around to get her things to head into the shower.

The multiple shower head coming from different directions hit every part of her body. The steam engulfed her and relaxed the tension from the night away. She washed her body with an organic body scrub that she found unopened in the bathroom's vanity. She thought to herself while she stood in front of the glass doors. She was trying to make sense of her actions while at the same time just wanting to be spontaneous. Sincere's rejection didn't help her feel any better but she wouldn't fault him, she was the one telling him nothing more would become of them. She could understand why he is being apprehensive at this moment. She was the one with the indecisive behavior. She washed the remaining body wash off, turned off the shower on the electrical pad and stepped out the glass doors. She dried herself off, lotion her body with the Chanel body lotion, she must admit whoever stocked the bathroom made sure there were luxurious items one could pamper themselves with.

The gold knee length satin nightgown was lying on the vanity's chair. She unclipped her hair and pulled the nightgown over her head. The bed looked comfortable as she pulled back the duvet and prepared to climb in. She laid there for almost twenty minutes and sleep still didn't come. Suddenly a small light shined into the room through the crack from the door. The door opened wider but the light was soon blocked by his muscular frame entering the room. She scooted up towards the head board waiting for him to move. He crossed the room to the other side of the bed. Her lungs began to burn from the oxygen she was holding. He reached for her and pulled her into his body, they laid side by side. Neither of them saying anything, just listening to each other's breathing. Lovely was sure he could hear her heart pounding she wasn't sure on what to do next, Sincere rolled over onto his side "Sin, listen I know-" he cut her off with a quick kiss to her plump rosey lips "Shh got to sleep, I have an early flight." With that he placed a kiss to her temple, and positioned his chin atop of her head. Lovely cuddled next to him with her head tucked between his collar bone, soon sleep found her as they laid together.

CHAPTER THIRTEEN

The ringing phone startled her out of her slumber. She lifted her head from under the covers and realized she wasn't in her bed; these weren't her Egyptian cotton bed sheets and the duvet didn't smell like her. The cellphone rang again, this time she saw that it was on the nightstand, she reached over to grab the phone. Glancing at the name on the caller id she wiped left. "Hello! I have been calling you for the past hour why aren't you answering the phone?" The caller exclaimed. Taking a deep breath before responding she looked around the room again, the curtains were slightly drawn back, she could tell the sun was crisp and was probably going to be a hot day.

"I know you hear me talking to you." Again, the caller stated.

"Damn girl I hear you, I just woke up let me get my thoughts together." She responded.

"Whatever, where are you I've called your house phone too and no answer."

"I can't remember at the moment."

"Oh my god what do you mean you don't remember, where are you so I can send a car to come and get you. Are you safe? Tell me something."

"Bih if I said I don't remember how in the hell am I going to tell you where I am. And obviously, I'm safe if I answered the phone and don't sound panic."

"Are you sure, do I need to do a GPS location on your phone? Cough once for yes and twice for no."

"Damn Love I'm good," Marisol giggled into the phone.

"Why are you blowing up my phone anyway?" Marisol asked.

"I was calling to tell you about my night."

"Well then spill the tea." As her friend began to talk Marisol noticed a picture on the nightstand, she reached over to get a better look at the people in the photograph all the while Lovely was still talking.

"You've got to be fucking kidding me." Marisol yelled

"What?!" Lovely asked, Marisol climbed out of the bed looking around for her clothes.

"Lovely I'm going to have to call you back, I remember where I am now." She told her

"Do you need me to send a car for you?" Lovely asked again.

"Send a car, why can't you come get me?" Marisol questioned.

"You didn't hear anything I said. I'm in the Hamptons that's why?"

"Hamptons, why? Never mind I'll call you back to get the tea." She disconnected the call as she continued to look around the spacious bedroom.

She was alone, it felt like déjà vu to her but she remembered she came to his house, she was sure he was still here, he wouldn't have left her in his home. She tossed the covers back and stretched her limbs, she had too many drinks last night. She sat for a few minutes trying to figure how she even ended up at his place.

~

Marisol opened the drawer to retrieve the automatic wine cork. It was a long day at the office. The campaign for the family owned jewelry company seemed to be more of a challenge then she originally laid out. With the pop of the wine cork she reached for her glass. The sound of the crisp wine flowing into the glass seemed to relax her mind just a bit. She placed the glass to her lips just as the buzzing of her cell phone grabbed her attention. The caller identification showed private; normally she would just swipe the decline button and let the caller leave a voicemail if it was important. She thought about it possibly being Mr. Braxtly's grandson, he was supposed to call to arrange a time for them to meet to go over the campaign's current progress. Marisol let out a deep sigh before picking up the phone to slide the green button to the left.

"Hello this is Marisol."

"Damn the way you said that made my dick hard." The deep baritone caused a shiver to run down her spine, she instantly knew who it was by the voice, she could not forget that voice if she tried. Marisol kept her tone cool and calm, she didn't want to give off her sudden pleasure of hearing from him.

"Usually when a person calls they state their name, and you have exactly three seconds to tell me who is calling my phone from a restricted number."

"Why is there so much unfriendliness in your voice? And why you frontin' you know exactly who this is." He said.

Marisol disconnected the call. Already stressed out from the day's work she didn't have time to play on the phone with anyone. The cell phone rang again with the same restricted caller identification on the screen.

"What is it that you want Rico?" She asked into the hand-held device.

"Aye don't be disrespectful, I don't play that hanging up the phone shit. Make that your last time."

"Who are you to be telling me what to do, it's obvious you can't follow directions, I clearly stated for you to identify yourself in three seconds or I would hang up. You thought I was bluffing."

"If you already knew who it was why did I need to identify myself ma." He stated.

"Again that is what normal people do when they call a person's phone. But clearly you aren't normal and you can't follow instructions. Now what is it that you want?" She sighed heavily into the phone taking another long swallow of her wine.

"I never got that dinner date and the last time we saw each other you seemed upset after you left. Even right now you seem upset, stressed, you should let me work that out for you." Marisol poured some more wine into her glass. She thought about his response and chugged down the liquid concoction.

"I wasn't upset, I was irritated there's a difference. But you really haven't told me why you are calling my phone again."

"Yo shorty you wildin." She rolled her eyes, she figured since he couldn't see her doing so, she would continue.

"Aight Pa, you ain't saying much, I'm about to get back to my wine."

"Come have a drink with me."

"Now why would I do that?"

"Because you shouldn't be drinking alone."

"I drink alone every night thank you very much."

"Damn ma every night. I might need to get you to an AA meeting."

"Fuck you Rico, I don't have a drinking problem. I just like to enjoy a glass of wine to unwind from the day."

"How about you come over so I can enjoy you, while we have a drink." Marisol sucked her teeth. She thought he was slightly smooth in trying to get her to come over, she knew he only wanted to get into her panties. The reminiscence of the night at the club made her body tingle, she wouldn't mind having his strong tempting body up against hers.

"Thanks, but no thanks, I'll continue to have my drink alone. I don't need to be anyone's drink and chill."

"You're something else, aight ma I'll get at you some other time."

"Am I wrong though? I mean that's the only reason you want me there, so we can drink and fuck." She heard him sigh into the phone,

"If I wanted to just fuck, I wouldn't be on the phone, a simple text message would suffice for some broads, but like I said I'll get at you some other time." With that Rico disconnected the call.

Marisol let out a frustrated scream. She wasn't sure of Rico, she was hesitant about doing anything further with him other than the night at the club. One moment he was tolerable, calm, fun and then the next he was a rude, condescending asshole.

"I bet he's a Gemini, he's sweet then sour. Just like a Gemini." The phone chimed indicating a text had come through,

917-555-6789: 2275 Parks Ave Suite 5, I'll leave your name with the doorman. She laughed at his arrogance, and continued to pour another glass of wine.

~

The door opened abruptly. He walked into the room as if he were the only one there. She took him in. He looked good in his distressed jeans that were pulled down slightly and his polo shirt, it was fitted around his biceps, the shirt was loose enough at the waist. Marisol noticed the glass in his hand as well as the bottle of aspirin.

"What happened last night?" She asked him as he sat the items on the table next to the bathroom.

"You came over to drink and chill," He said with a wink and a smile.

"Shit you were already tipsy when you came over here, I'm glad you took an Uber instead of driving yourself."

"I was already drunk and you took advantage of that and slept with me!"

"Nah I said you were tipsy not drunk. I ain't take advantage of a damn thing, but trust me ma any other nigga would have."

"You're so full of it Rico, why else do I not have my clothes on if we didn't sleep with each other?"

"Does your body feel like we fucked? You keep making accusation like I'm some fuck boy who's hard up on getting pussy." He responded to her accusation.

Marisol closed her eyes and tried to bring the events of the night to the front of her brain. Her body didn't feel any different, there were no soreness in between her thighs, she knew for a fact that if they did indeed sleep with each other she would have been sore, since Rico is well endowed.

"So, are you going to tell me why I have any clothes on?" He licked his lips and Marisol watched the action and wanted to lick them for him.

"I wasn't about to let your funky ass in my bed." Marisol gasped at his remark.

"Excuse you, nigga, what the fuck did you just say to me?" She was upset, Marisol knew she took care of her hygiene and there was no doubt in her mind that she would never go out smelling anything but feminine and fresh. He stood there with an expressionless face, no smirk or smile to indicate he was joking.

"I ain't got to repeat myself ma, you heard me." Marisol wrestled to get out of the covers, she was ready to get in his face and really tell him off.

"Settle yo little ass down, stop trying to get your panties in a bunch, no pun intended." He said with a smirk on his face while looking at Marisol's panties being ate up by her bodacious derrière.

"Who do you think you are speaking to me like that. I'm not one of these thots out here, you're mad disrespectful. I know damn well I don't have any body odor." He chuckled at her Brooklyn attitude, her Spanish accent poured out thick. Rico walked over to the couch area and sat down, he wasn't one for arguing so he had a decision to make. Either listen to her rant and yell or kick her out of his penthouse. He watched her tousled long hair sway back and forth as her neck twisted when she spoke. Her thick thighs slightly parted was getting his dick hard, as he remembered how she looked and felt last night with him standing in between them. The room finally became quiet, Rico looked up at her, she was sexy, her hair a mess, eyes blazing with annoyance.

"Are you done? I thought I was going to have to put something in your mouth to get you to shut up." Marisol's green eyes darkened as he spoke.

"Where the fuck are my clothes, I need to leave because if I stay it's going to become a domestic violence situation and I know I don't want to be in jail over no nigga." She walked around the room searching for her clothes. Her frustration was elevating since she couldn't find her items. She started towards the bedroom door to look in the rest of the house. Rico stopped her mid stride by her forearm.

"Your clothes aren't here."

"What do you mean they aren't here, where are they?"

"They haven't come back from the cleaners yet. I had them sent out."

"Why would you need to do that Rico?"

"If you calm down and listen I can tell you what happened last night." He removed his hand from her arm.

Marisol folded her arms under her breast pushing them up even more toppling over her bra. Rico's eyes stayed on hers. He was tempted to look straight down but he needed to make sure that he had her attention. She stood in the around the way girl pose waiting for him to give her the details about last night. He walked back to the couch and sat down. Marisol sucked her teeth and followed suit as she was about to sit her round ass down Rico grabbed her gently by the waist and moved her to his lap.

"I would have been fine sitting next to you not on you." She said. He shrugged his shoulders "Just have a seat and listen ma."

~

She walked into the spacious living room. He watched her walk into his penthouse, her full hips swayed side to side and her ass bounced when she walked. She sat down on the plush modern sectional, crossing her legs she flipped her hair then set her eyes on him. Rico couldn't tell if the glossy look in her eyes was lust or the alcohol.

"You aight ma?" He asked her.

"Yes I'm fine. Why?" Was her response.

"I'm just trying to make sure. I can't tell if you over there looking at me like that because you want to fuck or if you just got done smoking chief." Marisol rolled her eyes at his statement.

She licked her lips and ran her fingers through her hair.

"I didn't come over here to fuck, okay Rico." He nodded his head up and down.

"Aight then ma, why did you come over here?" She stood up on unsteady legs, he moved closer to her just to make sure he would catch her if she fell. She pulled down her bondage skirt as far as it could go which wasn't much.

"I came here to have a drink. I didn't want to drink alone." She responded.

"Nah ma I think you might have had three too many already and I ain't got nothing but strong drinks here. None of that Merlot bullshit."

"I can handle my liquor pa, I'm a big girl."

They were in the kitchen sitting at the island. Their drink of choice was Cîroc Apple. Rico initially suggested Hennessey, he wanted to gauge the type of woman she is. He knew a lot of strippers and ratchet women that took shots of Hennessey like it was water. Once Marisol declined the Hennessey Rico felt a slither of his uneasiness about her being in his home diffuse. Marisol was working on her second glass of Cîroc Apple and sprite.

The two were in a zone, talking and listening to the music. Marisol reached for the bottle of alcohol. Rico pulled it away from her, Marisol face turned into a scowl, "I think you've reached your limit." He explained. Marisol smacked her lips as she stood up.

"Where's the bathroom again?" She asked him he pointed her in the direction. He watched her as she tried to walk on steady legs a chuckle left his mouth causing Marisol to raise her middle finger as she continued to walk towards the bathroom. Rico finished off his drink in one gulp, he grabbed Marisol's glass and moved towards the sink to pour out the rest.

"Shorty is done, she can't even walk straight." He said to himself. He heard the clacking of her heels as she walked back into the kitchen area.

"Papí dónde está mi bebida?" He raised the glass in his hand to show her. He tipped the glass over the sink as the clear liquid poured down the drain. Marisol shrugged her shoulders and picked up the Cîroc bottle and tilted it to her mouth.

"What am I doing fuckin babysitting you," Rico walked around the island to where they were sitting.

"Yo shorty you wildin again. Ya ass could barely walk to the bathroom now you over here trying to get white girl waisted. Ya done ma." He tried to take the bottle away from her hand, the two went back and forth, one trying to keep the bottle in their possession and the other trying to take it. Rico decided to put an end to the childish act, he grabbed Marisol by the waist, lifted her off the ground and placed her on the kitchen island. He gave himself access in between her thighs the best he could, one hand was placed on her smooth thick thigh creeping its way up to her honey pot. The other hand was nestled on the back of her neck, Rico had her attention, the bottle was still in her hand with her fingers closed around it. Rico stared into her eyes as she gazed back into his cloudy gray orbs. His fingers slowly tickled her neck, but not in a ticklish giggly way. No, his movements were slow, deliberate, soft with a little bit of pressure on her pulse. Marisol inched her head back slowly as he worked his fingers around to the front of her neck. His head tilted towards hers as her breathing became choppy. Her stomach felt tight and her pussy muscles were clenching. He moved in, his breath on her neck.

The anticipation was exciting and dreadful at the same time for her. He set in with butterfly kisses from the side to the front, the hand on her thigh gradually moved towards her hand where she was holding the bottle. Without missing a step Rico was able to remove the Cîroc bottle from her fingers. He had a grip on the bottle as he pulled back from her neck, Marisol lifted her head up to see why he had stopped. The grin on his face said enough, and the bottle in his hand let her know she got played. The clenching in her stomach had stopped, she prepared to hop off the island.

"You good ma?" he asked her. She didn't lash out at him when he took the bottle from her, he was prepared for her slick smart mouth. She said nothing, she nodded her head up and down slowly.

"Listen I don't feel comfortable sending you home in an Uber. You have two options, crash here in the guest room or I drive you to your spot. Which one?" As she opened her mouth to speak her face twisted up a little bit, it threw Rico off he wasn't prepared.

"I'll --" was all Marisol was able to say before a spray of gut wrenching vomit unleashed from her mouth onto Rico's body. It seemed like it lasted for minutes, when it was only seconds that all the liquid exported itself. Rico had vomit strewn on his shirt and all the way down to his Gucci flip flops. He didn't have any warning to move out of the way. There was no gagging sound, Marisol didn't cover her face or hold her stomach to show any indication of regurgitation.

"What di blood clot."

~

The doorbell rang, Rico tapped Marisol's thigh indicating for her to lift up.

"This should be your clothes." He walked out of the bedroom to answer the door. A few minutes later he was walking back into the room with her clothes in a dry cleaners' bag. He handed her the clothes, "Thanks. How much do I owe you?" She asked him.

"Gone somewhere with that Marisol, a simple dry-cleaning bill ain't going to set me back mortgage money."

"I didn't mean it like that. I just, um, I'm just appreciative of the gesture of having my clothes clean."

"Ain't no big deal ma besides I couldn't have you walking out here with that funky ass smell that was in those clothes."

"Whatever Rico, I only saw my clothes in the bag what did you do with yours?"

"Oh, I burnt them. I don't think you understand the damage you did last night. Miss, I can hold my liquor." He said to her as she went off to put her clean clothes on.

"Hang with me today." He asked her, Marisol side-eyed him as she placed one foot at a time into the pearl colored Louboutin's.

"Time is money and I need to go and make mine." Was her simple reply.

He nodded his head up and down "Aight I understand that. I'll retain your services for the day. You own a marketing agency, right? I need some advertising done for my night club and gentleman's club." She stood up and walked over to where he was standing.

"You know I own a marketing agency, it was on the card that I gave you with my number, besides that's not how it works Rico. I have several projects that I'm working on right now. I wouldn't want to take on your business and not give it my full attention. Plus, I need to go home to change and freshen up." Marisol explained as she watched him pick up his keys and walked toward the door to head out of the bedroom.

"Just ride with me" Rico commanded.

~

"Who is Shannon?" She asked him as they zoomed throughout the light traffic. The slight skeptical look on his face held as he pondered on if he should answer truthfully.

"I am. My first name is Shannon. The only people who call me that are my mom, my sisters and sometimes the vendors I work with. Rico is my childhood nickname." He explained.

"Why'd they give you that nickname?"

"My father was Cuban, being from Kingston, Jamaica the people thought it would be humorous to call me little Rico, since my father was a hustler and we had money and it just stuck, as I got older I ditched the little part."

"A Cuban father and a Jamaican mother. That is definitely a unique match. Do you know how your parents met?"

"The same way a lot of island girls meet men. They see a dope boy making money and find a way to trap them." His blunt responses to questions intrigued Marisol. She was turned on from his authenticity.

"Can I call you Shannon?" She asked him putting on a big smile.

"You can call me Rico." He told her.

"Alright Shannon, I see that you're a businessman. But what I really need to know is how long you have been the business man." He looked at her perplexed by her question.

"I don't know what you're referring to Marisol. You've been with me all day and clearly you've seen how I'm handling myself." He was hoping his response would give him a clear insight on what she was referring to. He had an idea but like any true hustler, you speak once and listen twice.

"You're right I have been watching you all day handling business. I also have been observing you. You handle business like a hustler. Like a dope boy that graduated to the top status. You're not the only one in this car that's a product of poor girl meets kingpin. Before my father was killed, that was his lifestyle. He sold drugs in order for us to be able to have some nice things, like a nice brownstone in Brooklyn. A nice car, nice clothes. He graduated from corner boy dealings to being able to move some kilos in and out of state. I know a hustler when I see one, somebody that could talk me into buying that designer bag that I don't need is a hustler. I also know what a boss looks like too, he's the guy that doesn't need to say much for his presence to be known. He doesn't take orders from anyone, he gives them, my father was that type of man, the way you handle yourself reminds me a lot like my father did." Marisol hoped revealing that part of her would ease his tension and open up.

"Let me ask you something, how did you know so much about what your father was doing in the streets?" He asked.

"I was a daddy's girl. My father and I were really close. He told me a lot. He said it was his way to ensure that I survived in the world if he wasn't around to guide me."

"That's wassup I can respect that as a man."

"Are you going to answer my initial question?" He removed his fitted hat and rubbed down his waves. He turned his head to look at her.

"It isn't always best for the girlfriend to not know. You know so that she can have deniable plausibility." A smirk formed on his lips.

"Who said anything about me being your girlfriend?" Marisol questioned

"Shit with good pussy like that, I got to make you something." He said as he exited the car.

CHAPTER FOURTEEN

Three Months Later.......

The flashing blue and red lights were visible in his rear view mirror. The black low tinted unmarked SUV drove behind him. He looked to into his right-side mirror to see if any cars were visible before he veered into its lane, he exited the off the highway. He drove past the gas station, the lights continued to flash and the SUV's sirens sounded indicating to pull over. He stopped the car onto a back street, he parked and waited for the officers to approach.

The door to the SUV opened and two men stepped out. One tall white man with a lean frame. The other short, fat and slightly balding at the top of his head, the two were a typical looking cop duo. The lean cop walked up to the black CL 550 Mercedes Benz and knocked on the tinted window a signal for the driver to roll down the window. His hand was at his hip where his gun was holstered. The window slowly rolled down.

"License and registration." The tall white officer said.

"Why am I being pulled over?" He asked showing no signs of complying with the officer's request.

"I ask the questions not you. Now license and registration." The officer repeated.

The driver cut his eyes at the officer and began to reach for his wallet in his back pocket. "Easy there, as a matter of fact why don't you step out of the vehicle" The officer commanded.

The other officer just stood there waiting for the driver to exit the car. The driver opened the car door slowly. He didn't want to alarm the officer again as he was a black man and it was always open season on black lives for cops. He stepped onto the gravel covered ground.

"Step off to the side of the car." The officer instructed.

He did as he was told, "Turn around and place your hands on top of the vehicle." He turned around and placed his hands on the roof of the car. The officer began to search him for any weapons or drugs. The officer pulled out the wallet and handed it to his partner.

"My constitutional rights are being violated at this moment. I want to know why I was pulled over and asked to step out of my car." The driver said in a malice tone.

The officer looked him up and down before he spoke.

"What are you a lawyer or something? Your rights huh." The fat officer came back from the SUV.

"He has a warrant out." The tall white officer smiled at the information.

"Well mister, 'I know my rights' it looks like you're going with us. You have an outstanding warrant."

"Bullshit." Was his only response. The fat officer cuffed the driver.

"Damn do they have to be so tight?" All three walked to the SUV. The fat officer put the driver in the back seat and slammed the door. The tall officer went back to the driver's car and inspected the vehicle for any other items they could charge the driver with. He didn't find anything. He locked the car door and walked back to the SUV.

The drive to the precinct was quiet. Both officers in their own thoughts. The tall white driver took the exit towards their destination. A few minutes later they pulled into a warehouse. The passenger in the back looked around at his surroundings.

"Aye muthafucka this ain't the damn jail. Where ya'll pigs taking me?" Neither officer responded.

"Chill out homeboy. We just want to have chit chat with you." The fat officer chuckled as he exited the car.

The officer went to the back door to let him out. He stepped out of the SUV, he looked around again as he was led into the building. It was drafty, and had the familiar cold moldy smell, most abandon buildings had. The trio walked in further, the door closed loudly behind them. The tall white officer was in front leading him and his partner to a back room.

"Aight ya'll want to tell me what the fuck is going on and why I'm here and not the police station." They continued to ignore his question.

They stopped in front of old rusted sliding doors. The tall officer slid one half of the doors open to the room. He stepped aside and gestured for him to enter. Several eyes were on him when he entered the room, three men of different races looked back at him.

"Jeez guys are the handcuffs necessary?" One of the men in an off the rack suit asked.

"Mister I know my rights here, seemed like he wasn't going to cooperate if we asked him to come in nicely." The tall white officer responded. The suited man walked up to him to release the handcuffs.

"Nice to see you Laz." Said his boss and lead D.E.A agent.

"Yeah good to see you too boss, why did you send Barney Fife and Andy Griffith to pick me up. You could have called like normal." Laz asked the commanding agent.

"Well let's see. I have tried getting in touch with you on the private cell phone but every time I call I get a voicemail and text messages are not being answered as well. So, I decided to send a black and white to pick you up. Since we have the locator in the vehicle you're driving." His commanding officer explained.

"So what's up, you've gone through all the trouble to get me here? What is the reason?" The DEA agent looked at Laz for a few moments before responding.

"Didn't I just tell you why you're here?" He said calmly, Laz took a seat at the table that was set up with a few laptops, coffee cups and half eaten sub sandwiches.

"I'm undercover I can't be checking in every time you decide to call. I've also been very busy." Laz responded.

"Oh you've been busy, ok good, so you got some information for me?" Laz looked up at the ceiling, then back at his boss.

"Nah I ain't got nothing new." His boss slammed his hands down on the table.

"Dammit Alonzo, you're playing games, I knew I should have taken you off this assignment months ago when Sincere shot one of the guys in your crew, and you failed to report it to us." Laz just shrugged his shoulders

"I know Sincere shot him and I should have reported it, but did he die?"

"You've been undercover for almost a year. We're getting tired of no progress. Have you obtained anything that we can make a solid case against Sincere and Rico's operations."

"Listen Dean it's like I told you, when they collect the money or distribute the product they are never there. It's always King. He's the one that handles all of the dealings with the drugs and money. It just Sincere and Rico's business. This ain't no New Jack city times where the kingpin is standing in front of the buyers selling the dope. They delegate duties in this era, to ensure they are never caught on tape doing any dealings."

"Well then let's get King in here and get him to roll over on these two." Dean suggested.

"Man good luck with that. Unless you have something that will make that man talk he ain't about to snitch those two out. He's loyal to the soil to them. Shit their entire crew is." Laz shrugged his shoulders, he knew the probability of any of the men in their crew taking a type of plea deal was slim to none.

"What about you?" Dean asked as he looked his agent in his eyes

"What you mean what about me?" Laz sat up in his chair giving Dean an icy glare.

"Are you loyal to this operation, your job, or have you flipped on us and deliberately not giving us intel. You've been in the field for some time now. Touching more money than any of us will see in a year salary. You've got the nice car, living in the fancy house, with all these new women around. Are you loyal to them as well?" Laz stood up abruptly, his fist was balled up as he placed them on the table and leaned in towards his superior.

"Man get the fuck outta here with that shit. I'm loyal to the badge. Any money that I earn out there is turned over to the feds to help build a case. I'm an undercover agent so of course I have to keep up with the pretense. Ya'll approached me about this assignment and I am honored to take this on and take down a major drug empire. Don't ever question me again on if I've switched on this team. I'm here."

"Well then act like it. Get us some shit that will stick that we can use to take them down." Dean stated.

"What about the women we've seen them with. The tail that we put on Sincere shows him frequently visiting a woman." Dean picked up one of the folders that were scattered about the dull table. He thumbed through the file until he came across the photos. He laid the photos out in front of Alonzo.

"Her name is Lovely Daniels, from her profile she comes from a very well-off family. Father is a retired circuit judge and mother is a prosecutor. She's the Co-Owner of the financial management firm that she started with a law school buddy and it looks like she's handling the money from her beau's businesses. Can we flip her?" Dean inquired while looking at the black and white photos that were taking of Lovely with high powered camera lens. Several photos showed Lovely leaving her office, her home and Sincere's home as well. Dean's eyes stayed on one particular photo of Lovely standing in her window in a skimpy negligee, his eyes darkened with lust for the beauty.

Alonzo shuffled through the file he couldn't understand how a woman as educated and successful would be involved with a drug kingpin. But he knew the deal, good girls loved the bad boy. It's like their pussy yearned for it. Being undercover he has seen what the money would make the women do and how they would throw out all the good morals their mothers raised them with. He couldn't judge though he took full advantage of it as Laz.

"She's green Dean. I've only seen her once and when I did her face didn't read queen bitch, I bet my salary she doesn't even know Sincere's real dealings." Laz stated as he closed the folder and snatched the picture Dean was still ogling over.

"The way I see it. If she did know he was a drug trafficker he wouldn't tell her the intel of his business you know for plausible deniability."

"Get the fuck out of here Alonzo, there's no way she can't know. She's fucking laundering the money, she has to be." Dean exclaimed. Alonzo stared at the photo in his hand. He remembered the day he saw her and couldn't lie she was beautiful her honey eyes sparkled and she only had eyes for Sincere. He was out in New York on "business" and saw Sincere and Lovely coming out of a restaurant holding hands. Alonzo had called out to Sincere, Sincere had stopped while Laz walked over towards him and Lovely. Sincere briefly introduced him to Lovely as his lady and without so much words he knew not to talk shop in front of her.

"I'm telling you Dean she knows nothing, and if we brought her in and tried to flip her it would hurt us more than it would help us." The statement wasn't something Dean wanted to hear. He was getting tired of this operation and wanted it to come to an end. He could only see himself getting the top player in this takedown and the accolades he would reap from the takedown.

"Well it seems that we might have to go for gusto and use our confidential informant as a witness." The look on Alonzo's face was one of confusion, he wasn't aware of a confidential informant in the operation and more importantly what information they had that could take down one of the biggest drug rings since Escobar. Dean slid over a sealed manila envelope. Alonzo ripped it open and poured out its contents. He stared dumbfound at the information that was laid out before him.

"How the fuck did you get them to flip on the cartel?" He asked.

"Let's just say they got themselves in a whole heap of shit and the get out of jail free card was to become a C.I." Dean vaguely explained, Alonzo was still stunned, if what Dean said was accurate then they had everything they needed to take down not only Sincere and Rico but an entire Cartel.

"Get me a buy on video and that's all I need to start wrapping this shit up. I can go back home and you can go back to being Alonzo the desk paper pushing DEA agent." He grunted out.

CHAPTER FIFTEEN

"I feel like we haven't seen each other in forever." Lovely said to her best friend.

"Shit we haven't, you've been too busy dating this man that I still have not met by the way. I really think I need find a new best friend." Marisol said with a pouty face.

"You could never replace me Puchi so I don't even know why you would say something like that." Marisol just cut her eyes at Lovely. The friends were out doing some shopping around town.

"Besides you're one to talk, I know the last time we spoke on the phone you were going on and on about Shannon and I still haven't met him as well." Marisol laughed as she thought about her and Rico's interesting growing relationship. Marisol's phone buzzed in her purse, she retrieved the phone and saw the incoming text message. She smiled and bit her bottom lip as she read the text from her man. "Uh huh what's that grin for? Must be Mr. Rico Suave, are you about to ditch me for him. We are supposed to be having a best friend day out." Lovely asked her. Marisol thought about what Lovely said, today was as about them hanging out and catching up. She replied back to Shannon and put her phone in her purse.

"Nah girl we are still having our day. But since you did say you haven't met him why don't you come with me, he just sent me a text asking to stop by his office." She explained

"Girl that sounds like a booty call, not 'bring your home girl with you' and even if it was you know I don't do threesomes." Marisol laughed out loud at Lovely's statement.

"Bitch you don't even do sex, have you and Sincere even fucked yet or are you still holding out?" The question made Lovely slightly shift her stance. She and Sincere have been dating for the past three months, Lovely was enjoying getting to know him on a personal level. The apprehension of dating a client was still there, the thought of them together still gave her pause on a business level. Lovely wrapped her mind around this as being the real reason the two have not taken their relationship to the next level. They had come close on several occasions of actually sleeping with each other, but Lovely would always cut if off. Marisol stopped with her teasing implications, when she realized Lovely hadn't said anything.

"Lovely, my bad for teasing, I know that's a serious decision you have to make. Have you talked to him about it, I mean does he understand you wanting to wait to have sex?" Marisol waited for her friend's response.

"He doesn't know." Was Lovely's only response

"He doesn't know what?" Marisol said with a pointed look at Lovely

"He doesn't know that I'm still a virgin. Anytime we've gotten close to sex I have stopped him." Marisol's eyes widened at her friends' revelation

"Let me get this straight. You've been dating this man for three months and you have not told him that you're a twenty-seven-year-old virgin. This is what you're telling me Lovely?" Marisol shook her head from side to side. "Girl I don't know how you do it, I try to fuck Shannon any chance I get. I need to have that big thick dick inside of me. I'm aDICKted"

"It's not all about sex Marisol."

"Oh I know, Shannon and I talk when I'm not trying to ride his dick." She responded.

"Well it's not that simple for me, I'm actually into this man, he's amazing, fun, spontaneous. He's all the things I'm not, I'm such a controlled person and just being around him makes me relax. I never thought that I would be able to date someone who understands that I enjoy my career and that it's my priority. I mean he's just as busy as me with all of his business trips he has to take, but when we're on the phone we are just vibing, when we're around we just I don't know how to explain it, we just click. And I'm afraid that if I tell him, then it will change the dynamic of our relationship. I don't want him to be turned off, and I also don't want him to change up, like his main goal would be to deflower me."

"Deflower, who says that anymore. You just need to say you don't want his mind to drift from being focused on you to getting your cookie. But Lovely he's a man, at the end of the day his mind is always going to go back on getting pussy. That's just the way it is for men, that's how they think. I advise you to have that conversation soon, yeah things are good right now, you two are still enjoying each other's company like teenagers, I know my mind would be racing trying to figure out who he fucking especially if I'm holding out." Lovely looked at Marisol with unsure eyes, the thought has crossed her mind several times that Sincere could be sleeping with other women. The times they did see each other she was sure he left her sexually frustrated. Lovely didn't want to speak on her doubts.

"Where to next? Do you want to check out that new boutique in Soho?"

"Actually, can we take a shopping detour?" Marisol suggested.
"Sure where we going?"

"I'm taking you across town, I told Shannon that I would stop by and since you said you haven't met him, I think this is a perfect time."

"Marisol I already told you that the text was an afternoon booty call."

"Shut up its not, I told him I was hanging out with you, and I would be brining you along if he wanted me to stop by."

~

Marisol parked her car in front of the nightclub's door. She didn't see any of Shannon's cars so she sent him a text asking if he was inside the club. "His car isn't here. I'm texting him to see if he is still here." Marisol pulled down the visor to check her makeup to see if she needed any touch up. She applied a coat of matte lipstick. Her phone buzzed with a new text message; **Papí: I had to make a run, b back in a few, buzz the door Kam will let ya'll in.**

Marisol replied back; **Uggh we could be shopping right now not waiting on you.**

Papí: you should be waiting on me with your ass up and face down, but you brought your girl. You don't hear me complaining. The laugh that came out of Marisol startled Lovely. Once Marisol got her laughter under control she was able to show Lovely the text from Rico.

"I told you it was an afternoon booty call."

"I know but I didn't want to end our day because of him. He just got back in town yesterday. We haven't seen each other a lot this past month. Come on let's go inside Kameron will let us in." The ladies stepped out of the car and walked to the door. Marisol buzzed the intercom and waited. "Yo who is it?" a deep voice came through

"Hola Kam, its Marisol." The door unlocked and opened, Kameron stood off to the side of the door. Marisol greeted Kameron with a big smile, he just nodded his head back at her. "Yo who is this?" Kameron asked pointing at Lovely. "Oh my bad Kam, this is my best friend Lovely, Lovely this is Kameron he is head security at the club. Where did your manz go?" She asked Kameron "Shit I don't know, he just let me know you was stopping by and to open up for you if he wasn't back." Kameron stared at Lovely focusing on her face. The staring was making Lovely uncomfortable, she wasn't sure if he was sizing her up or trying to see through her soul. "He didn't the same thing to me when we first met, he's harmless though at least to me since I come to the club often when Rico isn't around. We're going to sit in the VIP area. I know his office is not unlocked." Marisol told him, he nodded his head up and down all the while still staring at Lovely.

"What's his deal?" Lovely inquired about Kameron and him staring without saying much. "Girl I don't know, he doesn't say much but when he does he's interesting to talk with. I can't wait for you to meet Shannon, oh and don't call him Shannon please call him Rico. He has a thing about people he doesn't know calling him by his government." Lovely just rolled her eyes. "Men always needing an alias, makes me wonder what he's up to." Lovely said with raised eyebrows. Marisol waved off Lovely's remark. They sat down on the plush couches in the VIP area, "I should have gotten one of the guys to make us a drink, fuck it I'll go behind the bar and make one, what do you want LiLi?" Marisol moved towards the bar and started making a panty wetter. Lovely declined a drink but Marisol made an extra one. "I told you I didn't want one." Lovely said "I am not drinking alone in the afternoon like some alcoholic." She said

"How does having a drink by yourself make you an alcoholic?"

"I don't know but since we're both here and there's a bar we are going to drink together, now here take this and sip." The pair sipped on their drink and continued top talk as they waited for Rico.

"Speaking of people from the past, you would not even believe who stopped me in midtown a few weeks ago. I can't believe I didn't tell you when it happened."

"Well who was it?"

"Jomari, Jomari fucking White, that's who." Lovely almost choked on her drink that she just had took a sip from. Marisol handed her a napkin so she could wipe her chin with from the little bit of drink that spilt out of her mouth.

"Yes bih pick up ya face, because that what I had to do when he stopped me."

"Oh my god, did he fall out of the sky. I mean damn you haven't heard from him for what almost five years."

"Yeah just about, and when I saw him so many different emotions came into place. I wanted to ask him so many questions but I played it cool. He spoke to me like he just didn't up and disappear out of my life years ago without so much as a goodbye or I'll see ya later."

"Have you heard from him since that day?"

"No, I hope I don't ever see him again. I can't bring the past into my future. Especially not now, shit this is my first serious relationship since Jomari and I'm not trying to bring the old in with the new. No Jomari needs to stay wherever Jomari came back from. I'm good over here." Lovely just looked at her friend. She was there when Marisol's ex-boyfriend just disappeared on her without any warning, Marisol tried various ways on locating him, his family was a dead end, the ones that were close to him wouldn't give her any information on his whereabouts or if he was even alive. Marisol's first love just vanished and it left her devastated.

"I see you've made yourself at home." The deep sexy voice said. Marisol and Lovely both turned around at the same time. To see Rico standing behind them, Marisol smiled and stood to greet her man. She walked up to him as her Giuseppe heels clicked on the floor, Marisol stopped in front of him. She was excited to see her man, they were almost eye level she still had to step on tip toes to place a kiss on his lips. She missed him and she showed it in her passionate kiss, Rico's hand was palming her ass as he deepened the kiss, biting on her bottom lip. The couple pulled away from each other, needing to catch their breath. Lovely looked on at the couple mostly looking at her best friend, she was happy for her because it looked like her friend might have found love again after the ordeal she went through with Jomari. "I'm being so rude, my fault LiLi, Lovely this is Shan- I mean Rico, Rico this is my best friend Lovely Daniels." Rico turned to face Lovely, a smile crept onto to his handsome face. Lovely thought he was very handsome with his deep mahogany skin and smoky gray eyes. He continued to smile at her as he stretched out his hand. "Nice to meet you ma, you can call me Shannon, you look familiar have we met before?" Lovely shook her head no "I never forget a face, I'm sure I'll place where I know you from later. I'm waiting on my manz to come inside, but he taking too long so we can head up to the office."

Lovely followed behind the couple, they were too cute in her eyes, Rico had his arm wrapped around her waist as they walked, they were leaned into each other whispering god knows what which was getting little giggles out of Marisol. Lovely just shook her head and smiled as they all stepped onto the elevator. The elevator reached the third floor of the night club. They all stepped out, Rico put the code into the keypad that was on the wall. The doors opened as Rico moved aside to let the ladies enter. Lovely took a seat in one of the chairs at the table that was set off to the side of the huge office. She looked on and admired the colors that were used to decorate the office. Marisol and Rico were seated on the couch close to each other. "What were you two doing before ya came this way?" He asked "We were shopping, actually having ourselves a best friend's day out" "Oh yeah shopping, you pick ya man up anything?" "Nah pa my man ain't leave me with no racks, I had to spend my own money on myself. Can you believe that." Marisol and Lovely laughed at the comment.

"You should always be thinking about your man when you're out." Rico said.

"Tuh was my man thinking about me when he was out on his business trip?"

"That's not the point shorty, I should always be on your mind." Marisol rolled her eye at his statement, she was about to respond when the door cracked opened.

"Damn shorty got a phat ass, I might need to stay here to see her audition, aye Rico I think you need to hire her for the strip joint, she could be your new money maker, damn. Aye nigga why you ain't wait for me downstairs, I thought you was introducing me to shorty and her friend." He walked completely inside the office, he saw Rico sitting on the couch next to Marisol. Rico shook his head at Sincere's entrance. Rico stood up and looked over at Lovely who hadn't said too much since they came into the office. Lovely had a bewildered look on her face. Rico and Sincere dapped each other up, Sincere turned around to take a seat at the table, he paused when he saw her sitting there.

"What are you doing here beautiful?" Sincere approached asking Lovely. "I was going to ask you the same but I wasn't sure if you were done being distracted by shorty's phat ass." Sincere started to laugh but the look on Lovely's face told him not to. He stood her up for a hug and a kiss. Lovely turned her face so that he could only kiss her cheek. "Is that how we doing it beautiful?" Lovely just raised her eyebrow at him.

"Wait, is this Sincere, Lovely?" Marisol asked her best friend, Sincere turned around when he heard his name, he checked out the woman that was hanging all over his best friend, she was a ten in the beauty and body no doubt about it. Sincere moved toward Marisol to shake her hand. "You must be Marisol, nice to meet you I'm Sincere." Marisol and Sincere shook hands. "Well it seems like we all know each other but just never met, so Sincere you're the man my friend decided to break all of her rules for, well almost all of them." Marisol said to him

"I knew I would remember where I've seen you before, the dealership, right. Yeah my mans was straight thirsty that day." Rico deep voice cut in.

"Man, wasn't nobody thirsty I was admiring her beauty." Sincere replied

"That's not how I remember it, you damn near tripped over yourself trying to get downstairs." Marisol laughed at the two going back and forth she noticed Lovely stood with her arms crossed "You okay LiLi?"

"Yes I'm fine, I'm actually ready to leave but I know you want to stay here with Shannon, so I'm going to wait downstairs for an Uber." Sincere's head tilted at Lovely's comment, he felt like she just disregarded him in front of his friend and hers. "Love, what's the deal, you see me right here if you need a ride, you know damn well I'm going to take you, later for that Uber."

"No I can wait for the Uber, I wouldn't want to hold you up for that audition." Both Marisol and Shannon looked at each other with Oh shit expressions, Marisol was ready to curse Sincere out, she could see that Sincere words earlier had indeed upset Lovely. Lovely walked over to Marisol to give her a hug "Don't let that upset you, you need to show him that shit don't affect you." Marisol whispered in her friend's ear. Lovely turned to Shannon to shake his hand, Shannon embraced her with a side hug. "It was nice to finally meet you Shannon, take care of my girl." She said to him.

"No doubt, I'm sure we'll see each other again soon." He told her.

"Of course, you're dating my best friend, I'm sure we will." Lovely pulled out her iPhone 6 to connect to the Uber app, she walked past Sincere and headed to the door. Sincere gently grabbed Lovely by the arm to stop her.

"Aight Love, I can see you're upset, and if you want to talk about it we can on the way to your place. I'll be the one taking you home." Sincere said with finality in his voice. Lovely slipped out of his hold and walked out of the office, Sincere turned back to the couple in the room. "Aight son I'll get at you later, Marisol it was nice meeting you, you're just as beautiful as my manz said you were." "And you're just as charming as Lovely described, I hope that helps when she gives you silent treatment on the ride to her place."

"Yeah I already know what I'm in for with shorty." Shannon laughed at Sincere and Marisol eyes turned into thin slits at his remark. Sincere walked out of the office to Lovely waiting at the elevator.

~

Marisol waited for Rico to come back into his office. When Rico finally told her about his illegal dealings she was able to make the choice on if she was going to continue with their relationship. She decided that it wasn't an issue for her. She understood, her beginnings were humbling. She wasn't born with a silver spoon in her mouth, her father was a drug dealer who started at the bottom of hustling. He did what he had to do to survive and to make sure his kids were able to live comfortably. Marisol accepted this part of Rico. He never discussed any part that particular business with her. The door to the office opened "What's that look for?" Rico asked her "Nothing." She responded with a shrug of her shoulders. Rico just waited, he knew she would tell him what was wrong, she had no problem doing so before. Marisol tapped her manicured finger on the arm of the chair.

"You and Sincere have been friends for how long?" she asked him

"we've been friends since we were shorties. Why?"

"Well this is my first time meeting him and you always referred to him as you boy never by name."?

"Ok so what's your point ma, what is it you're trying to say?"

"What I'm asking is if Sincere is your business partner?" Shannon wasn't sure how he wanted to respond to her question. He made it a point to keep her out of the loop when he did his illegal dealing, he didn't want to expose her to anything so she could never be hemmed up by police or the feds. She would never have anything to use against him, to the world she was the girlfriend to a business owner to successful night clubs and several five-star restaurants. Shannon was never comfortable about telling her that he was one half to a multi-million drug empire, but without even telling her, Marisol somehow knew based off her past with her father. Shannon enjoyed being around her, their chemistry was electric when they were around each other. Shannon sat up in his chair, his eyes focused on her. "Why are you asking me that ma?"

"Well Shannon I just found out that your friend is dating my best friend. And I'm a hundred percent sure she has no idea that he is a drug kingpin." Shannon gestured with his finger for Marisol to come to him. She walked over and leaned on the edge of his desk, Shannon pulled his self towards her in the chair. "That's none of my business ma, however Sincere and your friend's relationship is set up isn't my concern. I told you what I was about simply because I felt that you would understand. You're not like these thots out here where I would have to sleep with one eye open if they knew my pockets is deeper than the ocean. No, you ma, you're different, and I hope I won't regret letting you in like this so soon." Marisol bent down to give him a small kiss, Marisol let out a moan when she felt him tug on her bottom lip. Her mouth opened to receive his tongue, he licked her top lip before the tips of their tongues touched. Marisol's body started to heat up, Rico grabbed her by the hips and placed her on his lap. Marisol started slow grinding against him when she felt his long hard dick through his jeans. Shannon let out a growl, before he smacked Marisol on her ass. He stood up with Marisol legs wrapped around his waist. "You already know what it is ma, face down ass up." Marisol purred as she unwrapped her legs from his waist, she stood on her feet, turned towards the desk and bent over putting a deep arch in her back.

CHAPTER SIXTEEN

The oncoming headache was not what I needed at the moment, the back and forth trips between to Houston the past month have been exhausting, the only thing I wanted to do was go see my woman and take her out, just spend time with her. The excitement was no longer there, I'm feeling like this life is starting to get old.

I remember when my father started grooming me for this position, for the takeover of our highly lucrative but highly illegal family business. I couldn't wait to be at the top, running shit, making so much money it had to be placed in off shore accounts and Swiss banks. The lifestyle was ruthless but it also had it rewards if you played your cards right. But after these last few trips to collect our product, the risk almost caught up with me and Rico. Our entire empire could have crumbled right before our eyes. People's greed was starting to get the best of them, and it was jeopardizing my freedom. Man, I think it's time we start throwing in the towel. I have more money than I could spend in this lifetime, I have several successful businesses that I could fall back on. And then there was Lovely, I'm really feeling shorty, she's smart, successful and beautiful; her ambition is a turn on, she's sensible which is pleasant because I for sure thought she was going to be a high maintenance with the way she was making me chase. I know shorty ain't going to blow through racks of money on bullshit, I also know if I want shorty to be with me, I'm going to either have to tell her the real about me or be completely out of the game. And since being out ain't happening no time this year, I know I got to come clean with Lovely, shit she might be my future.

Even though I just got into the office and there are several items that needed my immediate attention I wasn't going to be able to focus on them, Lovely has been on my mind heavy since I landed back home. The last time we saw her, I can admit I put my foot in my damn mouth, shit had I known she was in the office at the club, I wouldn't have walked in the same way. She claimed when we made it to her place that she wasn't upset, but I could tell what I said bother her. We haven't spoken since then only because I've been out of the country handling business. I needed to go see her and make sure we really are good. "Mr. Riz you have a visitor." My assistant buzzed through the intercom. The visitor was unexpected and I ain't have time for it right now, I needed to catch Lovely before she leaves her office. "Tell who ever it is that they need to set up an appointment. I don't do walk ins." I relayed to Michele, I was about to head out when I heard the commotion at the door "Miss you can't go back there, Miss wait." The door swung open and the visitor walked in. Michele was right on her heels, trying to block her from entering.

"Sincere you know I don't like being told what to do." To say I was surprised to see her would be a lie, to say I was happy to see her would be an even bigger lie.

"It's alright Michele, I'll handle it from here, go ahead and take the rest of the day off." Michele nodded and closed the door behind her. My visitor walked in further into my office, I had to admit she still looked beautiful, one would think her face should be gracing the covers of magazines for vogue, GQ, or Esquire. She still had her signature five-inch heels on since she was only a mere five foot even. Now I have the burden of finding out why she was here, because even though she was beautiful, she is also poison. Carmen De La Cruz is the daughter of Rafael De La Cruz,

Don to La Muerte Mexican drug cartel, she is also my ex-girlfriend.

"I would say it's nice to see you again Sincere. But I don't want to start off this visit by lying."

"What are you doing here Carmen?" I asked her, as I sat back down in my chair.

"Well I would say I made this trip for pleasure but I'm here on business. I also heard that you had an incident down in Mexico a few days ago." Of course, she knew about the incident that could have had me seeing football numbers in prison.

"On business, huh, shorty you and I have no business together so I don't even know what made you decide to come to my place of business."

"There is no need for hostility Sin, I'm simply here to talk business. I'm here on behalf of the Don, La Muerte needs one of your investment companies to use as a front." I looked at her to see if she was serious in what she just told me. When her eyes didn't flicker and her breathing stayed even, I knew she was serious.

"Let me get this straight your father, who has one of the biggest drug empires and I'm sure legitimate businesses around the world where he can filter money, asked you to come to New York to see me about turning over one of mine to the cartel. Is that right?" I laughed this had to be a joke, the Don and I have no love lost between us. The last time we were in the same room he vowed that if we ever crossed paths again I wouldn't be breathing. The only reason why my family and his aren't at war is because the other Dons stepped in and knew a war between both organizations would bring the attention of feds and profits would diminish.

"Look at you, those eyes still showing what your mood. You know it's said the eyes are the window to the soul." Carmen said as she touched the side of my face.

"Yeah and what does your eyes say about you, el diablo, look ma my answer is no, The Don and I have no business to tend, I played my cards with him before and I ain't about getting fucked again, by him or by you."

"Sin I was not asking you, I'm telling you. I'm going to use one of your businesses as a front. You owe me this, don't forget I'm the one who stopped Papa from almost killing you." When she said that I had to stop myself from grabbing her by her throat. She was the reason why I almost lost my life. I knew she didn't come alone and that her goons were outside my office door.

"A lot of shit went down between us Carmen and I know it's not good for us to work with each other again. Find another way shorty and leave me out of it." She shrugged her shoulders as she walked to the door.

"You've got forty-eight hours to get it set up. I'll contact you to set everything in motion."

~

I called ahead to Lovely's office to see if she was still there, Sasha informed me she had already left for the day, I called her phone but she wasn't picking up. So, I was making my way to her house, I needed to see her. Carmen's visit today only meant trouble, and with Carmen it was soon to follow. She was no good, by the time I realized that it was too late, we were already involved beyond business. I had turned onto Lovely's street; her house was settled in the rear. My baby was doing well for herself I couldn't even lie, she was a determined levelheaded business woman. Initially seeking out her company was just a play to get close to her, I had to admit it was a good decision on both personal and business. I pulled into her driveway and saw her car and another parked, I parked behind hers. I knocked on the door and waited for her to answer, the red Aston Martin in the driveway made me think back to when I first saw Lovely. When I heard the door opened I turned around and saw her, a feeling of comfort took over. The ordeal in Mexico, Carmen showing up to my office any and all worries vanished when I saw her standing in the door way.

"May I come in?" I had to ask, she was still in the doorway, and I know she had a guest but I have to be in her presence. She slid off to the side, "I called your office and Sasha let me know you were gone, I called your phone on the way over just to let you know I was coming over." I explained to her some of her hair was in her face and I pushed it back behind her ears, my eyes wanted to see all of her. "My phone is upstairs, I didn't hear it. Is everything ok?"

"Yeah ma everything's okay I just wanted to see my lady, I can do that can't I?" I teased her, she broke out into that bright smile that I enjoyed seeing on her face. I pulled her in close to me and bent down to give her a kiss. It was meant to be a quick peck, but my mouth and tongue had other plans. I needed to feel her close to me, my hands were all over the place, caressing her neck, to palming her ass. "Sin, wait." I heard her say, her palms were on my chest like she was trying to push me away, I removed her hands as I backed her up against the wall. I had her hands locked between mine, and pinned against the wall, "Sin wait my-" I cut her off again with another kiss. If being addicted to drugs felt like this than I know why that shit is hard to kick. "Lovely is everything alright, who is that at the door?" I heard the voice behind me, I lifted my head up and turned around to see who the voice belonged to. Lovely stepped from around me, the woman and Lovely features favored and she had my lady's exact eye color, I immediately know who she is.

I stepped up to her and extended my hand to introduce myself. "It's a pleasure to meet you I'm Sincere Riz." She looked back and forth between me and Lovely, I still had my hand out waiting, for a minute I thought she was going to play me by not shaking my hand since she just saw me basically trying to freak her daughter down in the entryway. She walked over to me and shook my hand "Teresa Daniels, I'm Lovely's mother, so Sincere, I haven't heard about you, and seeing how you and my daughter were just slobbing each other down, can I assume that you two are together and the reason I haven't seen my baby girl in almost two months?" I let out a chuckle at her remark and Lovely's face was something to laugh at as well. I held my hands up in defense "I can say that Lovely and I are together, as far as not seeing her I can't answer that, you'd have to ask her that."

"That's what I was doing before you arrived. Love you have some explaining to do." She addressed Lovely, who just stood there like she was being chastised, this was amusing, this was a first seeing Lovely timid. I wrapped my arms around her waist as she stood in front of me, she placed her hand on mine, and her mother's eyes looked on at us.

"Mom we can talk later about this, I promise to call you later." Lovely said to her mom.

"Are you trying to get rid of me Lovely Marie Daniels?" she said with a devious smirk on her face. The two looked so much alike, it was like seeing into the future of what Lovely would look like in her early fifties.

"Since I'm being kicked out, I want to see you tomorrow at dinner at the house, seven sharp. And Sincere make sure you're there as well." Lovely tried to protest her mom and her invitation but she wasn't having it. Lovely walked her mom outside to her car. When she came back in she walked towards the living room where I was seated. I pulled her down on my lap, "So that's mom dukes huh." She just nodded her head up and down. I tilted her head to face mine, "Babe are we good?" I had to ask, I wanted to make sure that she was ok after the last time we seen each other. She stared at me and I did the same, "Yes we're good Sin."

"Good, because I missed the hell out of you." I told her, she smiled in my face before she placed a kiss on my lips, she pulled back before I could get anything started. "I missed you too." I smiled at her, "So I'm meeting the folks tomorrow, you know what that means right?"

"No, what?" she asked

"That means it's time for you to hop on this dick." she punched me in my arm, I had to laugh at her attempt to hurt me, it was like a poke, I need to show my woman how to throw a jab. "I'm just messing with you Love, but on the real, it means I ain't going nowhere, you're stuck with me. Especially if I hit it off with Pops. I can tell Mom dukes already feelin ya man."

"Whatever Sincere, you may be charming, but you're not that damn charming, my parents are going to interrogate you like you're on the witness stand." Damn was I ready for all that, I watched her as she spoke, her lips were drawing me in again, I needed a fix. I wanted to hear everything she had to say, but right now she was talking just a little bit too much. I wanted feel her and the way that my mind was going another part of me wanted to feel her too. My dick was staring to get hard, Lovely was moving around on my lap absentmindedly shorty ain't even realize she was giving my dick some grinding action. I knew she wasn't ready for that part, every time we got close she would stop us. I wasn't in the mood to get shot down especially with everything going on, me beating up some pussy would alleviate my stress for the time being. I picked her up and she instinctively wrapped her legs around my waist. "Where are we going?" she asked

"To the kitchen ya man's hungry I didn't eat a damn thing when I got off the jet. Plus, you making my dick rise with all that moving on my lap. I know you ain't ready for what it wants to do to you." I walked in the kitchen and sat her on the island, I went to the refrigerator to find something to cook. I found some items I could use to make a pasta dish "Babe where your noodles at?" I asked her as I was going through the cabinet. I didn't get a response so I turned around making sure that she was still there. She had a gloom look on her face. "Are you ready?" was all she said, I placed the food in my hand down on the counter. I made sure our eyes were connecting, I wanted her to know that what I was about to say was real. "Lovely I'm ready when you're ready."

"Okay" she walked over to me and wrapped her arms around me.

"Whatever it is you're about to cook I want a big ass plate of it." She said with that bright smile as she looked up at me.

CHAPTER SEVENTEEN

The Maybach crept slowly into the cul de sac where the Daniel's residence was nestled. The ten thousand square foot Mediterranean style mansion was a jewel bestowed in New Jersey. Bennie parked the car in the roundabout driveway. Lovely and Sincere waited for Bennie to step out to open the car door. "Is this the house you grew up in?" Sincere asked Lovely. "No, my parents moved up here when I left for NYU. We're originally from Maryland, my father was a circuit judge for almost 20 years before he retired a few months ago, he was the one who I bought the Aston Martin for." Bennie opened the door for the couple, Sincere was clad in charcoal black dress pants and a gray button-down dress shirt. Lovely was dressed in an off the shoulder burgundy above the knee dress. Sincere grabbed her hand and interlocked their fingers as they walked to the front door. Lovely opened the door without waiting, her parents were expecting her so she knew the door would be unlocked.

They entered the foyer, her heels tapped on the limestone floor. "They might be in the sitting room." Lovely pulled Sincere in the direction of the sitting room. She heard her parent's voice, her mother was sitting on the Venetian style couch, and her father was on his cell phone talking. Lovely's father spotted the couple enter the doorway. He winked at Lovely, who smiled in return. His eyes then zeroed in on Sincere. He was still talking on the phone when he pointed in their direction. Teresa looked behind her and saw the couple standing there. Teresa stood up to greet her daughter and Sincere, she embraced Lovely as if the two didn't just see one another yesterday. Sincere went to shake her hand instead Teresa bypassed the hand shake and gave him a short hug as well. Lovely's father finished with his phone call and took his side by his wife, "Hey baby girl, I've missed you." Her father bent down to hug his only daughter. Lovely's bond with her father was strong, she was indeed a daddy's girl through and through, the two normally talked on a weekly basis, Lovely felt bad that she hadn't been keeping up with their ritual for the past few months. Sincere looked on at Lovely and her father, the pair separated and Lovely's father turned to him. Neither men moved to introduce themselves, Sincere stared at Lovely's father just as he was staring at him. "Who are you?" Lovely's father asked with his arms crossed, Teresa swatted her hand at her husband, for being rude. "Sincere please excuse my husband, Marcus this is Sincere Riz, Lovely's boyfriend, Sincere this is my husband and Lovely's father Marcus Daniels." The two still didn't move, Sincere wasn't intimidated by any man, and he felt that this was Lovely's father's intention. "Oh, cut the crap Marcus and shake the man's hand, how often do I get to see my daughter bring a man home for dinner." Marcus cut his eyes at Teresa but did as she said, he extended his hand to Sincere and they finally shook.

"Sincere are your parents still married?" Teresa asked, he wiped the corners of his mouth with the dinner napkin. "Yes, my mom and dad have been married going on twenty-five years." He told the entire table. Teresa nodded her head, "That's wonderful, any siblings or are you an only child like Love?" she continued to ask.

"Actually, I'm the oldest I have two younger sisters. I can tell you it isn't easy growing up with sisters, I prayed that the last child my parents had was a boy no such luck there." Everybody laughed at his teasing.

"But in truth I love them and would protect them with my last breath."

"And what about my daughter, would you do the same for her?" Marcus asked Sincere, it was his first time addressing him since that sat down at the table, mostly the conversation had been light and the parents were catching up with Lovely. Sincere sat back in his chair, he looked from Marcus to Teresa and back. He grabbed Lovely's hand that was under the table and interlocked their fingers.

He looked at her before he spoke "I want to be everything she needs, I know she's ambitious and she's taking a risk with our relationship, unsure of the outcome, but I want her to know that I wouldn't do anything to ever give her any doubts that this risk wasn't worth taking. To answer your question Mr. Daniels, I would give anything for her even my last breath." Teresa was pleased with Sincere's response, she looked on at the couple and saw the connection the two had, it reminded her of herself and her husband in their early stage of dating. Marcus cleared his throat and the two broke eye contact "Do you smoke Cuban cigars, I have some of the finest Cohiba, come on down to the cellar with me." Marcus told Sincere. The two men excused themselves from the table.

They stayed at the Daniels's estate for several hours, after Marcus and Sincere came back up from the cellar, Teresa went about asking more questions to Sincere, wanting to know what he did for a living, if he attended college, what his future goals were, she had indeed put him on the stand like the lawyer she was. Lovely cut off her mother's interrogation, she was sure her father asked him the same questions if not more down in the cellar. The two got ready to leave, Teresa and Marcus walked the couple outside to the Maybach where Bennie was waiting with the door ajar. Lovely hugged and kissed her father, she went to hug her mom "I like him, keep him around, I'm so happy for you." Lovely let out a small laugh "Alright mom." She waited for Sincere to finish speaking with her father before she walked off to the car. Sincere let her enter the car first, just as he was about to get in he heard Marcus say

"Don't forget what we talked about Sincere."

"I got you Mr. Daniels." Sincere said before he got into the car and closed the door. The Maybach purred to life as Bennie drove off.

~

The music played in the background as the car continued to drive to its destination. Lovely's head was rested on the headrest, their hands were still together. Sincere moved to kiss the back of her hand, "What's on your mind baby girl?" he asked her

"I was just thinking about what my father possibly threatened you with down in the cellar." She said, Sincere let out a sigh "Aye your father is something else, but just like I said I have sisters so I understand being protective. Now as far as what was said between us, that's for me to know."

"Did you mean that, what you said at the table?" she looked over at him. Sincere let up the partition in the car so they could have some privacy, he turned down the music so they could hear each other better. "I meant it, the real question is do you believe me. I ain't putting any game on you Lovely. I'm really feeling you ma, these past few months have been a reality check. I've been with women who only want to use me for their gain and on some real shit I've only used them for sex, nothing meaningful. With you it's different, I don't want anybody but you, I want to be that man you can depend on, I want to see that smile on your face and know that I'm the one that put it there. Now I'm not saying everything's going to always be good between us, I know there are going to be times when shit might seem like it's too much, but like I said I wouldn't do anything to intentionally hurt you. I know niggas cheat and lie but every man ain't me. If you're willing to let your guard down with me, for us, I'm letting you know here right now I'm not going anywhere and it's us forever." Lovely sat there and listened to his words, she asked herself if she was willing to let go of her inhibitions for this one man. She remembered what he said to her when she took him on as a client, he left his previous management company because they weren't willing to take risks with him. She looked up at him and saw sincerity in his eyes, which was funny in a way. "Sin if you're ready for this than so I am, no walls, no inhibitions on my part. I'm ready for us." He pulled her in for a kiss, "Good because I wasn't letting you go anyway."

The two were talking for so long they didn't realize that they had arrived at her house. Bennie parked the car, Sincere opened the door deciding not to wait, he stepped outside and on instinct checked his surroundings, he noticed a black car parked not too far down the street from Lovely's house, Lovely stepped out the car as well and stood next to Sincere. "What's wrong babe." She asked him, Sincere figured it was no big deal and decided not to waste too much time thinking about it. "It's nothing ma, let's get you in the house, you were doing all that damn yawning in the car." They walked inside her house, Sincere checked around like he always did, just making sure nobody was waiting on her. He needed to get her some scanners installed to sweep her house for any devices, he would have to get them in without her knowing. Sincere walked up to the bedroom checking everything in there as well. "Why do you do that, I have an alarm system, I would know if anybody broke into my house."

"Shit ma, you never know and what kind of man would I be if I just let you walk inside and not make sure there ain't nobody in here trying to knock you over the head."

"I don't have any enemies like that baby so that's not something I'm too worried about." Sincere thought about what she had just said, true she might not have any enemies, but he did, and now that they were together, he knew firsthand what could happen to girlfriends, wives or baby mothers of drug dealers. He knew he needed to tell her soon about his other lifestyle. "Aight Love, everything looks good, I'm about to head out and let you get some rest. I'll talk to you in the morning." He moved towards the bed where Lovely was laying down on her back, she still had her dress on she only removed her heels. Sincere hovered over her, one hand placed on each side of her near her head, Lovely's arms reached out and wrapped around his neck, she pulled him down for a kiss, she nibbled on his bottom lip, while lightly pecking, Sincere swiped her lip with his tongue, "Stay." She told him. Sincere heard her speak, he reached behind him to remove her hands from around his neck, he sat her up on the bed. "Are you sure Lovely? I mean I'm straight with the way things are right now." she bit on her bottom lip her amber eyes was filled with passion, she was ready for him. "Yeah I'm sure."

His hands caressed her neck as he kissed her from her lips and nibbled on the spot behind her ear, her moaning turned him on. Her pulse was erratic, he applied a small amount of pressure to her throat. Lovely gasped, he looked up into her amber eyes that seemed to be glowing with her growing arousal. He stepped back and admired her, his body was feening for hers "Take your clothes off." He told her, Lovely reached for the side zipper and slowly let it down, her dress slowly fell to the floor. She stepped out from the dress, her full breast was rising and falling with each breath, her round hips made her panties look like they were specially crafted for her frame. Sincere licked his lips, he had to calm himself down, he needed to go slow with her, he knew there had to be a reason why she waited until now to share her body with him. As bad as he wanted to put her on the bed and fuck her, he knew her body needed time and attention and that's exactly what he was about to give to her. His fingers traced her arms, he moved in closer, one hand behind her back and the other tracing her lips. He unhooked her bra, and watched it fall. He looked down at her beast, her nipples were hard pebbles, his mouth watered ready to suckle on the caramel colored rounds. He backed her onto the bed, she scooted further back. Sincere came out of his shoes and started unbuttoning his shirt removing it and the undershirt from his muscular frame. Lovely watched on as his chiseled chest and abs were on display, Sincere began undoing his belt, he pulled down his zipper and in one motion removed his pant and boxers. His thick long dick was standing at attention and pointing in her direction. Sincere absentmindedly started stroking his dick, as he looked on at Lovely laying on the bed.

He gently opened her legs wider as he crawled in between them, he zoned in on her breast as his hand caressed one and he placed his mouth on the other. She gasped as his tongue lavished her nipple, his hand squeezed and tweaked the other. He flicked his tongue around her harden pebble as it grew. Her hands caressed her neck "mmhmm" she moaned. He moved his mouth to her other nipple to give it the same attention. Sincere's hand snaked its way down towards her awaiting pussy, he moved his fingers inside her panties. His finger played with her pearl, Lovely could feel her pussy muscles clenching as his fingers played with her clit. Her hands were everywhere as he continued to suck on her breast and tease her pearl. Sincere's finger went even further as he placed a finger inside, her wetness turned him on, he stroked one finger in then two, the tightness that wrapped around his finger made his dick jump. He moved his mouth from her breast and kissed her. Lovely's hips were winding, Sincere started kissing her from her neck, down to her stomach. He placed tiny kisses at her navel, he grabbed her legs and placed them on his shoulders. She watched as he took her panties off, Sincere's eyes went from hers to her pussy. He was ready to dive in, he pushed her legs back towards her chest and went in like a starving man. Sincere's mouth sought out her pearl and started sucking on it. Lovely squirmed from side to side as he put in on her clit. His tongue did figure eights as his hands held up her legs. She clenched onto the duvet as she rotated her hips, Sincere worked his way to her opening, tasting her sweet nectar, his tongue spread wide not wanting to miss any drop of her arousal. He inserted two fingers into her as far as her tightness would allow, he rotated them back and forth as her juices flowed down his knuckles.

He tried to insert them deeper, her body rejected the motion as she flinched back, her legs instinctively tried to close around them. Sincere went back to her tantalizing clit and flicked his tongue in the same motion as his fingers, he could feel her pussy pulsing around his fingers, he wouldn't let up until he tasted her cream. "Sin wait baby, mmhmm." She moaned as she tried to scoot away. Sincere wrapped his forearm around her thigh to try and keep her in place. He had her pinned to the bed unable to move backwards, feeling her oncoming orgasm, she grabbed the back of his head and grinded her pussy on his face. Her stomach tightened, her legs started to shake, she could feel the tingling in her toes, as it shot up to her walls. Her voice felt strained as she moaned his name, he worked faster as he felt her heat up, her pussy locked in on his fingers as he exploded. He licked at her cream as it flowed preciously from her body. Her legs were still shaking as he gently placed them back on the bed, his bulbous head teased at her pussy when he raised up to look at her. "You taste damn good, love." His dick was hot rubbing against her pussy, she closed her legs around his waist. The friction was making him harder, she reached down between them and grabbed his dick, she rubbed the head around her lips letting her cream moisten the tip. "Fuck Love, that shit feels good." Sincere was ready to push through and feel her tightness and her warm pussy wrapped around his dick.

He tongued her down, letting her taste her juices from his tongue. His dick was aligned with her opening, his shaft continued to try to creep into her sex. "I'm not on birth control." She said as he pulled back from the kiss. *Damn* he thought to his self, he was ready to risk it all, but he was sure that getting pregnant was not in her plans at least not anytime soon. Sincere got off the bed and went to his pants, he retrieved his wallet and pulled out the condom. He ripped it open with his teeth and rolled the condom onto his shaft, Lovely watched on. With his dick sheathed with the condom he walked back over to the bed. He picked Lovely up from the bed, he pulled back the duvet and sheet. Sincere placed her down, and climbed onto top of her. Her legs spread wide letting him nestle his body between hers. He sucked on her breast that were now sensitive from the orgasm, she moaned and arched her back. Sincere dick was drawn to her heat in between her legs, he slowly slid inside as he lifted one of her legs onto his waist. He felt the tension as he tried to move in deeper, he didn't want to pull back her tightness was painful but a pleasurable pain. "Love your tight as fuck, damn ma." Sincere pushed further in, Lovely's nails were digging into his back, as he continued to move. "Love baby the nails, you got to ease up." He looked down at her, her eyes were closed tight, she biting her lip so hard he thought she was going to draw blood. "Lovely look at me." She opened her eyes and stared back into his blue green orbs.

"You okay, do you want me to stop?" she shook her head no.

"Nah ma let me hear you, do you want me to stop Lovely."

"No Sin, please don't stop. I'm just a little nervous."

"It's aight babe I got you." He kissed her to try to ease her
nerves, with her leg still wrapped around his waist, he rotated his
shaft and moved in again, he could feel some of the tension start
to break away. Sincere became distracted by her warm tight pussy
that his body started moving on its own, he plunged all the way in
until he was able to move back and forth freely. Her breath caught
in her lungs, Lovely's entire body froze when he broke through.
Sincere stopped moving when he felt her body stiffen. He looked
down at her waiting for her to open her eyes. She started
breathing again normally, her pussy slowly started adjusting to his
girth. She wrapped her other leg around his waist, he started
moving again slowly stroking her walls. The pain she felt melted
and soon became pleasure she massaged his back as his strokes
started to smooth out. Her body felt like it was on fire, his dick
was hitting against her walls searching for the soft sponge. Lovely
moaned in his ear as she started moving her hips under him.
"Yeah that's it babe, it's just you and me here, fuck your man
back." She felt encouraged as her hips winded against his dick. She
placed kisses and licks on his chest, he hiked her legs up higher
around his waist. "Oh my god Sin." She screamed out, the head of
his dick found her g-spot. Her juices flowed even more around his
dick, the sound of their bodies coming together was like music to
his ears. The feeling of her juices running down the base of his
dick made him swell even more inside her. He stayed drilling her g
spot until he felts her pussy flex around his dick, she was grabbing
onto the sheets, and pushing her pelvis further into his when he
stroked down. The intense build up feeling between her legs
suddenly felt like she had to pee Sincere kept hitting her spot. Her
legs started to shake, "Sin I have to pee, we have to stop." She
told him, he was enjoying the feeling of being inside her that he
didn't hear what she said, she tapped his shoulder and he looked
at her, Lovely repeated to him what she said. Sincere didn't stop
moving it was feeling to damn good to him. "Nah babe that's not
what that is. Trust me, just go with it." He sped up his movements

knowing she was close to coming. He slid his fingers down and started playing with her clit. Lovely was unsure what to do, the sensation never went away, Sincere went from long deep strokes to short strokes only hitting her spot with the head of his dick. "Damn, love you're so damn wet, that shit feels good." She felt the onset of her orgasm again, her body heated up, her stomach clenched as she throbbed around the head of his penis.

He stroked his fingers faster with the rhythm of her pulsing, and then he felt it. Her legs spread open a little wider, her hips came off the bed, he kept plunging into her. She came hard and fast, her body shivered, she felt his lips on hers as he kissed away her scream. Sincere's hands were placed under her ass, she continued to throb even after coming. Sincere couldn't hold out any longer, he felt his nut at the tip of his dick. He stroked her as she clenched and unclenched her pussy. His hips moved faster and faster as his orgasm reached its peak. His nut flowed into the condom as he came, he laid on top of her with his dick still nestled inside of her warmth. The moaning in his ear caused his dick to reflex and slightly harden again. He lifted his body weight off of her and moved to the side of her. She laid there trying to even out her breathing. She felt fatigued, Sincere placed his arm around her shoulder moving her closer to him. Her head laid on his chest, he reached for her hand an intertwined their fingers. "You ok?" he asked her, she nodded her head up and down, he moved her unruly hair from her face. He kissed the top of her head. "Are you tired, do you need anything?"

"Yes I'm tired and no I don't need anything."

"Aight get some rest baby girl." He got up to leave the bed.

"You're not leaving, are you?" she asked him as she pulled the sheet over her body.

"Nah ma, I told you I ain't going anywhere. I need to flush the condom and let Bennie know to come back in the morning for me." He went over and placed a kiss in her lips, to ease her mind.

CHAPTER EIGHTEEN

Somebody was laying heavy on the doorbell that woke Sincere out of his sleep. He was hoping the person would go away seeing as how no one was getting up to answer. He looked over at the clock on the nightstand and read the time, it was still early for a Saturday morning. Lovely was snuggled right up under him. The doorbell stopped but then there was the loud knocking soon to follow. He rubbed his face up and down and got out of the bed. He put on his pants from the night before not even bothering to button them up. He knew it wasn't Bennie because he would have called to inform him that he was outside. Sincere walked down the winding staircase. He opened the door just as the person was about to knock again. When Sincere saw who was at the door and the time of day, his head tilted to the side.

"Aye what's with all the loud knocking and laying on the doorbell and shit." Sincere asked, the visitor was taken aback by his remarks. When he arrived at her house he needed to talk to her about something important regarding one of the accounts. He had tried to reach her yesterday but she took the day off and wasn't answering her cell phone. He decided to show up to her house. To say he was shocked to see a man answer her door would be an understatement. He looked at Sincere with no shirt on, half put on pants and the look like he was just woken from his sleep, no Desmond was pissed. His face must have shown his disdain with Sincere answering the door. Because the next words out of Sincere's mouth were less than welcoming "Son you looking at me as if there's a problem?" Desmond straighten up his stance "No, no problem I wasn't expecting for you to answer the door, umm is Lovely home?" he inquired.

"Yeah she's here, but she's asleep right now, maybe you should try calling her later." He told him as he was about to shut the door. Desmond put his hand out to stop the door from closing, "If you don't mind can you go and get her please." Desmond said, he was trying to be as polite as he could. He was not pleased with Sincere trying to shut the door in his face. Sincere was about to reply when they both heard her voice as she came down the stairs "Sin, is there somebody at the door?" She walked down in a silk thigh high robe. Sincere thought she looked beautiful in her morning after glow, he wasn't too pleased with her choice of cover up since Desmond would be seeing it as well. She walked up to him and he bent down to kiss her cheek, she looked around and saw Desmond at the door. Her hand instinctively went to her robe belt and tightened it even more. She looked down at the shortness and wished that it had been longer. "Des, what are you doing here?"

"May I come in?" He asked, she stepped back to let him inside the foyer.

"Of course come in, is everything okay?" she asked as she closed the door and walked towards the living room. Both men followed behind her, Sincere did not plan on leaving her around him with that short robe on, he knew she had nothing underneath when he saw her ass jiggle when she walked towards the living room. He was ready to tell her to go upstairs and put some clothes on, she must have felt his thoughts, before she sat down she told Desmond that she would be right back. She went upstairs to change into some joggers and a t-shirt. The two men were seated on the opposite couches, neither saying anything, Lovely entered back into the room. Sincere was okay with her choice of clothing all expect for the shirt she had no bra on and her full perky breast was sitting high, her nipple was hard and round you could see them through the shirt. Sincere felt that if Desmond even looked down at her breast he was going to be all over him.

"I actually need to talk to you in private it's about one of our accounts. I called several times yesterday but I never got a response back." Lovely looked over at Sincere "Babe can you excuse us for a moment." She said to him, Sincere got up and placed a kiss on her lips as Desmond looked on. "It's cool I have a few calls to make." He said to her before heading up the stairs. Desmond watched him retreat up the stairs, like he was living there. He looked too comfortable in her home.

"How long has this been going on?" Desmond asked her, Lovely gave him the head tilt look, she knew he couldn't have just asked her that as if he had the right to know.

"Des that's not your concern, but you did say that you needed to speak to me about one of our accounts."

"I do, but what happened to not mixing business with pleasure, I mean with the way he's walking around your house. I can damn sure bet that you two aren't going over financials."

"Again Des, that's not your concern."

"Was it because my skin it too white, is that the real reason why you didn't want to give us a chance?"

"You're out of line right now Desmond, and before this questioning goes any further and you say something even more absurd, I'm going to ask you to leave. Whichever accounts we're having an issue with bring it up in our weekly meeting and we'll go from there." She stood up to walk him to the door, he followed behind. Before leaving he turned around and said "You need to be careful with who you decide to lay up with." With those words Lovely closed the door. She let out a deep sigh, as she rested her head against the door.

He was on the phone when she entered the bedroom, he still had his pants half way undone, his back was to her, the muscles in his back flexed when he raised his hand to the back of his head. Her pussy jumped, she walked over to him and placed a kiss on his shoulder. She heard him say to the caller that he would call them back later. "You didn't have to get off the phone." She said to him, he turned around and tilted her chin to kiss in her soft full lips. The light in the room reflected off the side of her face, her amber eyes were shining bright. "I felt you before you touched me and you already had me distracted." He said with a wink. "Everything alright?" he asked truly concerned "I don't know we didn't even get to talk about the accounts."

"Why not, that's the reason he came over knocking on the door at eight in the morning like he was the jakes."

"He started talking about other things that doesn't concern him, so I asked him to leave." He nodded his head understanding what she was saying "Is he going to be a problem? I mean were you and him ever together?" she sighed, she knew what Desmond was getting at when he said mixing business and pleasure, she had told him that it wouldn't be best if the two of them were together in a relationship outside of business.

"No babe, I mean I hope not, I don't want to lose my business partner over something so juvenile."

"You won't ma, you're the boss you make up the rules. And if you want to date your client you can, fuck him." He said as he swatted her on her ass. "ouch Sin that hurt, I'm really sore down there. When I woke up I thought for sure I wasn't going to be able to move."

"Yeah ma let me run you a bath, so you can soak. It's not every day you lose your virginity." She looked up at him her wide eyes looked like a deer caught in headlights. "Yeah I know, well at least I knew when I discarded the condom last night. Then when I walked back to the bed I saw the blood. That's why I moved you to the other bedroom, I put the sheets and covers in the laundry room." She felt embarrassed, her head cascaded down, he lifted her chin back. "It's aight ma, I actually feel good that you shared that with me.

Let me get this bath started, you got bath salts or anything like that." Lovely told him yes and where to find them. She undressed as she walked into the bathroom. "Love where they at?" he asked regarding the bath salts, she put her robe on but didn't tie it. She nudged him out of the way as she bent over in search of the item. "You know one way to get rid of soreness is to work through it, I only got to hit it once last night. I need to finish breaking that pussy in." Sincere said while rubbing on her ass, "Don't be thirsty babe." She teased him. "Thirsty, nah you got it wrong, I just marked my name all over that ass. That shit is mine. I can't be thirsty over my own pussy." Lovely turned around and slapped his shoulder; "So it's yours huh." He wrapped his arms around her, their faces were so close their lips were almost touching. "That's what I said, so can I hit it in the morning?" she laughed at his J. Cole reference he knew that was her favorite rapper. "You got any more condoms?" she asked him, it was like the mood slowly waned "nah I don't have any more on me. You got any?" she shook her head no "You better not, what your virginal ass needed with condoms anyway."

Lovely had pushed the weekly meeting back almost three weeks, she sat in the conference room at the round table with Desmond to her left, Sasha taking notes on her right. The three other colleagues and Desmond's assistant were seated at the table as well. The group were going over their accounts making sure everything was in top shape. Making sure no one was losing any money or those who had new investments were seeing some financial return. Lovely was about to call the meeting when Desmond spoke up; "I think we need to look further into the accounts of Mr. Riz mainly the ones that I've seen the last quarter that have gained an immense amount in the last month or so.

Lovely sharply turned her eyes on Desmond, she didn't know what type of games he was trying to play, she was about to nip it in the bud quick. "Why are you looking into Mr. Riz's accounts, if I'm not mistaken I'm the lead financial manager over his accounts." Desmond adjusted his neck tie "Yes you are, but as your business partner we agreed that we would cross check major accounts such as this one. Making sure nothing was out of place, keeping ourselves in line so nothing seeps through the cracks."

"So are you saying something is slipping through the cracks with his accounts, and more specifically which ones. I know he just brought on a business venture with our newest client Carmen De La Cruz, is this account you're referring to?"

"Possibly that one as well, but the one I'm referring to is his investment with SJ Realty. If you take a look-" she cut him off as he tried to hand her over the files, files she already looked over beforehand "I already know what's on the papers Desmond, what I don't understand is why you're bringing them up. I've gone over everything with a fine tooth comb." She was getting upset she felt like he was making it personal.

"If you would just get out of your feelings regarding your boyfriend you would understand what I'm referring to. I've been trying to tell you this for weeks, but I kept getting blocked with your so called meetings and important phone calls whenever you're in the office these days." The entire room went quiet, the shade that Desmond just spoke out against Lovely took the entire table by surprise. Lovely could see Sasha trying to avoid eye contact with her.

"Everybody out now." Lovely commanded; the room cleared like a scene from the Color Purple. Sasha shut the door behind her as she was the last one to leave.

"Who the hell do you think you are trying to call me out in front of the staff?" she was pissed her hands were balled into tight fist.

"Listen I'm just trying to get you to put aside the fact that you and Sincere are together and-"

"I don't need to put that aside anything, you need to, you're the one making this personal." She cut him off again.

"Dammit Lovely I'm not, okay. I need you to take a look at the financials again but with open eyes. I don't care about the fact that you're fucking the man or that you're contradicting yourself with the whole no getting involved with clients. We need to cover our business on this one." He said calmly. She tapped the pen on the table, she had to think about her business first. The two had built it from the ground up and she didn't want anything to jeopardize it.

"Alright I'll look them over again. But before I do, answer this for me. What made you decide to delve in further into these accounts?" She waited for a reply, for a few moments he didn't say anything.

"The night we went out to dinner, I saw the two of you by the restroom. At first I thought it was just a guy hitting on you, then when he came into the office the first time I figured it was no coincidence and then you took him on as a client. The real confirmation though was of course seeing him half naked answering your door." Lovely shook her head, she packed up her leather writing pad, grabbed her folders and proceeded to walk out. She turned around and walked back in; "So like I said this is personal."

Lovely threw her items on her desk. The tension in her neck became more prominent, she settled down at her oversized glass desk. She moved the mouse to turn on her computer, she had work to get done and she needed something to distract her mind. Her cell phone chimed next to her. She looked at the caller id and saw it was Sincere. She swiped to answer; "Hey babe." She greeted him, she tried to get her voice to sound as normal as possible, her hand tried to rub the tension away. "Wassup baby girl. How's your day going?" she thought about the throw down in the conference room, she didn't want to alert him in anyway until she was sure that Desmond's accusations had any merit and wasn't strictly just get back. "Uggh so far not good, but it's nothing I can't handle." She told him, "Damn babe, sounds like we both are having an uneventful day." They stayed on the phone for a few more minutes, she told him she had to get ready to go for a conference call in a few minutes and she wanted to go over her notes again.

"Aight babe I'll let you go, but here's something I want you to think about and give me an answer when I see you tonight." He said "Okay what is it?"

"Shit since we're both stressed, I think we need to get away for a few days. Just you and I, someplace where neither one of us has to worry about business."

"Sin, baby I have so much work that needs my attention now, I can't just get up and go."

"Why can't you, it's your company, and what good is being successful if you can't enjoy it. Just think about it Love. Besides your man needs a few uninterrupted days to dig in them guts." He laughed in her ear "Sin is that the only thing you think about?" she said with a smile in her voice. "Shit when it comes to you yeah, shit I was visioning when you were bent over the table and you throwing that tight wet pussy back at me, before I called you. Who taught you that anyway, I know I didn't." he teased her. "Oh my gosh Sin, you're such a freak." "Yeah you like it though, I don't hear any complaints when my tongue is giving you back to back orgasms." She bit her tongue as she too thought about their last sex session. "Just think about it, aight." "I will, but do I have much of a choice?" "You always have a choice with me Lovely, besides if you say no, I'm just going to kidnap your ass."

CHAPTER NINETEEN

I hadn't spoken to or seen Shannon in weeks. To tell you the truth I was more pissed off, than concerned. I couldn't understand how he could be in a relationship with someone and doesn't even think to pick up the phone and call and simply state "babe I'm ok". No, that's so hard for him to do; I didn't even know what to do at this point. I had invited Jomari over for dinner at my house, we've been catching each other up on our lives. To say that I am still shocked that he just popped up after all this time. Now the timing is not right but it's still great that we can be cordial and re build our friendship. I looked in the oven to see how the food was coming along; I had about fifteen more minutes before everything was done. I went into the dining room to fix the plate setting and put the wine glasses down. He should be arriving in a few so I had enough time to slip out of my cooking clothes and into my attire. I put the pot on the stove on a simmer so that the green beans wouldn't burn.

Walking up the stairs to my bedroom I went into the closet to get out my outfit for the evening. I wasn't too sure how I wanted to dress so I just decided on a high waisted pencil skirt and a crop top. It was casual but cute, it wasn't like I was going out, it was just dinner between old acquaintances. I applied my eyeliner and some mascara, a little perfume here and there. As I was finishing up my make-up I heard the door bell and went to put on my heels and walk down the stairs to answer the door.

Jomari was leaning up against the frame when I opened the door. His caramel skin was glowing, if that was even possible for a man. He was equally casual in some denim jeans and Royal blue Ralph Lauren Polo shirt. His biceps were defined and on display as well as the tattoo of praying hands with a rosary woven through them. I went to greet him with a side church hug and gestured for him to come in. "Hey Puchi, you look nice." Jomari said. "Thanks, so do you. Dinner is almost ready, would you like some wine or anything?" I asked him. His eyes wandered from my eyes down my body, I knew that look from when we used to date so I knew exactly what he was thinking. I decided to put a stop to that, I still consider myself in a relationship even if Shannon has gone missing in action. My feelings for Shannon were strong, our chemistry was insane. When I was around him I didn't want to leave his presence. But with his actions lately, I'm not sure if he is even feeling me the same way. It's not like I can ask him since we haven't spoken in weeks and when I do call he doesn't pick up. I didn't want to get Lovely involved by asking her to ask Sincere about his boy. I was so happy for my friend, she was happy in her relationship and I didn't want to cause in turmoil in theirs. She and Sincere were in Saint-Tropez the past few days, my girl was living it up and relaxing with her man and I wasn't in the slightest mad at her.

I can't even lie I do miss Shannon something crazy and I'm craving my man's dick but I can't deal with the entire pop up one day gone a month game he's playing. I looked at Jomari and just stared for a brief moment to see if any feelings that I had felt for him all those years would resurface. I felt myself comparing him and Shannon but there was no comparison that I could see on the outside and I knew for sure they had different personalities.

I shook my head at Jomari and walked into the kitchen, you could smell the different aromas from the food. "Dinner should be ready you, can have a seat and I'll bring over the dishes." I told him. "Nah I don't mind helping, you don't need to serve me. Now if I was your man then by all means, please do." He left that open statement at that. "But you're not Jomari so I guess you can help bring the dishes to the table." I said with a slight attitude while cutting my eyes at him.

I thought we had an understanding but I guess I needed to remind him again of the platonic relationship.

I could feel his eyes watching me move around the kitchen, yeah I looked different from when we used to date. Hell we were young; I know my full hips was swaying from left to right in my fitted skirt as I moved around. I had definitely filled out over the years. I shook my head to get the thoughts out of my mind. Jomari followed me into the dining room and placed the dishes on the table. Jomari looked at the spread which consisted of Broiled steaks, baked potatoes with all the fixings, grilled shrimp and vegetables kabobs and green beans. Nothing to intricate but it still looked delicious. I could always cook my ass off and I'm sure he knew this meal was no exception. Jomari pulled out my chair for me to sit down. He then pulled the chair that was seated across from me and pulled it up closer to mine. I gave him a puzzled look trying figure out why felt the need to rearrange my damn furniture. I bowed my head to say Grace, Jomari did the same. He knew how I was; don't touch the food until you have given thanks. My mother used to reach across the table when my brothers would try her, I knew not to play with my mother when it came to blessing the food she prepared. As I finished up the prayer, I gave a silent prayer for Shannon a safe return from wherever he was and for God to shine some type of light on our relationship. I began to pass Jomari different items to place on his plate as we began to eat; it was quiet at first no one saying anything. It was as if the elephant in the room was apparent.

I wanted to ask him since I've seen him, I needed to know the reason why he left, well why he just up and vanished. I wasn't sure if I wanted to open those old wounds but I guess since I had him here he should divulge the information. I looked up at him and got the courage to ask. "Jomari I need to know why? Why did you leave all of a sudden, with no type of contact you just up and disappeared?" Jomari leaned in and grabbed my hand, as I waited on him to speak, I realized that Jomari and Shannon might have one thing in common the two liked to disappear with no contact. I mean look at Shannon, gone for weeks no contact, nothing. I just realized in that moment that I had an uncertainty when it comes to relationships. I was waiting on Jomari to answer when his head snapped towards the entrance way of the dining area. I turned around to see what he was looking at and when I saw him I wanted to just die right then and there. I was happy, pissed, and nervous all at the same time. He stared at me for a brief moment then his eyes turned to Jomari.

They stared at each other neither one looking away. I had lost the thought of speech, I knew this didn't look good at all, me eating dinner with a man by candlelight and he was still holding my damn hand. After a long pregnant pause, finally words were able to come from my mouth "Babe ...umm you're back." I knew all hell was about to break loose his face showed no expression as he looked at Jomari, his eyes never even met mine when I spoke. He didn't need to say a word to me I felt the anger rolling off him. His almond shaped eyes had turned into slits; they slowly turned to me before he opened his mouth "Am I interrupting something?" I stood up to walk towards Shannon, in my head I was trying to figure out how to make sure nothing escalated between these two. I really was glad to see Shannon, my body started tingling the closer I got to him. I could smell his signature cologne mixed with his natural essence as I felt a smile creep upon my face. Damn I really missed him, I wrapped my arms around his neck and hugged him, he didn't hug me back. I felt snubbed so I stepped back I was trying to will him to look at me but he was still focused on Jomari. The movement behind me caught my attention, it was a good thing before I decided to go off on Shannon for his rudeness. Jomari was standing off to the side of us; "Hey what's up, I'm Jomari White." He had his hand extended for a shake, Shannon still didn't take his off of him or even move. Jomari retracted his hand, "Uh Puchi, I'm going to go ahead and go. Sorry I couldn't answer your question maybe I can another time. Thanks for dinner though."

"Yes I thinks that's best, I'll umm I'll call you." I walked Jomari to the door, he tried to give me a hug but I shook my head no. I could feel Shannon's eyes on us. Now I really wished that I hadn't wore this tight ass skirt, shit ain't no telling what he over there thinking.

"Jomari that's ya ex, right ma?" he asked the question but I knew it was rhetorical, what I was trying to figure out was how he knew. I hadn't spoken of Jomari to Shannon, "You were so busy talking to Lovely you ain't even realize I was behind ya'll, that day you stopped by the club. What I'm trying to figure out though shorty is why the fuck that nigga in your crib sitting down at ya table with a meal fit for a king holding ya hand and shit."

"Shannon it wasn't even like that. I did invite him over but it was just to talk."

"Yo ma you tripping, what the fuck you need a nigga in your house just to talk. And not the next nigga nah you got the ex nigga in here. What kind of shit you on Marisol." I didn't like his tone, it seemed like he was trying to imply some shit and I wasn't here for it. Hell he's the one that need to be talking about why I haven't heard from him.

"You need to calm down and stop trying to make it out to bigger than what it is. Like I said he was here to talk and that's it. It's not like when I pick up the phone to call you, you answer."

"Yo you on some get back shit Puchi, you trying to get back at a nigga for out here grinding. You act like you don't know what I'm out here doing, I'm out here moving weight and you mad cause a nigga ain't picking up the phone."

"No I'm not mad a nigga ain't picking up the phone, I'm pissed that my so called man can't even fucking pick up the phone to tell me he's okay, I know your lifestyle Shannon I understand what you're out here doing. But I also feel like you forgetting that you're in a relationship."

"How the fuck am I forgetting I'm with you Puchi? You ain't walk in on me entertaining no other bitches." I had to refrain from rolling my eyes at his response "Can we just sit down and talk Shannon I really did miss you and seriously I think we need to get a better understanding at what it is that we're doing."

"Nah you got a phone call to make clearly that nigga got all the time in the world to talk, gone head and chat it up with him, I'm good over here I can't have my woman out here trying to talk to exes just because she ain't heard from me in a few days."

"What are you saying Shannon?"

"I said it, do you ma. We over." I couldn't believe it, he actually broke up with me. I watched him walk out the door, I was paralyzed in place. My mind told me to go after him but I couldn't move.

~

"I'm glad we out in the middle of the ocean. Shit with the way you were screaming last night, I know somebody would have called one time on us." I was nibbling on his ear when he said that. I was loud last night, but I couldn't help it. The way he worked over my body it was as if my body couldn't get enough; it wanted more and that's exactly what Sin did he gave me more and more. He had me laid on the edge of the bed with my legs wrapped around his neck as he his dick slowly penetrated me. He was torturing me when he fucked me with just the head of his dick, and to top it off he did it slow so I could feel every bit of his bulbous head. My body shivered thinking about last night and this morning when we were out of the deck eating breakfast. He had me on top of the table with my legs spread wide as he ate out my pussy. The last three days have been so relaxing I didn't want it to end.

Sincere's phone had buzzed again, he picked it up and looked at it and put it back down. He had been doing that a lot on the trip. I know we said no business calls while we were here but damn it seemed like his phone would go off every few minutes. I wanted to ask him to turn it off for the last day of the trip.

"Babe if you need to take the call go ahead. We're on our last day here so its fine." He shook his head no "Nah ma it's you and I remember. No business. Besides its nothing that can't be handled by the many other people that I employ." He said as he placed a kiss on my cheek. We were on the lower deck taking in the sun I had wanted to tan with no bra on and Sin told me the only way he would allow that is if we were low enough where the Captain and crew couldn't see my breast. I laughed because I was sure they weren't even paying attention to us. The staff only came to talk to us when the food was prepared. Other than that they left us to ourselves to enjoy Saint Tropez and its beautiful body of water.

I was absently playing with Sin's ear when I saw him shift his manhood in his swimming trunks. I knew that his ear was one of his hotspots and the growing erection was a dead giveaway that he was turned on. I had been talking myself into doing oral sex on him since day two of our trip. I was nervous, I have never given head to anybody and I didn't want my first time to be horrible. He shifted again, I saw this as my chance, I said a little prayer right before I straddled his lap. He was laying down on his back. His hands instantly went to my hips. He had that naughty look in his eyes "You ready for some more dick babe. Look at you I got you out here ready to ride this dick." He said as he squeezed my ass. I licked my lips and bent over to kiss him. I was trying to remember all of the pointers I was given, my hand traveled down his chest and his wash board abs. I loosened his ties on his trunks and slipped my hand inside. His dick was resting on his thigh, it was semi hard, I began to massage it giving it a little squeeze. I rubbed on the tip that was slightly moist. I sat on his thighs and used the other hand to fully untie his trunks. I pulled out his dick, I used the precum from his dick to moisten my hand "Babe get the condom out of my pocket." I looked him in the eye and shook my side to side. I moistened the inside of my mouth the best I could, I licked the top of his dick, my tongue swirled around the head. I followed it up by licking further down, my tongue trailed the base of his dick then back up to the top, I tried to let as much wetness as I could so my hands would easily glide up and down. My hands jerked up and down as I put pressure on his shaft. I opened my mouth as wide as I could and took him in, he reached the back of my throat as I tried to relax. "Oh shit, Love." Was all I heard.

I bobbed my head up and down and continued to swirl my tongue on his dick. He kept hitting the back of my throat causing my stomach to heave. I remembered what she told me about controlling my gag reflex, I started breathing through my nose. My mouth popped off his head, I swear it felt like his head grew almost three sizes. I mean it's already wide but when it came out of my mouth it looked magnified. My saliva trailed down his shaft, I swiped it with my hand and continued to jerk him up and down. Sincere's eyes were closed so I was unable to tell if I was doing okay. I went back to work and put it back inside my mouth. I started making vibrating noises as I moaned, he tasted damn good from the precum that was on my tongue. "Fuck babe, do that again." I repeated the action and I felt his hand grab at my hair. I remember this part she told me would happen, I braced myself for what could possibly happen next. His hips started moving up and down. I suctioned my jaw as I tried to keep up with his grinding and not choke. The grip on my hair got tighter, I didn't want to stop but I didn't want to be bald either. I reached behind my head and placed my hand on top of his. I guess he got the message and loosened his grip. I got back to work sucking and licking.

A few minutes later I felt him pulling my head off of him. I was perplexed as to why he was stopping me. I became nervous thinking maybe I had scrapped him with my teeth or maybe he was bored with it. I wiped my mouth with the back of my hand. The smell of his arousal was an aphrodisiac, my pussy was wet. He moved so fast it caught me off guard. Sin had flipped me on my back so that he was on top of me and my legs were touching my chest. He moved my bikini bottom to the side, his dick entered me hard and swift. "Oh babe" I moaned, there was some pain but that soon diminished. I was still getting accustomed to his shaft. He moved inside me with so much force I thought we were going to fall off the lounger. His hips pumped back and forth, making my juices flow heavily down his dick. He told me when my pussy made the sound like stirring good creamy mac and cheese he knew he was hitting it right. And that's exactly how it sounds at the moment. I bit my lip trying to stifle my moans I was getting louder as he started fucking on my spot. The position I was in didn't allow me much movement, I was stuck to receive any stroke he decided to give me. My inner walls started pulsing I knew I was about to come "That's right come on this dick Love. I feel you. Fuck" I couldn't tell you if it was the way he said the words or if it was knowing that he was enjoying my body that set me off. My pussy started contracting as I gushed on him. He fucked me through my orgasms and I could feel his dick pulsing inside of me. It felt so damn good against my walls that I had to tighten them even more around his dick. "Ugh fuck, shit." He pulled out and I could feel hot wetness on my inner thigh. Sincere was hovered over me stroking his manhood, I was able to put my legs down on the side of him as best as I could since they were still shaking. Sin was panting hard trying to get his breathing under control. My hands were rubbing on his chest he finally laid back on the lounger. He gestured for me to come towards him, he kissed me gently at first then it intensified we were battling our tongues trying to get as much as we could. We were interrupted by the clearing of one of the staffers throat. The junior butler let us know that dinner would be ready in an hour. Sin had his arms covering me as we were chest to chest. We laid there for a few more minutes. I thought to myself in those moments I couldn't believe I was here laid up on a one hundred foot yet half naked with my man and his semen running down my thighs.

I heard him yelling when I walked out of the bathroom. "Listen I didn't want to work with you in the first fucking place. Whatever problems you got Carmen are yours and yours alone, leave me the fuck out of it." I didn't want to ease drop on the conversation, so I went back into the bathroom. I didn't really know much about Carmen, when Sincere asked me to see if I could take her on as a client to help build her portfolio I was accepting. He gave me some background on their joint business venture and he wanted to make sure her money was handled right. I was hoping everything was ok, because I sure didn't want to be caught in the middle of client versus client beef. He disconnected the call I opened the door again "Sin is everything alright?" I was out of concern not to be nosey. My man looked tense in just those few moments. "Yeah babe, everything's good. Damn Love you look beautiful." He said as he admired me in my gold satin slip dress. I could feel the heat rise up on my cheeks, no matter how any times he told me I looked beautiful it still made me blush. I walked over to him, I know he told me everything was okay, but his eyes told me differently. Before I could say anything dinner was announced. We walked out of the cabin and took the elevator to the top deck where we were eating. It wasn't completely dark yet. The sun was setting and it looked magical against the water. Sin pulled my chair out so I could sit. I was going to complement him on his chivalry but his hand slapping my ass before I sat down put a stop to that.

"Is everything alright between you and Carmen?" I asked

"Yeah, ma everything is good. It's nothing that she and I can't handle business wise." He responded

"Okay, I was just asking because she is a client of mine too and having to dissolve a business between two mutual clients can be a pain in the ass and long hours." I said with slight humor in my voice. He chuckled as well. "Nah ma, it ain't even that serious though."

"How long have you two known each other. I mean for you to ask me to take her on, with her having little to none she's basically a startup with you backing her. You know our clientele are more established and understand the risk with investments and money management."

"We're childhood acquaintances, our fathers have known each other for years. Whenever we were in the same town we would link up to kill time and shit like that while our father's handled business." It was in the back of mind to ask him if the two had ever been together intimately. When I met Carmen I was immediately drawn to her beauty, she had the exotic look most men went after. Beautiful hazel green eyes, high cheekbones, long thick jet black hair. And her body oh my gosh if I was insecure I wouldn't want Sin anywhere near her. I looked up at the sky, the stars were bright it was beautiful and I didn't want to leave it.

"What I want to know is who the hell taught you how to give head like that." I looked down at him and my hands covered my face.

"Nah ain't none of that bashful shit Lovely, answer the question."

"Marisol." I responded "I asked her to give me some pointers on how to do it and she did." His hands rubbed up and down on his goatee "My nigga Marisol out her giving head lesson, ha." I was not expecting that response "Shit if she teaching you that, I understand now why that nigga Rico always trying smash that ass."

"Uggh Sin, really" he could be so crass at times, it made me forget who was I talking with. He laughed, I wasn't about to entertain his shenanigans

"On some real shit though my boy really feeling her. Shit this the first time I've seen him with a shorty longer than a couple of weeks." I had to agree Marisol was definitely into Rico, the two of them together showed a strong connection. The times that all four of us were together Marisol was attached to Rico and vice versa. "Aye did she teach you how to do it with no hands? If not I'm about to."

CHAPTER TWENTY

The two were sitting inside Lovely's office. Marisol wanted to meet at the nearby café but Lovely was unable to leave with all the work that had piled up while she was away. Marisol had brought some chai tea, they sipped and talked. "Why was he even at your house Puchi?" Lovely asked Marisol as she picked up her phone.

"Didn't I just tell your ass why, he was there because I needed to know why he left." Marisol said.

"Yeah but why? I didn't even know you two were back talking; the last time you mentioned him you said he could stay where ever the hell he came back from."

"Whose side are you on?" Marisol questioned

"I'm on your side but I'm not about to lie to you. There was no reason for him to be in your house, you could have met him somewhere other than your place. And when did Shannon have a key to your house, I knew you two were serious but I didn't think you both were at that stage in your relationship." Marisol sucked her teeth, she felt like her friend was siding with Shannon and not understanding the reason why she had Jomari at her house.

"For your info hoe, he and I didn't exchange keys. One night he was over there and had put it on me something crazy I couldn't even attempt to move out of the bed until the next day. I told him to take the spare key to lock up when he left since he had to catch an early flight. I just never asked for it back."

"Have you tried to talk to him since he left?"

"Nope, fuck Shannon, he wants to be in his feelings about the situation then that's on him. Shit I don't understand why he ain't getting it, forget the fact that Jomari was in my house. I shouldn't feel like I'm in a relationship by myself. If he's not out of town on business, then he's busy in meetings or running around the damn city. I couldn't even get a lunch date with my own man."

"Oh my god" Lovely said as she looked at her best friend "You're in love." She said

"Tuh what gives you that idea?" Marisol aske Lovely

"Girl you are really over here sad about a man not being able to spend time with you. Normally you wouldn't care you'd be on to the next one or handling your business. I've never seen you like this over a man Marisol. You're in love with Shannon, just admit it."

"See now I know you done soaked up too much of that Saint Tropez sun, you over here talking reckless about somebody in love and shit. I just enjoyed the dick." Lovely laughed at Marisol as she scrolled through her phone.

"Get the hell out of here Puchi, you like more than that man's extended ligament. And besides Sin told me this is the longest he's ever seen Shannon involved with a woman. Maybe you are the one he wants to be with. Are you still going to go to his birthday party?"

"Lovely did you not here me say he broke up with me. Why would I just show up at the man's birthday party like a basic thirsty ex-girlfriend."

"Yes if you want your man back. You go in there with your freakum dress on, face beat by the gods and you slay, so that at the end of the night whatever female he brought with him is taking an Uber home alone and you're in the back of the Bach telling the driver to roll up the partition." Marisol tried to hold in her laugh but it was no easy task, "Did you just give me a damn Beyoncé lesson on how to get my man back, who are you? Looks like Sin opening up that pussy got you out here wildin'." Lovely giggled as she typed on her IPhone.

"What are you over there doing anyway?" Lovely showed Marisol her Instagram page after she replied to a comment Sincere had placed under the picture, she scrolled through the recent pictures with her and Sincere in Saint Tropez " Oh ya'll cute or whatever." Marisol stated sarcastically. "You over there with damn hearts in your eyes, looks like you might be the one in love."

"If I were I would not be afraid to admit it at least to myself." With that statement Marisol knew her friend didn't know the full truth about Sincere, she was going to have to talk to Sincere and let him know he needed to come clean with Lovely. "Just be careful who you give your heart to Love."

"Why is there something that I don't know?" Marisol felt it wasn't her place to tell her, but if Sincere didn't, Marisol told herself she would. She only wanted her friend to be happy and safe and if that was truly with Sincere then she needed to know what she might be up against.

"Nah Love I'm just talking, what do I know, I just got dumped." Marisol packed up her things to leave, she didn't want Lovely to start asking more questions. "Alright Love let me get out of here and actually do some work. I know you have a ton since you've been gone getting your chocha dug out." The women laughed, Lovely opened the door to walk Marisol to the elevators. Marisol stopped mid stride which caused Lovely to crash into her from behind. "Damn did you forget how to walk. Why did you stop?" Marisol just shook her head at the two people coming off the elevator. Lovely stepped around Marisol she finally saw the reason Marisol stopped.

"I know this has to be some type of joke, what the hell are you doing here Heather?" Marisol had dropped her bag on the accent chair that was not too far from the reception area. Out of her peripherals she saw Marisol removing her earrings, they were still in her office building and Lovely didn't want to be seen in an all out cat fight in her office. Heather's face held a smirk, she was pleased that she was able to see the look on Lovely's face when she entered the office. She walked over to the two of them just as Desmond was rounding the corner from his actual office. His eyes were wide, he wasn't expecting Lovely and Marisol to be finished catching up for at least another hour or so.

When Marisol arrived in the building her and Desmond were on the elevator. Marisol had let out that she and Lovely were probably going to be a while catching up. Desmond figured that he would be able to meet Heather down in the parking garage but she insisted on coming upstairs. Desmond stepped in between Heather and Lovely. Lovely looked like she was ready to claw Heather's entire face. Marisol had somehow managed to secure her hair into a top knot on her head. "Ladies let's remember where we are, okay." Desmond said to all three women. "I know exactly where the fuck I am Des, the question is why is she here. I know damn well I didn't invite her." Lovely said she was trying to keep her voice calm, she didn't want to alert the other staff. "Funny you said invite because I was invited here by my handsome beau." Both Lovely and Marisol looked at Desmond as if he had lost all the sense he was given. Lovely couldn't comprehend why Desmond would one invite someone he knows she despised to her place of business, but also why he would be dating her as well. Lovely was exhausted she was still jet lag from her trip, she didn't get much sleep on the trip with Sincere stamina and she had accounts that she needed to go over. Lovely was in no frame of mind to fight with Desmond, she felt that he was taking a serious jab at her. Lovely just pushed past the two "Come on Marisol." She directed to her friend. "You sure Mamí, because I got bail money I can put these hands on this heffa for you." Lovely continued to walk to the elevators.

~

Across town Sincere was on the burner phone speaking in code with one of his over searers in Mexico. There was a shipment set to depart from the Gulf of Mexico into the Port of Houston. With the issues that happened with the last shipment Sincere was weary. He had to eliminate one of his own because of the mishap that could have put him in prison or dead. Sincere had to find someone he trusted as much as he trusted Rico to get the kilos off the boat without any hitches. He knew one person who could do it but he was no longer in the game. Sincere wrapped up the call and placed the phone on the desk. He picked up his personal phone and scrolled through the contact list. He sent a text to the number telling them to call asap.

His doorbell rang, he walked to the door and looked on the small screen that was on the wall. "Wassup Kid." He dapped up Rico as he stepped back to let him in. "Kid? B I'm a grown as man, gone somewhere with that kid shit B." Sincere laughed as he mushed Rico in the back of the head. "That's right yo old ass about to be thirty in a couple of weeks. You ready for that old life. You get a checkup yet, make sure everything still working." Sincere joked, "Nigga I know everything work over here, shit I'm ready for the next chapter in my life." Sincere just smirked and shook his head at Rico. "Well stay ready for it baby boy. Because after this you might need to make some serious decisions about what next for you." Rico nodded his head up and down as he went to sit on the couch. "Man well I'll worry about all of that once I hit the big three oh, aye you make sure all the baddest freaky bitches are at my party. I need straight freaks, not thots, I'm trying to smash everything before midnight like Cinderfella." Sincere spit out the water he was drinking at Rico's comment. "Nigga you trying to get us both killed. Marisol ain't going for that shit you not about to have me getting the nigga you ain't shit stare all night from her or Lovely."

"Oh that's right wifey going to be there so you can't play how you want to."

"Shit Marisol gone be there too so what you saying. She ain't about to let that shit go down."

"Nah shorty uninvited." Sincere was about to respond when his phone rang, he picked it up knowing who it already was on the other line. "Deejay wassup man." The caller on the other end gave a short reply. "Listen I need to call in that favor." "Sin mayne you know I don't get down like that anymore." Deejay responded.

"Nigga I know but I wouldn't be calling if I didn't think anybody else could get it done and make sure it's right." Sincere briefly explained what he needed done. Deejay agreed after a few minutes of convincing that the transaction would go smooth. Sincere disconnected the call, "Deejay, you called Deejay. You couldn't think of anybody else in Houston that could do it."

"Not anybody that I trust as much as you. I'll send King down there as well to give him extra back up. This is a bigger than normal shipment. But back to what you were saying before Deejay called, why isn't the Wifey invited again?" Rico side eyes Sincere for the wifey comment. He went on telling Sincere the incident that happened at Marisol's house. After Rico left Sincere headed to the in home gym, he had worked out for about twenty minutes when the door buzzed. He grabbed a towel and wiped off the sweat that had gathered on his face, neck and chest in the short time. Looking at the monitor on the wall, he did a double take. The door buzzed again, he sighed he wasn't in the mood for oncoming headache he knew would come from whatever the person at the door had to say. He unlocked the door and stood in the doorway. "How did you get pass the doormen, your name damn sure isn't on my list." He asked her, "I can be very persuasive when I want to be are you going to let me in." Sincere stepped back and let her in, he had an instinctive feeling that he would soon regret it.

"Make that your last time you come to my place unannounced. This ain't your shit and it's real disrespectful. Yo ass can call just like anybody else. Now why are you here?"

"I told you I had a problem and it needs your attention." Carmen said as she walked around the first floor of his penthouse. "Nice place Papí, I see drug money is treating you well." Sincere ignored her comment.

"And I told you ma, your problem ain't my problem. You want to be big and bad and strike out on your own, trying to create your little mafia. You need to handle whatever the fucking problem is like a big girl or like any other leader would." Carmen watched him move around as his muscles flexed, his bare chest was turning her on his tattoos were glistening from the sweat, his sweatpants were riding low on his hips, his v cut on display. Carmen licked her lips remembering the times that they were together. She could admit that Sincere was one of her best lovers. Carmen wanted Sincere back in her life, the two could be the power couple of the underworld. She had the backing of the Cartel, Sincere's family's name is respected in the game. "Now I gave you my answer, you need to leave."

"You know you should be bending backwards trying to assist me. If it weren't for me you'd be just another afterthought. You should be begging me." Sincere rushed her and before he could think his hand reached out and grabbed Carmen's throat. He applied pressure to her neck, Carmen's hands reached up trying to pry his hand loose. "Beg, bitch I don't beg even when you're father and his punk ass men had me with in an inch of my life. You should know that, you were there." His grip tighten, the more she clawed at his hand the more he applied pressure. "You see what it feels like don't you, knowing somebody else has your life in their hands. That one person can seal your fate. Beg for your life Carmen." Her face started turning dark red, Sincere released her neck from his grip. She gasped for air when he let go, she started choking trying to get air into her lungs. Carmen gained her composure after a few moments, she knew this side of him, and she'd seen it before. "You must be crazy to put your hands on me." Sincere's head slightly tilted to the side, "Carmen if you don't want black roses and your head sent to your father with my regards I suggest you leave." Carmen's eyes turned into slits with his threat, she huffed and picked up her purse that had slipped out of her hands. She headed towards the door "I'll be seeing you soon

Sincere." Sincere shook his head as he closed the door. Some people were good for your life and some people just weren't. He knew he needed to pull out of this business with Carmen, before he killed her and started a war between families.

CHAPTER TWENTY-ONE

Lovely slipped in her Chiffon backless crème colored dress for the second time. They were running late for the party, Sincere didn't seem to mind as he was still taking his time putting on his clothes. The party started at least an hour ago, sure it was a club and people were still arriving but Sincere and Lovely were supposed to be there to walk in with the birthday boy. "Sin can you please hurry up, we've already missed his entrance." "Babe, trust me that nigga ain't worried about us missing his grand entrance. I'm sure he in there wilding with bottles of Ace, Dussé and Henny everywhere and bitches surrounding him." Lovely rolled her eyes at his comment, she still tried to convince Marisol to show up to the party but she was still being stubborn. Sin stood up and ran his hand over his waves, he checked his appearance in the mirror again. When he was satisfied with his look he glanced at Lovely "Aight ma I'm ready. You ready?" Lovely just shook her head at him, "Sin with the way you keep checking to make sure you look aight, I would think you got some females waiting on you at the club." She commented, "Cut that out ma, you know I'm only flexing for you." Sincere kissed her on the cheek, they walked hand in hand to his door. They took the elevator downstairs, the doorman greeted the couple as he called on their car.

The matte black Rolls Royce Ghost pulled up to the club. Lovely looked out of the tinted windows at the crowd of people waiting to get inside the club. The line was wrapped around the building. People were dressed to the nines with the strictly enforced dress code. If you weren't dressed like you were going to meet President Obama at a White House gala then you weren't stepping inside the club. Bennie opened the door to let the couple out. Sincere stepped out and buttoned his suit jacket, his hand reached out for Lovely as her Oscar de le Renta heels touched the pavement. They walked up to the front door, the bouncer had the doors opened immediately when he saw the Rolls Royce pull up and Sincere step out of the car.

The bass was pumping through the speakers, the club was packed from wall to wall. Lovely looked around at all the people there to celebrate Rico's birthday. "I didn't realize Shannon was so popular, look at all these people here Sin." Sincere laughed at her comment, he thought to himself *if she only knew the truth about Him and Rico she would know most of the people in attendance were perpetrators trying to come up or people showing fake love*. The real family and friends were in the VIP section which had heavy security, not for Sincere or Rico, but for their siblings and family. Sincere knew his enemies could possibly try to get at him when they think he's the most vulnerable. Both Sin and Rico's sisters were in attendance, this was the first time people were seeing Sincere and Lovely together (those that weren't close friends). As they continued to walk towards the VIP, Lovely could see that she was getting stared down by the females and lustful looks from some of them that were bold enough to keep their eyes on her longer than five seconds.

"Am I going to have a problem in here tonight Sincere I keep getting stared down by these females?" Sincere looked around a bit; he saw the stares of the women and he just pulled her closer to him.

"You know how it is ma, bitches hate on others when they want something they can't have."

"So you're telling me I'm getting salty ass stares because all these women want you." She asked him with a little sass in her voice. He stopped and turned her towards him and leaned in to her ear, "What they want is your beauty, something they can't obtain with any makeup or brush. They want that gorgeous smile of yours that lights up any room. And what you need to do right now is smile at these hoes with your man on your arm." Sincere's mouth connected with hers, the kiss was passionate, sensual the two didn't care that they were standing in a room full of people, Sincere was putting a claim on his lady in front of everyone.

"You late Casanova." Rico said as Sincere and Lovely approached him. Rico had two women draped under his arms like Ice T in New Jack City. The only thing he was missing was the Kango hat and shades. Sincere and Rico exchanged the brotherly hug, "My bad it was Lovely's fault though she was tempting a nigga with that dress on, so I decide to oblige." Lovely slapped Sincere on the shoulder for the half-truth, yeah they did have sex before they left but it was Sincere who started it. Lovely mugged the women that were still standing next to Rico. "You look beautiful ma." He said as he winked at Lovely before he hugged her. "Happy birthday Shannon." She said, "I 'preciate it ma, but where's my gift. You show up late and empty handed, what part of the game is that Love." Rico teased.

Sincere worked his way around the room. He dapped up his boys that were in the VIP section, he introduced Lovely to some of the people on his team that hadn't met her. Kameron came up to the couple and dapped up Sin, he hugged Lovely. Sincere spotted his sisters dancing off the side with some other females he didn't know. He figured they were some of Rico's groupies for the night. One of the sisters looked up and saw her brother, smiled and waved. Sin gestured his head signaling for them to come over, the sisters walked up to their big brother and embraced him in a hug "Why you got this short ass dress on Nyla around all these thirsty ass niggas." His sister gave him a sour look for appraising her outfit. The baby sister Bella giggled at her brother's chastising forgetting the fact that his sisters were grown women. "You must be Lovely." Bella said "Yes I am, I didn't know you two were twins." Lovely said looking at the sisters whose features were identical to one another, "We get that often, but we're not, I'm Bella the youngest and this is Nyla. It's nice to finally meet you. I don't understand why my big bro has been hiding you." Lovely went in for a handshake instead Bella opened her arms for a hug. "You are more beautiful than my brother described." Nyla told her, Lovely blushed at the comment. She noticed Sincere had ventured off towards the other side of the VIP. When she spotted him she also seen Rico with three women surrounding him vying for his attention. She rolled her eyes and took out her cell phone. She snapped a picture of Rico with one woman sitting in his lap with his hands on her ass, the other whispering in his ear, she pressed send and tucked her phone back into her clutch. "I saw that." Lovely turned around at the deep baritone voice, she smiled at Kameron, "You saw what?" she asked him his tall lean frame was clad in a black Gucci suit with a red dress shirt and Gucci Elanor bit style loafers "You working for TMZ or Marisol. I hope it's the latter, my mans over here thinking he foolin somebody, maybe everyone else but not me. He misses that woman." Kameron stated "Well let's hope they both come to their senses. He seems to be enjoying his party though." She said looking at the two friends joke around with each other.

Kameron chuckled as he shook his head. "Oh yeah, well then tell me why he keeps looking at the entrance to the VIP every few minutes." He said before he walked away. Lovely sighed she wasn't going to harbor on it she felt if the two were going to be stubborn then she was going to leave herself out of it. The DJ started playing the intro to Young M.A. single, the dancefloor was packed. The beat dropped and 50 Cent stepped onto the stage, the crowd went wild, money started flowing from the VIP onto the crowd below as 50 rapped his part, Young M.A. joined the stage she shouted out Rico as she finished off the song. 50 Cent's track *I'm the Man* was performed, the crew in the VIP started popping Ace of Spades bottles spraying them towards Rico. The girls around him scattered not wanting to get their weave wet or smell like alcohol all night. After the performance the DJ went back to mixing he was still riding the wave of 50 cent as he mixed in *No Romeo No Juliet*.

Lovely was dancing with Sincere's sisters when she felt a pinch on her butt. She turned around quickly to see who it was, Sincere stood there looking mischievous. Lovely and Sin was grinding on each other as they danced; One of the security guards tapped Sin on the shoulder and spoke in his ear. Sin nodded his head up and down, he went back to dancing with his woman. Sin saw her enter the VIP section, she looked around room, she spotted Sincere and Lovely and headed towards them. Marisol tapped on Lovely's shoulder, her head turned around she screamed in excitement when she saw Marisol. The two hugged, "You came to get your man after I sent you the picture, it took you long enough." Lovely stated. "I was actually on my way when I got your text, Rico's sister Eilanna had sent me a text telling me to come get my man before she and I quote 'shot a thot'." Lovely had met Rico's sisters as well, they both were beautiful but very hood, and they had the Brooklyn attitude down to the tee. "He's not in here he's in the office, he had to change they doused him with bottles of champagne." Sincere had called for Kameron to come over, when he saw Marisol standing there he smiled and hugged her. Sincere told him she was looking for Rico, Kameron led Marisol to the back of the club to the elevator.

~

These niggas were having too much fun at my expense, dousing me with bottles of champagne messing up a five thousand dollar costumed suit jacket. I just so happened to have a suit in my closet, I needed to change, the damn clothes were starting to stick to me. I left the office area and went into the bathroom to take a quick shower to wash the alcohol smell off my body. I only stayed in there for ten minutes, I left them broads in the office and I didn't want them getting to familiar with my shit. I heard the door open as I pulling up my pants, only two other people had the code to the door, but I went over to the dresser for my gun just in case these bitches decided to be bold and set a nigga up at his own shit. I heard that sultry voice tell the others they needed to leave. I put the gun back in the dresser and continued to put on the rest of my clothes.

"Oh I see I need to snatch wigs and edges in order for you bitches to understand that I'm serious." Marisol said, she was reaching in her purse and the ladies immediately got up and started heading for the door. I just shook my head at her, one moment she could be the classy, sexy independent woman and the next she was ready to throw hands like a true Brooklyn thug.

"What you doing here shorty?" she turned her head from the door to look at me; "I'm cleaning house, but these bitches so scary, all I was doing was getting a hair tie." I just stood there, I was waiting for her to really answer my question. I had a mundane expression on my face I wasn't here for the bullshit, she must have figured it out. "I came to talk to you and to celebrate your birthday."

"This ain't the time to talk Marisol, I'm about to get back to my party."

"And those bitches, you about to get back to them too."

"Yeah ma and the bitches too." I moved towards the door and she jumped in front of me trying to block me.

"Wait, wait okay. I am sorry Shannon. Just hear me out please." I waited for her to continue. I wasn't intentionally trying to make it hard for shorty but like I said I wasn't up for the bullshit.

"I was wrong for having Jomari over my house, I can admit that. I'm not trying to make any excuse but if you knew the history, I just felt that I really needed closure on the past with regards to him. I could have handled it differently and for that I am sorry. I feel that you also need to own up to your part in this too."

"What part Marisol?"

"The lack of communication Shannon, I shouldn't be wondering if you and I are together are not."

"Did I ever give off the notion that we weren't. It's like I said already you already know how I'm getting it out here. Me not calling or checking in is something that I don't do when I'm conducting my business. I'm trying to make sure I make it home not in a box or in handcuffs." There as a long pause her head cascaded down.

"I understand." She said, I lifted her chin so that we were looking eye to eye.

"Do you, because I don't want to have this conversation again, I need to be able to trust you when I'm out of town, just like you need to trust me."

"Are you saying you're willing to give us another try?"

"Yeah, I was just waiting on you to your shit together."

"Whatever Shannon, I'm always together."

"Nah ma you was straight trippin having a nigga in your crib. You had to be on something. And if I had my piece on me at the time, ole boy's face would have been on an obituary, real shit. If I ever see you like that again I'm straight bodying that nigga." She rolled her eyes at me. I missed her sassiness it always turns me on. I hugged her she smelled good, I moved my hands down her back to grab her ass. She started giggling and moaning near my ear.

"Mmm I missed those hands Papí." I squeezed her ass cheeks again.

"Oh yeah what else you miss?" I asked, her hands were running up and down my chest.

"I missed you Shannon." I looked down at her into those clear green eyes, the look she gave me assured me that she was the one I needed.

"Let's finish celebrating my birthday ma." She pulled away and turned towards the door. "Aye where you going, I said we about to finish celebrating my birthday."

"I know I was about to go back downstairs to the party."

"Nah ma, I ain't had that pussy in almost two months, you know what I like. Face down ass up shorty." She laughed but I was dead serious.

"Is that right Pa. You're lucky I love you otherwise you'd be over there with blue balls."

"So you love me huh." She started biting on her bottom lip. Something I noticed she does when she gets uncomfortable.

"Yes I guess I do." That wasn't good enough for me.

"Ain't no guess Marisol either you do or don't"

"Then yes I do love you and yes I'm in love with you Shannon."

"That's good to know, since I love your feisty ass too." I was about to pick her up and put her on the closes thing to us which was he table, when I saw the lights come on inside the club. I checked the monitors and saw the place had some new guest. "Fuck we got to go."

"Why what's wrong." I turned her around and showed her the screen.

"Oh shit, is that the DEA?"

~

The music stopped abruptly, everyone was looking around trying to figure out what had happened to the music. Suddenly the club's lights came on, the club became filled with what seemed like almost two dozen people. Everybody kept looking around as they were surrounded by men and women in FBI and DEA jackets.

Sincere was sitting down with Lovely on his lap when the music stopped and the lights came on. He tapped her leg for her to get up. When he looked over the balcony of the VIP he saw the agents storm in. They had guns drawn, and were filtering in from different directions of the club. "What the fuck." Sincere said out loud. Kameron came over and saw the agents down below, he had his gun tucked into the back of his pants. He knew if the FBI and DEA were here it wasn't for any code violation, they were there to hand out federal time. Kameron reached for the gun, he wasn't going to shoot but he knew if they searched him he would be going back to the pen for possession a firearm with a felony record. He felt someone at his back, he turned around and saw Eilanna remove his gun and place it in her purse. She mouthed to him "I got you." He nodded his head in acknowledgement. The crowd below was being detained by NYPD as the agents searched the club for their perps. Rico and Marisol exited the elevator trying to find a way to get to the VIP area.

"Oh my god Sin what's going on?" Lovely asked when she looked down and saw the agents. He turned to her and saw the distress in her face. He was about to speak when Lovely's hand cover her mouth "They're arresting Shannon, Sincere, why are they arresting him!?" She could she Marisol trying to hang on to Rico, Rico was yelling at the cops to not touch Marisol.

The agents made their way to the VIP area with their guns still drawn they had them pointed at majority of the men in the room. Lovely's hand searched for Sincere's as she interlocked their fingers. A tall man with a DEA jacket and vest walked up the stairs almost like he wasn't in any rush. He looked around the room and spotted Sincere. A cocky smirk appeared on his face. He smoothly walked over to Sincere, "Sincere Riz I have a warrant for your arrest. Turn around and place your hands behind your head." Sincere's muscles in his jaw flexed, he didn't care for the smirk on the agents face but most importantly he knew that his other lifestyle was about to be exposed to Lovely before he got the chance to tell her. He did as the agent stated, he let go of Lovely's hand and turned around. The agent placed him in handcuffs and he did a mediocre pat down. "Why are you arresting him, what are the damn charges?" Lovely interrogated the agent.

"What you don't know? Your boyfriend over here is a drug kingpin, but tonight he's being arrested for money laundering." The DEA agent said in a condescending tone. "What!? Was Lovely's response. "Yeah Ms. Daniels and I'm going to have to ask you to do the same. Please turn around and place your hands behind you hand." Lovely was shocked she couldn't believe the words that just came out of the agent's mouth. "Lovely Daniels you are under arrest for money laundering, you have the right to remain silent, anything you say can and will be used against you in the court of law."

"Aye yo get your hands off her, she ain't got nothing to do with this" Sincere shouted at the female officer who was hand cuffing Lovely. The agent finished reading her the Miranda rights. "Escort these two down the vehicle. Put them in the same car, I'm sure they have a lot to talk about." He looked at the hurt on Lovely's face "Well judging by her face they might not." He chuckled, a path was cleared as they walked the two down the stairs. Marisol saw Lovely being escorted outside the club in handcuffs and it set her off. She started cursing and trying to break through the cops that barricaded themselves around the partygoers. She kept yelling for them to let Lovely go, and cursed Sincere's entire name. Marisol was furious, she didn't know why her friend was being arrested but she knew that she was the innocent party.

The scene outside the club looked like a movie to Lovely. There were dozens of cop cars, unmarked cars, a swat van parked outside of the club. It made her think, *who the fuck where they coming to arrest John Gotti's they have enough back up like they were going to be in a shootout.*" She looked back at Sincere her eyes welled up with tears. The back door to the Escalade opened, she stepped up and slid into the car Sincere followed.

"Who are you Sincere! Who the fuck are you! Im sitting in fucking handcuffs in the back seat of a car waiting to be taken to jail for money laundering."

"Babe not here not right now. Just stay quiet and ask for a lawyer when you get inside. I promise I will make this shit right." Sincere said

"Don't fucking tell me what to do. My mother is a fucking criminal lawyer, you don't think I know not to fucking talk to the cops when I'm arrested for a got damn crime." She yelled "I can't believe this, this isn't happening right now. A drug kingpin Sincere, really. I put my trust in you."

"Promise me you'll let me explain when we get out of here. Lovely promise me." Sincere wasn't going to say much, there was a cop in the front seat.

Lovely willed herself not to shed any tears, she turned her head and looked out the window at the scene, red and blue lights, people in jackets with FBI and DEA, the crowd of people on the side of the street watching. The sound of Sincere's voice faded into the background, the noise outside seemed deafening to her, she saw Marisol on the phone the cops were holding her back; she was trying to get to the car that Sincere and Lovely were being held in. The driver door to the car opened, the arresting agent slid into the seat and started the ignition. The sirens sounded off as the black escalade pulled off into the street.

LOVE
And
PAIN

CHAPTER ONE

I couldn't even begin to think how I was going to put my entire career back together. I should have never trusted him. I should've never took that risk. I should've have ever fell in love with Sincere. Now look where I am, hiding in my parents' house like a child. I had to constantly keep my phone on do not disturb. If it wasn't the reporters or lawyers calling my phone asking me questions; it was Sincere calling and texting or Marisol wanting to know why I wasn't speaking to her. I shut every one out. It's been a few weeks and the I keep replaying the entire night in my head. No matter how much I wanted it to be a dream it was real, that night really happened. I was taken away in handcuffs read my rights and told I was being charged with money laundering.

I had no idea who I was standing next to, the man I had come to know was a façade, the DEA agents continued to read off his charges and he just stood there with a blank face. No words came out of his mouth and for some reason I couldn't take my eyes off him. That walk out of the club had to be the most embarrassing moment of my life. Cameras were flashing everywhere, people standing off to the side with their phones out recording what would be ultimately played on social media feeds and news outlets.

The room door opened without as much as a knock. It was okay I knew who it was. My mom entered the room looking graceful and poised like always. It was hard to believe this woman is a no non-sense prosecutor from Maryland. She came over and sat on the edge of the bed. I just stared at her as she looked at me. I wondered what she saw when she looked at me. Did she weaknesses, did she see defeat, was she able to see my broken heart and my anger.

I bit my bottom lip trying to control myself. I didn't want to cry, I knew it wouldn't help. How would I explain that the tears weren't because my successful career was ruined, no the tears would be because of him? She came closer to me and tucked a piece of hair behind my ears. I gave her a small smile which probably couldn't been seen if you weren't up-close.

"Love have you eaten anything today? She asked me. I tried to eat just to appease her and my father, I didn't want them to worry about my health let alone my mental state. I just shook my head yes in response. I had something to eat earlier when I went to walk outside the property. Thank goodness, my parent's estate was heavily guarded and upheld it residents' privacy. I didn't have to worry about any paparazzi or news cameras.

"Baby girl I know this isn't good time but someone is here to see you." My mother stated, my heart had begun to race. I told my parents that I didn't want to speak or see anyone no matter how persistent they were. I silently prayed that my parents didn't let a certain person into this house because not only would I be in court for money laundering but second-degree murder as well. My mother must have read my mind she shook her head "No it isn't him. Your father and I wouldn't do that to you." A soft sigh escaped from my lungs, I was grateful for my parents. I don't know what I would do without them, when we arrived at the DEA's building the first words that came out of my mouth were phone call. I called my mother and explained to her that I needed her and dad to come down and I would need a lawyer. I know traffic was heavy that time of night but somehow my parents made it from the outskirts of New Jersey to Midtown New York in a matter of minutes.

As I sat there in the investigation room waiting, I tried to put the pieces together and I tried to figure out how I could have gotten into this situation. My mind kept going over Sincere's accounts and nothing seemed out of the norm. The door to the investigation room opened and walked in a tall white man in an impeccable suit. The suit looked too pricey for a government official so I knew he wasn't one of the DEA or FBI agents. He had introduced himself and informed me that he was there to represent me for counsel. I was confused because I didn't call him and I knew my parents were on their way and my mother would be my counsel. When he further explained that he was contacted by Sincere and he wanted to ensure that I had proper legal counsel. The laughed that escaped my mouth didn't register as normal, hell it scared me. I explained to the Jewish lawyer whose retainer fee I was certain is thousands of dollars by the hour, that I didn't need his legal representation and to inform his real client that I plead the fifth amendment and I didn't need anything from him. After a few moments of silence, the lawyer understood what didn't need to be said and walked out of the room. I was back alone with my thoughts waiting for my real legal counsel, even though I was innocent I knew that this was not going away easily. I knew I had a fight on my hands.

"Whoever is downstairs tell them I'm sleeping." I told her, I still didn't want to face the world. The only person on the outside I contacted was Desmond. He told me we had loss several high-profile clients and he was trying to retain the few that haven't pulled out of business with us. I was grateful to him for trying to keep the business afloat and most of all for not throwing anything negative in my face about Sincere and I.

"Love I know this I hard but you are going to have to put your extra big girl panties on and tackle this. You know your father and I are here to back you up with any and everything. But I can no longer see my baby locked up in a room, giving up."

"What do you want me to do mom, am I supposed to go out and pretend that I haven't loss everything; that everything that I worked and sacrificed for just wasn't snatched away from me."

"I want you to get up and reclaim what is yours. I want you to stop feeling sorry for and stop accepting defeat. You are innocent and we will fight this." The confidence in which she spoke made it sound so easy.

"Ok Mom, let's say I get up and get things in order. I go back into the office, pick up the phone and fight for the business I loss. I regain the trust of my clients and slowly start getting business back to normal. Then we fight these charges and my name is free and cleared. How do I go about putting the pieces back for my heart, how do I begin to trust another man?"

"I can't tell you how to feel, I can only tell you what I know and from experience I know that this too shall pass."

I had met this guy we were in the same class, he looked older than some of the students in the class so I figured he was probably a police officer trying to obtain his law degree. Any way he projected himself as a know it all, he had an arrogance that for some reason gotten under my skin. During mock trials somehow, we would always be on the opposing counsel and our cases were always linked. It had gotten to the point where the entire class would become entertained at us going back and forth. I finally had enough and was going to confront him and find out what his issue was with me. Before I got the chance to do so our professor had informed me that I had been selected as junior counsel on a case alongside two others and he was one of them. Before trial started we had to get together to go over the evidence, witnesses, jury selection and how we would approach the opposing counsel. He and I were partnered together to collect research on the case.

Anyway, we got to know each other on a personal level now that we were working so closely. I learned that he was worked his way through college and was working his way through law school. His parents couldn't afford much of anything let alone a college education for their son. We were two different people with different backgrounds. As time went by and the trial was wrapping up, I had realized that he and I wouldn't be spending anymore late nights with each other just talking about whatever. I realized that I didn't want that to end that I wanted to be around him as often as I could. We started dating shortly after and let me say I was in love, open with my head in the clouds. No one could tell me anything wrong or bad about him. I was happy, he made me happy.

One night we were out and we had just left this nice casual restaurant. It was so cold that night and I was rubbing my hands together trying to get some heat generated. I had remembered I'd left my gloves in his car a few days ago so I went to open the glove compartment in search for them. When I opened the compartment, a small clear bag fell out and hit the floor. I immediately went to pick it up and when I saw it contents. I froze, I didn't notice the car had stopped and we had pulled over. My eyes were still on the bag. He took the bag out of my hand and placed it back inside the glove compartment. The things that were going through my mind at that time. I didn't understand why he would have crack inside his car. I looked over at him just focusing on him looking at his features he didn't look like a user, didn't show any signs of a user so I concluded that he was selling the drugs. I don't know what came over me but my hands reached up and I slapped the shit out of him before I exited the car. During that time crack was an epidemic and anyone caught selling was getting major time. There wasn't any type of explanation that he could give or any that I would want to hear.

Let me tell you when I got home I was devastated, I didn't understand how he could have put me inside of a car he knew had drugs in them. Anything could have happened that night; we could have been stopped by police for no reason and even though we knew the law anything could have still occurred, we were still black and we were in a nice part of the city. Days went by he tried to call, I ignored them all. He would try to talk to me after class and I would walk away. He had finally finagled his way into my tiny apartment begging me to listen to him. I gave him the opportunity to explain, after several minutes he explained that he was selling the drugs and yes, he knew the risk and the only reason why he was selling was to pay for law school. He apologized for having me in the car with the drugs, he explained that he was in a rush trying to get to me for our date and forgot to drop them off. I had so many questions for him but I just let him talk, he promised that he would never put me at risk like that ever again and begged me to give him another chance.

I was confused and torn between the love I had for this man and my morals. Here I was a law student studying to become the definition of upholding the law and prosecuting people that broke the law. I had a decision that I needed to make whatever decision I made I needed to be okay with it and not regret it. I didn't let this one incident stop me from seeing the good in a man or to give up on love. I'm telling you do not give up on love, do not let this stop you from finding your true happiness and remember whatever decision you make own it." I had listened intently to the story and understood the message my mom was giving me. She stood up and grabbed my hand and pulled me up as well. She held me tight as she whispered in my ear that she loved me. I loved her with everything in me and was glad she was here by my side non-judging, being protective. She walked to the door and before she opened I had to know, "Mom what did you decide?"

"Like I said I didn't give up on love and to this day I don't regret my decision." She told me, I patiently waited for her to elaborate.

"We married shortly after we both passed the state bar and I have been by his side for the last twenty-five years. He has made good on his promise, he never put me at risk like that again and he has continued to make me a happy woman." To hear this about my mother and father's relationship is surprising. The two of them were perfect for each other in every way.

"How did you get him to stop selling?" I asked her.

"I didn't get him to stop, he did that on his own, it took some time. I worried about him all the time, I didn't want to see him locked away just because he was trying to better himself. It did put a strain on our relationship, but I knew he had to want to do it on his own." My mom placed her hand under my chin and lifted my head eye level with hers. I was trying to hold back the tears, but they slipped away.

"Lovely, I know you're hurting and that isn't going to go away anytime soon. I don't ever want to see your in pain or hurt like this and I can only fix one part of the situation the other part you are going to have do on your own. When you brought Sincere to dinner and as I watched intently at the both of you and not to sound cliché but I could see the sparks going off. Sincere's life decisions although morally wrong, I honestly don't think he meant for it to cross paths with you." She wiped my eyes and kissed me again on the cheek.

"Get yourself straighten up I'll tell your company you'll be down shortly."

I walked down the winding staircase holding my breath. I still wasn't sure who was downstairs waiting on me. Whomever it is surely didn't take no for an answer or they convinced my mother that they needed to see me. I passed the grand room and didn't see anyone in there so I made my way to the sitting room. The voices were low but I could easily recognize them, my father laughed lightly at something that was said. I entered the room fully and the conversation abruptly stopped. My father stood up and came toward me with arms open wide. I walked into his embrace and he held me tight. He placed a gentle kiss atop of my head, "Glad to see you out of the room baby girl." He said to me.

"Well today Mom didn't give me a choice." I told him, his throaty chuckle set off one of my own. My dad stepped aside, "I'll give you two some privacy. Good to see you again Marisol." My dad said as he left the room.

"Mami how are you doing? I've been calling your phone for days. I figured you didn't want to talk but I had to make sure that you were okay," Marisol explained all in one breath.

"I thought I was going to have to do some mission impossible shit, the guard didn't want to let me through. After convincing moms that I just wanted to make sure that you were okay, I finally got the okay to come through." It was comforting to know that she was here, we've been the best of friends for years and to know she would go to no ends for me was reassuring. We both sat down on the couch, her eyes continued to peer at me like she was inspecting me.

"I was going to call you soon, I just needed time to get things into perspective. Figure out my next move." I explained to her.

"It's okay Love, I know this is a difficult time for you, but just know that I'm here for you if you need anything." Again, I was grateful for our friendship. We'd been through some difficult situations before and we always prevailed through the adversity. We had people telling us both that we wouldn't become successful in our field of work because it is dominated by the opposite sex or due to the fact that our skin wasn't the right shade that could persuade the masses to trust us with their finances or business. But we overcame, we became the success that we were told wasn't guaranteed and we did that together as friends and as sisters.

We sat there making small talk but we both knew were averting around the elephant in the room. My mind repeatedly asked the question but I forced my mouth to not speak the words. I needed to focus on other important issues, I needed to get myself back together and start handling this as I would if it weren't me on the receiving end but one of my clients. I needed to get back to Lovely Daniels and sitting and hiding in my parents' house and wallowing in self-pity was not the answer.

"Listen Love, there is something that I need to get off my chest. I have been trying to figure out the best way to tell you and I came to the conclusion that I just needed to keep it all the way real with you like I always have."

My body went on alert, the tone of her voice told me that I wasn't going to like what I was about to hear. I gave her my full attention. She looked a little nervous which is something I rarely saw from her. I braced myself for whatever I was about to hear and I prayed to myself that whatever it is I could handle it. Marisol swiped her tousled long bangs from her in front of her face. She tucked her long tresses behind her ear, she cleared her throat as she let her truth flow from her mouth.

"I went to see Sincere a few weeks after he and I were introduced that day at the club, you remember that day when he burst into Shannon's office and made that stupid remark," I nodded my head I remembered the day she was referring to. After the entire ordeal inside the office and the remark Sincere had made, it was later on that night after he dropped me off at home, I had decided it was time for me to take our relationship to the next level.

"I dropped by his office one day, you know how I am I'll pull up on you without warrant, demanding my time. Anyway, after seeing you and him together and seeing the chemistry ya'll have I had to make sure he was serious about you and the relationship. I also wanted to let him know that if he hurt you in anyway that he would have to deal with me. You know I'm not above lacing up the timbs, slashing some tires and putting them jakes in a nigga's life for the ones I love. But the main reason why I went to see him was to tell him that he needed to be honest with you. That day after the you and Sincere left Shannon's spot I confronted Shannon about who he conducted his business with, I had already known how Shannon made his money but I didn't know that Sincere was his best friend and business partner. So, I went speak to Sincere and told him that he needed to tell you who he really is."

"Why didn't you tell me this before?" I asked her.

"He gave me his word that he would tell you soon. He said that it was something he was going to do in order for the two of you to move forward and I believed him, then everything that was going on around me personally, I actually put it on the back burner. Mamì I'm sorry I should have come to you as soon as I found out." Her hand reached out to grab ahold of mine. At this point I don't think anything else could make me numb. It seems like enough people knew about the wolf disguised in sheep clothing but me.

"It wasn't your responsibility to tell me about Sincere. There's nothing for you to be sorry for girl." I told her. I embraced her in a hug, I didn't fault Marisol for not knowing who I was dealing with.

She had finally asked me the question, the one I didn't want to answer, "Have you spoken to him since the party?"

My head just shook side to side absently, "He calls from different numbers but I haven't answered. He leaves voicemails that I have not listened to. I've placed him on the block list so I don't see any text messages. I think about what I would say to him if I did pick up the phone. Would I let him explain to me how he got me caught up in this mess? Would I ask him if he was just using me, were the feelings ever real or am I just a pawn in this damn game of his. Then I think about would I become a different person and become violent, angry, yell out my frustration. Would I want to hit, and slap him?" Marisol giggled at the last remark, I guess she knew just like I did that I wouldn't muster up the strength to become violent.

"Mami you're better than me I can say that much," She said, "I did all of the above when I encountered Sincere last week. Soy bonita, pero empaco un poderoso gancho de derecho, Sincere now knows I pack one powerful punch. And if Shannon wasn't there to hold me back I would have tried to claw those damn eyes out of his skull. Shannon had to restrain me and carry me out of his office because I went the fuck off. I called that nigga every name in the book in English and Spanish. I better not see him on the street no time soon or else it's on and poppin." Marisol was a character but she is a real as it gets as a friend. I don't condone domestic violence but it was amusing to hear she went hard on my behalf. We both shared a laugh, it felt good to know people had my back. Between the conversation with my mom and Marisol I knew it was time to pick myself up and get my business in order.

Looking at my friend and noticing her glow made my heart smile. Before I came down stairs I stood in the mirror and looked at my reflection. What stared back at wasn't me, it wasn't because of the dark circles from lack of sleep or the puffy red eyes from the unshed tears. The image that was being reflected back in the mirror was a broken-hearted woman. The pep talk I had to conjure up just to will myself to head downstairs was one of unanswered questions. Is this how this is supposed to feel? Am I supposed to feel this gut wrenching animosity at the same time feel in love? Is this what people mean when they say love is pain.

Author's Note

I want to thank you for taking the time out to read this story. It took me almost two and half years on and off to write and complete my first novel. I hope I was able to deliver an exciting, page turner book for you to enjoy, although this is my first published novel I am not new to writing. I've loved creative writing since primary school. I am an avid reader from fiction to non-fiction I indulge in it all. I won't take up too much space writing out my sentiments but I am grateful for your time, I hope you like it enough to share with other avid readers of urban romance. Again, thank you and look out for the next chapter for Lovely Daniels and Sincere Riz, lord knows I need to figure out how to get these two back together.

Tempestt Luckett, Author

IG/Twitter/FB: tluckwrites

Don't forget to subscribe to WWW.TPPUBLISH.COM for updates and my blog.